COLLECTED STORIES

JAMES SALTER

COLLECTED STORIES

PICADOR

First published 2013 by Picador
an imprint of Pan Macmillan, a division of Macmillan Publishers Limited
Pan Macmillan, 20 New Wharf Road, London N1 9RR
Basingstoke and Oxford
Associated companies throughout the world
www.panmacmillan.com

ISBN 978-1-4472-3938-3

CONTENTS

INTRODUCTION

Nothing in literature is more difficult than the depiction of commonplace reality. Only the greatest have succeeded in the task. In the novel form we think immediately of Flaubert, of the opening sections of Joyce's *Ulysses*. Among short-story writers there is Chekhov, of course, and Joyce again in *Dubliners*. These wonderful artists do not write *about* reality: their work *is* reality itself. Reading them, we forget that we are experiencing a highly wrought and mediated version of the world. Emma Bovary dying; Leopold Bloom serving his wife breakfast in bed; the lady with the little dog falling haplessly in love and out and in again; Gabriel Conroy staring into the snowy wastes of his marriage and of his selfhood— all this strikes us with the force of lived life, immediate, graspable, at once mundane and sublime.

James Salter is probably best known as a novelist. Two of his books, *A Sport and a Pastime* and *Light Years*, are classics of the form. This year, at the age of eighty-seven, he has published *All That Is*, a big ambitious novel about war and the life of soldiers after war, about writing and publishing, about America and Europe, about love and the loss of love. It is a spellbinding work that a writer half Salter's age would be proud of producing. And now, too, comes this magnificent collection of his short stories, drawn from two slimmish volumes, *Dusk and Other Stories* and *Last Night*, published in 1988 and 2005 respectively. There is also, as a splendid treat, a brand-new story, 'Charisma', on which the ink is hardly dry. In these stories Salter shows himself to be a master chronicler of quotidian lives.

He was born James Arnold Horowitz in 1925, in New Jersey. His father was a real estate broker and a former soldier. Young Horowitz, following his father's distinguished example, entered West Point military academy at the age of seventeen. That was in the summer of 1942, when the world was hard at war. He was an assiduous student and graduated with honours in 1945. The story here, evocatively titled 'Lost Sons'—the opening of which strikes an eerie echo with Joyce's tale of youth's wildness, 'After the Race'—evokes with staccato pointedness and dispatch a West Point reunion:

> In the reception area a welcoming party was going on. There were faces that had hardly changed at all and others like Reemstma's whose name tag was read more than once. Someone with a camera and flash attachment was running around in a cadet bathrobe. Over in the barracks they were drinking. Doors were open. Voices spilled out.

This is the kind of writing Salter does superlatively well. The pace is headlong but at intervals a detail will spring up—Reemstma's name tag being 'read more than once'—on which the reader's attention snags, like a fingernail snagging on silk. It is not only Reemstma's awkward name that sets him apart. Having left the academy he became a painter, and now, returned briefly to the old school, he reflects with brooding melancholy upon the life that might have been: 'A wave of sadness went through him, memories of parades, the end of dances, Christmas leave. . . . It was finished, but no one turns his back on it completely.'

Salter is that rarest of phenomena, a man of action turned successful, more than successful, artist—his is the career that Hemingway could only dream of. At West Point he trained as a pilot, was stationed in the Philippines and Japan, and after post-graduate studies at Georgetown University, he was assigned to the Tactical Air Command. A couple of years later he volunteered to serve in the Korean war, and underwent training in flying the F-86 Sabre fighter jet. In Korea he flew more than a hundred combat missions. His first two novels, *The Hunters* (1957) and *The Arm of Flesh* (1961), drew on his wartime experiences. These books were prentice work, and in later life he was scathingly critical of them—although he republished *The Arm of Flesh* in 2000, under the new title *Cassada*.

In all, Salter served for twelve years in the Air Force, and a further three or four in the Air Force Reserve, before quitting the military life to become a full-time writer. That must have been a tough decision. He was a born flyer, and the thrill of combat was in his blood. Also he was married, with two young children. His early work was not well received either by publishers or the reading public—he was already acquiring that most dreaded of labels, a 'writer's writer'. Despite this handicap he threw himself into the marketplace, and began to write films. As for so many of his predecessors and peers, this proved a dispiriting experience. The story 'The Cinema', with its sardonically portentous title and jump-cut style, catches the disenchantment perfectly—'Yes, notes, make notes,' a director urges his leading man, 'I am saying some brilliant things.' A script that Salter had written for Robert Redford was rejected, and the author turned it into a novel, *Solo Faces* (1979). It was an apt metamorphosis, and marked the end of Salter's time in the movies.

The years in which Salter gave up the life of action in favour of literature marked a fascinating transformation in America at large. The excitements and certainties of wartime had been exchanged for the harsh realities of civilian life. Women, who during the war had enjoyed hitherto undreamed-of freedoms, in the workplace, in the home and in bed, had to be got out of dungarees, real and figurative, and back into gingham and high heels. Hollywood was one of the moving forces in this normative drive—think of Doris Day, and all those musical comedies replete with white telephones and red-blooded leading men such as Rock Hudson.

Salter writes about this post-war world with insight, exactitude and wit. The earlier stories, from the 1960s through the 1980s, have a jazzy rhythm and the glossy, brittle sheen of the world of *Mad Men*. The characters are edgy and streetwise, and they use each other up. It is the latter half of the American century and the Twin Towers are just being planned. What can go wrong? Yet pretty well everything does. In 'Twenty Minutes', one of Salter's most celebrated stories, a rich woman is thrown by her horse and as she lies dying she reviews random moments from her past which somehow do not add up to a life. 'There were all the things she had meant to do, to go East again, to visit certain friends, to live a year by the sea. She could not believe it was over . . .'

Salter's characters are at once vague and instantly memorable. He is particularly good at writing about young females, a skill he has retained right up to the present day—see the opening of 'Charisma', in which two bright young women at a New York party are discussing the painter Lucien Freud, whom one of them has glimpsed looking at the pictures in the Metropolitan Museum of Art:

> "How does he do it all?"
> "I don't know," Cecily admitted.
> They thought about it.
> "I'd fuck him, though," she said.
> "You would?"
> "In a minute."
> "I would, too."

Very many of Salter's stories carry a high-voltage erotic charge. In the unending war between men and women his characters take their positions early at the battle front and go at it toe to toe. Mostly the fighting is dirty. In 'American Express' a couple of lawyers, Frank and Alan, successful, crass and hungry for the world, take an extended vacation together in Italy. Driving through Arezzo they pick up a schoolgirl at a street corner and Frank takes her to his hotel room. 'At one point she seemed to tremble, her body shuddered. "Are you all right?" he said.' Later the trio travel together, to Florence, to Spoleto, other tourist towns. Inevitably Alan develops a desire for the girl, and Frank, ever the sport, casually offers to share her. This is what buddies do, after all. The girl, the child, is of no consequence, is virtually an object. Here, in a short space of pages, Salter fashions what might be a Henry James novel in miniature: Americans in Europe, the abuse of innocence, the strangely contingent feel of life passing by. 'He didn't know what to do. Apart from that, it was perfect.'

In another story, 'Am Strande von Tanger', another trio of travellers, a young American and two German women, spend time together in Barcelona. Nothing much happens, on the surface: the significant action is submerged, or takes place in the spaces between words. The story is a bravura performance, a triumphant exercise in the art of saying little but conveying much. At the end a pet bird dies and, we understand, much else dies with it. The closing sentences create a chilling bleakness out of the most banal material: 'She has small breasts and large nipples. Also, as she says herself, a rather large behind. Her father has three secretaries. Hamburg is close to the sea.'

Here, as so often elsewhere, Salter deploys the objective correlative to brilliant effect. In one of the most moving and forlornly beautiful stories in the collection, 'Dusk', Mrs Chandler, a divorced woman of a certain age and social position—'She knew how to give dinner parties, take care of dogs, enter restaurants'—is visited by her half-hearted lover, who tells her he has healed the rift with his wife and is going back to her. For Mrs Chandler it is a loss among losses, the hardest of which was the death of her young son. She prays for the child: 'O Lord, don't overlook him, he's very small . . .' The story is no more than eight pages long, but its power is immense, especially in the perfectly pitched, heart-rending close. Throughout, images recur of wild geese brought down by hunters, and as dusk turns to night the woman feels the darkness encroach upon her own heart:

> Somewhere in the wet grass, she imagined, lay one of them, dark sodden breast, graceful neck still extended, great wings striving to beat, bloody sounds coming from the holes in its beak. She went around and turned on lights. The rain was coming down, the sea was crashing, a comrade lay dead in the whirling darkness.

In 'My Lord You' the erotic element is fused with the disruptive power of art. A middle-class dinner party is invaded by a drunkard and failed poet, Brennan, who lives in the neighbourhood. One of the guests, a young woman named Ardis, is alarmed and fascinated in equal measure by the man's disruptive presence. Next day, returning from the beach, she makes a detour to Brennan's house. There seems to be no one at home except a huge, silent dog, which follows her home—'He was trotting awkwardly, like a big man running in the rain'—and attaches itself to her, sleeping in the grass beyond the house. She leads the dog home to Brennan's house, and finding it empty she goes inside to explore. It is a strange, unsettling experience for her, and she hardly credits her own behaviour. 'Deliberately, without thinking, she began to remove her clothes. She went no further than the waist. She was dazzled by what she was doing.' Eventually the dog disappears from her life, 'gone, lost, living elsewhere, his name perhaps to be written in a line someday though most probably he was forgotten, but not by her.'

A phantasmal version of the poet's dog lopes through all

these stories, an emblem of menace and mysterious power, a silent, biding reminder of life's wildness and unassuageable yearnings. James Salter is a magician, and his marvels are exquisitely wrought yet exert a muscular grasp on the everyday realities of life. Again and again in these pages he succeeds in what John Updike stated as the writer's duty, to 'give the ordinary its beautiful due.' In fulfilling that duty, Salter shows the ordinary for what it really is: the marvellous.

JOHN BANVILLE, 2013

AM STRANDE VON TANGER

Barcelona at dawn. The hotels are dark. All the great avenues are pointing to the sea.

The city is empty. Nico is asleep. She is bound by twisted sheets, by her long hair, by a naked arm which falls from beneath her pillow. She lies still, she does not even breathe.

In a cage outlined beneath a square of silk that is indigo blue and black, her bird sleeps, Kalil. The cage is in an empty fireplace which has been scrubbed clean. There are flowers beside it and a bowl of fruit. Kalil is asleep, his head beneath the softness of a wing.

Malcolm is asleep. His steel-rimmed glasses which he does not need—there is no prescription in them—lie open on the table. He sleeps on his back and his nose rides the dream world like a keel. This nose, his mother's nose or at least a replica of his mother's, is like a theatrical device, a strange decoration that has been pasted on his face. It is the first thing one notices about him. It is the first thing one likes. The nose in a sense is a mark of commitment to life. It is a large nose which cannot be hidden. In addition, his teeth are bad.

At the very top of the four stone spires which Gaudi left unfinished the light has just begun to bring forth gold inscriptions too pale to read. There is no sun. There is only a white silence. Sunday morning, the early morning of Spain. A mist covers all of the hills which surround the city. The stores are closed.

Nico has come out on the terrace after her bath. The towel is wrapped around her, water still glistens on her skin.

"It's cloudy," she says. "It's not a good day for the sea."

Malcolm looks up.

"It may clear," he says.

Morning. Villa-Lobos is playing on the phonograph. The cage is on a stool in the doorway. Malcolm lies in a canvas chair eating an orange. He is in love with the city. He has a deep attachment to it based in part on a story by Paul Morand and also on an incident which occurred in Barcelona years before: one evening in the twilight Antonio Gaudi, mysterious, fragile, even saintlike, the city's great architect, was hit by a streetcar as he walked to church. He was very old, white beard, white hair, dressed in the simplest of clothes. No one recognized him. He lay in the street without even a cab to drive him to the hospital. Finally he was taken to the charity ward. He died the day Malcolm was born.

The apartment is on Avenida General Mitre and her tailor, as Nico calls him, is near Gaudi's cathedral at the other end of town. That's a working-class neighborhood, there's a faint smell of garbage. The site is surrounded by walls. There are quatrefoils printed in the sidewalk. Soaring above everything, the spires. *Sanctus, sanctus*, they cry. They are hollow. The cathedral was never completed, its doors lead both ways into open air. Malcolm has walked, in the calm Barcelona evening, around this empty monument many times. He has stuffed peseta notes, virtually worthless, into the slot marked:

DONATIONS TO CONTINUE THE WORK. It seems on the other side they are simply falling to the ground or, he listens closely, a priest wearing glasses locks them in a wooden box.

Malcolm believes in Malraux and Max Weber: art is the real history of nations. In the details of his person there is evidence of a process not fully complete. It is the making of a man into a true instrument. He is preparing for the arrival of that great artist he one day expects to be, an artist in the truly modern sense which is to say without accomplishments but with the conviction of genius. An artist freed from the demands of craft, an artist of concepts, generosity, his work is the creation of the legend of himself. So long as he is provided with even a single follower he can believe in the sanctity of this design.

He is happy here. He likes the wide, tree-cool avenues, the restaurants, the long evenings. He is deep in the currents of a slow, connubial life.

Nico comes onto the terrace wearing a wheat-colored sweater.

"Would you like a coffee?" she says. "Do you want me to go down for one?"

He thinks for a moment.

"Yes," he says.

"How do you like it?"

"*Solo*," he says.

"Black."

She likes to do this. The building has a small elevator which rises slowly. When it arrives she steps in and closes the doors carefully behind her. Then, just as slowly, she descends, floor after floor, as if they were decades. She thinks about Malcolm. She thinks about her father and his second wife. She is probably more intelligent than Malcolm, she decides. She is certainly stronger-willed. He, however, is better-looking in a strange way. She has a wide, senseless mouth. He is generous. She knows she is a little dry. She passes the second floor. She looks at herself in the mirror. Of course, one doesn't discover these things right away. It's like a play, it unfolds slowly, scene by scene, the reality of another person changes. Anyway, pure intelligence is not that important. It's an abstract quality. It does not include that cruel, intuitive knowledge of how the new life, a life her father would never understand, should be lived. Malcolm has that.

At ten-thirty, the phone rings. She answers and talks in German, lying on the couch. After it is finished Malcolm calls to her, "Who was that?"

"Do you want to go to the beach?"

"Yes."

"Inge is coming in about an hour," Nico says.

He has heard about her and is curious. Besides, she has a car. The morning, obedient to his desires, has begun to change. There is some early traffic on the avenue beneath. The sun breaks through for a moment, disappears, breaks through again. Far off, beyond his thoughts, the four spires are passing between shadow and glory. In intervals of sunlight the letters on high reveal themselves: *Hosanna*.

Smiling, at noon, Inge arrives. She is in a camel skirt and a blouse with the top buttons undone. She's a bit heavy for the skirt which is very short. Nico introduces them.

"Why didn't you call last night?" Inge asks.

"We were going to call but it got so late. We didn't have dinner till eleven," Nico explains. "I was sure you'd be out."

No. She was waiting at home all night for her boyfriend to call, Inge says. She is fanning herself with a postcard from Madrid. Nico has gone into the bedroom.

"They're such bastards," Inge says. Her voice is raised to carry. "He was supposed to call at eight. He didn't call me until ten. He didn't have time to talk. He was going to call back in a little while. Well, he never called. I finally fell asleep."

Nico puts on a pale grey skirt with many small pleats and a lemon pullover. She looks at the back of herself in the mirror. Her arms are bare. Inge is talking from the front room.

"They don't know how to behave, that's the trouble. They don't have any idea. They go to the Polo Club, that's the only thing they know."

She begins to talk to Malcolm.

"When you go to bed with someone it should be nice afterwards, you should treat each other decently. Not here. They have no respect for a woman."

She has green eyes and white, even teeth. He is thinking of what it would be like to have such a mouth. Her father is supposed to be a surgeon. In Hamburg. Nico says it isn't true.

"They are children here," Inge says. "In Germany, now, you have a little respect. A man doesn't treat you like that, he knows what to do."

"Nico," he calls.

She comes in brushing her hair.

"I am frightening him," Inge explains. "Do you know what I finally did? I called at five in the morning. I said, why didn't you call? I don't know, he said—I could tell he was asleep—what time is it? Five o'clock, I said. Are you angry with me? A little, he said. Good, because I am angry with you. Bang, I hung up."

Nico is closing the doors to the terrace and bringing the cage inside.

"It's warm," Malcolm says, "leave him there. He needs the sunlight."

She looks in at the bird.

"I don't think he's well," she says.

"He's all right."

"The other one died last week," she explains to Inge. "Suddenly. He wasn't even sick."

She closes one door and leaves the other open. The bird sits in the now brilliant sunshine, feathered, serene.

"I don't think they can live alone," she says.

"He's fine," Malcolm assures her. "Look at him."

The sun makes his colors very bright. He sits on the uppermost perch. His eyes have perfect, round lids. He blinks.

The elevator is still at their floor. Inge enters first. Malcolm pulls the narrow doors to. It's like shutting a small cabinet. Faces close together they start down. Malcolm is looking at Inge. She has her own thoughts.

They stop for another coffee at the little bar downstairs. He holds the door open for them to go in. No one is there— a single man reading the newspaper.

"I think I'm going to call him again," Inge says.

6

"Ask him why he woke you up at five in the morning," Malcolm says.

She laughs.

"Yes," she says. "That's marvelous. That's what I'm going to do."

The telephone is at the far end of the marble counter, but Nico is talking to him and he cannot hear.

"Aren't you interested?" he asks.

"No," she says.

Inge's car is a blue Volkswagen, the blue of certain airmail envelopes. One fender is dented in.

"You haven't seen my car," she says. "What do you think? Did I get a good bargain? I don't know anything about cars. This is my first. I bought it from someone I know, a painter, but it was in an accident. The motor is scorched.

"I know how to drive," she says. "It's better if someone sits next to me, though. Can you drive?"

"Of course," he says.

He gets behind the wheel and starts the engine. Nico is sitting in the back.

"How does it feel to you?" Inge says.

"I'll tell you in a minute."

Although it's only a year old, the car has a certain shabbiness. The material on the ceiling is faded. Even the steering wheel seems abused. After they have driven a few blocks, Malcolm says, "It seems all right."

"Yes?"

"The brakes are a little weak."

"They are?"

"I think they need new linings."

"I just had it greased," she says.

Malcolm looks at her. She is quite serious.

"Turn left here," she says.

She directs him through the city. There is a little traffic now but he seldom stops. Many intersections in Barcelona are widened out in the shape of an octagon. There are only a few red lights. They drive through vast neighborhoods of old apartments, past factories, the first vacant fields at the edge of town. Inge turns in her seat to look back to Nico.

"I'm sick of this place," she says. "I want to go to Rome."

They are passing the airport. The road to the sea is crowded. All the scattered traffic of the city has funneled onto it, buses, trucks, innumerable small cars.

"They don't even know how to drive," Inge says. "What are they doing? Can't you pass?

"Oh, come on," she says. She reaches across him to blow the horn.

"No use doing that," Malcolm says.

Inge blows it again.

"They can't move."

"Oh, they make me furious," she cries.

Two children in the car ahead have turned around. Their faces are pale and reflective in the small rear window.

"Have you been to Sitges?" Inge says.

"Cadaques."

"Ah," she says. "Yes. Beautiful. There you have to know someone with a villa."

The sun is white. The land lies beneath it the color of straw. The road runs parallel to the coast past cheap bathing beaches, campgrounds, houses, hotels. Between the road and the sea is the railroad with small tunnels built beneath it for bathers to reach the water. After a while this begins to disappear. They drive along almost deserted stretches.

"In Sitges," Inge says, "are all the blonde girls of Europe. Sweden, Germany, Holland. You'll see."

Malcolm watches the road.

"The brown eyes of the Spaniards are irresistible to them," she says.

She reaches across him to blow the horn.

"Look at them! Look at them crawling along!

"They come here full of hopes," Inge says. "They save their money, they buy little bathing suits you could put in a spoon, and what happens? They get loved for one night, perhaps, that's all. The Spanish don't know how to treat women."

Nico is silent in the back. On her face is the calm expression which means she is bored.

"They know nothing," Inge says.

Sitges is a little town with damp hotels, the green shutters, the dying grass of a beach resort. There are cars parked everywhere. The streets are lined with them. Finally they find a place two blocks from the sea.

"Be sure it's locked," Inge says.

"Nobody's going to steal it," Malcolm tells her.

"Now you don't think it's so nice," she says.

They walk along the pavement, the surface of which seems to have buckled in the heat. All around are the flat, undecorated facades of houses built too close together. Despite the cars, the town is strangely vacant. It's two o'clock. Everyone is at lunch.

Malcolm has a pair of shorts made from rough cotton, the blue glazed cotton of the Tuaregs. They have a little belt, slim as a finger, which goes only halfway around. He feels powerful as he puts them on. He has a runner's body, a body without flaws, the body of a martyr in a Flemish painting. One can see vessels laid like cord beneath the surface of his limbs. The cabins have a concrete back wall and hemp underfoot. His clothes hang shapeless from a peg. He steps into the corridor. The women are still undressing, he does not know behind which door. There is a small mirror hung from a nail. He smooths his hair and waits. Outside is the sun.

The sea begins with a sloping course of pebbles sharp as nails. Malcolm goes in first. Nico follows without a word. The water is cool. He feels it climb his legs, touch the edge of his suit and then with a swell—he tries to leap high enough—embrace him. He dives. He comes up smiling. The taste of salt is on his lips. Nico has dived, too. She emerges close by, softly, and draws her wetted hair behind her with one hand. She stands with her eyes half-closed, not knowing exactly where she is. He slips an arm around her waist. She smiles. She possesses a certain, sure instinct of when she is most beautiful. For a moment they are in serene dependence. He lifts her in his arms and carries her, helped by the sea, toward the deep. Her head rests on his shoulder. Inge lies on the beach in her bikini reading *Stern*.

"What's wrong with Inge?" he says.

"Everything."

"No, doesn't she want to come in?"

"She's having her period," Nico says.

They lie down beside her on separate towels. She is,

Malcolm notices, very brown. Nico can never get that way no matter how long she stays outside. It is almost a kind of stubbornness as if he, himself, were offering her the sun and she would not accept.

She got this tan in a single day, Inge tells them. A single day! It seems unbelievable. She looks at her arms and legs as if confirming it. Yes, it's true. Naked on the rocks at Cadaques. She looks down at her stomach and in doing so induces it to reveal several plump, girlish rolls.

"You're getting fat," Nico says.

Inge laughs. "They are my savings," she says.

They seem like that, like belts, like part of some costume she is wearing. When she lies back, they are gone. Her limbs are clean. Her stomach, like the rest of her, is covered with a faint, golden down. Two Spanish youths are strolling past along the sea.

She is talking to the sky. If she goes to America, she recites, is it worthwhile to bring her car? After all, she got it at a very good price, she could probably sell it if she didn't want to keep it and make some money.

"America is full of Volkswagens," Malcolm says.

"Yes?"

"It's filled with German cars, everyone has one."

"They must like them," she decides. "The Mercedes is a good car."

"Greatly admired," Malcolm says.

"That's the car I would like. I would like a couple of them. When I have money, that will be my hobby," she says. "I'd like to live in Tangier."

"Quite a beach there."

"Yes? I will be black as an Arab."

"Better wear your suit," Malcolm says.

Inge smiles.

Nico seems asleep. They lie there silent, their feet pointed to the sun. The strength of it has gone. There are only passing moments of warmth when the wind dies all the way and the sun is flat upon them, weak but flooding. An hour of melancholy is approaching, the hour when everything is ended.

At six o'clock Nico sits up. She is cold.

"Come," Inge says, "we'll go for a walk up the beach."

She insists on it. The sun has not set. She becomes very playful.

"Come," she says, "it's the good section, all the big villas are there. We'll walk along and make the old men happy."

"I don't want to make anyone happy," Nico says, hugging her arms.

"It isn't so easy," Inge assures her.

Nico goes along sullenly. She is holding her elbows. The wind is from the shore. There are little waves now which seem to break in silence. The sound they make is soft, as if forgotten. Nico is wearing a grey tank suit with an open back, and while Inge plays before the houses of the rich, she looks at the sand.

Inge goes into the sea. Come, she says, it's warm. She is laughing and happy, her gaiety is stronger than the hour, stronger than the cold. Malcolm walks slowly in behind her. The water *is* warm. It seems purer as well. And it is empty, as far in each direction as one can see. They are bathing in it alone. The waves swell and lift them gently. The water runs over them, laving the soul.

At the entrance to the cabins the young Spanish boys stand around waiting for a glimpse if the shower door is opened too soon. They wear blue woolen trunks. Also black. Their feet appear to have very long toes. There is only one shower and in it a single, whitened tap. The water is cold. Inge goes first. Her suit appears, one small piece and then the other, draped over the top of the door. Malcolm waits. He can hear the soft slap and passage of her hands, the sudden shattering of the water on concrete when she moves aside. The boys at the door exalt him. He glances out. They are talking in low voices. They reach out to tease each other, to make an appearance of play.

The streets of Sitges have changed. An hour has struck which announces evening, and everywhere there are strolling crowds. It's difficult to stay together. Malcolm has an arm around each of them. They drift to his touch like horses. Inge smiles. People will think the three of them do it together, she says.

They stop at a café. It isn't a good one, Inge complains.

"It's the best," Nico says simply. It is one of her qualities that she can tell at a glance, wherever she goes, which is the right place, the right restaurant, hotel.

"No," Inge insists.

Nico seems not to care. They wander on separated now, and Malcolm whispers, "What is she looking for?"

"Don't you know?" Nico says.

"You see these boys?" Inge says. They are seated in another place, a bar. All around them, tanned limbs, hair faded from the long, baking afternoons, young men sit with the sweet stare of indolence.

"They have no money," she says. "None of them could take you to dinner. Not one of them. They have nothing. This is Spain," she says.

Nico chooses the place for dinner. She has become a lesser person during the day. The presence of this friend, this girl she casually shared a life with during the days they both were struggling to find themselves in the city, before she knew anybody or even the names of streets, when she was so sick that they wrote out a cable to her father together—they had no telephone—this sudden revelation of Inge seems to have deprived the past of decency. All at once she is pierced by a certainty that Malcolm feels contempt for her. Her confidence, without which she is nothing, has gone. The tablecloth seems white and dazzling. It seems to be illuminating the three of them with remorseless light. The knives and forks are laid out as if for surgery. The plates lie cold. She is not hungry but she doesn't dare refuse to eat. Inge is talking about her boyfriend.

"He is terrible," she says, "he is heartless. But I understand him. I know what he wants. Anyway, a woman can't hope to be everything to a man. It isn't natural. A man needs a number of women."

"You're crazy," Nico says flatly.

"It's true."

The statement is all that was needed to demoralize her. Malcolm is inspecting the strap of his watch. It seems to Nico he is permitting all this. He is stupid, she thinks. This girl is from a low background and he finds that interesting. She thinks because they go to bed with her they will marry her. Of course not. Never. Nothing, Nico thinks, could be farther from the truth, though even as she thinks she knows she may be wrong.

They go to Chez Swann for a coffee. Nico sits apart. She is tired, she says. She curls up on one of the couches and goes to sleep. She is exhausted. The evening has become quite cool.

A voice awakens her, music, a marvelous voice amid occasional phrases of the guitar. Nico hears it in her sleep and sits up. Malcolm and Inge are talking. The song is like something long-awaited, something she has been searching for. She reaches over and touches his arm.

"Listen," she says.

"What?"

"Listen," she says, "it's Maria Pradera."

"Maria Pradera?"

"The words are beautiful," Nico says.

Simple phrases. She repeats them, as if they were litany. Mysterious repetitions: dark-haired mother . . . dark-haired child. The eloquence of the poor, worn smooth and pure as a stone.

Malcolm listens patiently but he hears nothing. She can see it: he has changed, he has been poisoned while she slept with stories of a hideous Spain fed bit by bit until now they are drifting through his veins, a Spain devised by a woman who knows she can never be more than part of what a man needs. Inge is calm. She believes in herself. She believes in her right to exist, to command.

The road is dark. They have opened the roof to the night,

a night so dense with stars that they seem to be pouring into the car. Nico, in the back, feels frightened. Inge is talking. She reaches over to blow the horn at cars which are going too slow. Malcolm laughs at it. There are private rooms in Barcelona where, with her lover, Inge spent winter afternoons before a warm, crackling fire. There are houses where they made love on blankets of fur. Of course, he was nice then. She had visions of the Polo Club, of dinner parties in the best houses.

The streets of the city are almost deserted. It is nearly midnight, Sunday midnight. The day in the sun has wearied them, the sea has drained them of strength. They drive to General Mitre and say good night through the windows of the car. The elevator rises very slowly. They are hung with silence. They look at the floor like gamblers who have lost.

The apartment is dark. Nico turns on a light and then vanishes. Malcolm washes his hands. He dries them. The rooms seem very still. He begins to walk through them slowly and finds her, as if she had fallen, on her knees in the doorway to the terrace.

Malcolm looks at the cage. Kalil has fallen to the floor.

"Give him a little brandy on the corner of a handkerchief," he says.

She has opened the cage door.

"He's dead," she says.

"Let me see."

He is stiff. The small feet are curled and dry as twigs. He seems lighter somehow. The breath has left his feathers. A heart no bigger than an orange seed has ceased to beat. The cage sits empty in the cold doorway. There seems nothing to say. Malcolm closes the door.

Later, in bed, he listens to her sobs. He tries to comfort her but he cannot. Her back is turned to him. She will not answer.

She has small breasts and large nipples. Also, as she herself says, a rather large behind. Her father has three secretaries. Hamburg is close to the sea.

MY LORD YOU

There were crumpled napkins on the table, wineglasses still with dark remnant in them, coffee stains, and plates with bits of hardened Brie. Beyond the bluish windows the garden lay motionless beneath the birdsong of summer morning. Daylight had come. It had been a success except for one thing: Brennan.

They had sat around first, drinking in the twilight, and then gone inside. The kitchen had a large round table, fireplace, and shelves with ingredients of every kind. Deems was well known as a cook. So was his somewhat unknowable girlfriend, Irene, who had a mysterious smile though they never cooked together. That night it was Deems's turn. He served caviar, brought out in a white jar such as makeup comes in, to be eaten from small silver spoons.

"The only way," Deems muttered in profile. He seldom looked at anyone. "Antique silver spoons," Ardis heard him mistakenly say in his low voice, as if it might not have been noticed.

She was noticing everything, however. Though they had known Deems for a while, she and her husband had never been to the house. In the dining room, when they all went in to dinner, she took in the pictures, books, and shelves of objects including one of perfect, gleaming shells. It was foreign in a way, like anyone else's house, but half-familiar.

There'd been some mix-up about the seating that Irene tried vainly to adjust amid the conversation before the meal began. Outside, darkness had come, deep and green. The men were talking about camps they had gone to as boys in piney Maine and about Soros, the financier. Far more interesting was a comment Ardis heard Irene make, in what context she did not know,

"I think there's such a thing as sleeping with one man too many."

"Did you say 'such a thing' or 'no such thing'?" she heard herself ask.

Irene merely smiled. I must ask her later, Ardis thought. The food was excellent. There was cold soup, duck, and a salad of young vegetables. The coffee had been served and Ardis was distractedly playing with melted wax from the candles when a voice burst out loudly behind her,

"I'm late. Who's this? Are these the beautiful people?"

It was a drunken man in a jacket and dirty white trousers with blood on them, which had come from nicking his lip while shaving two hours before. His hair was damp, his face arrogant. It was the face of a Regency duke, intimidating, spoiled. The irrational flickered from him.

"Do you have anything to drink here? What is this, wine? Very sorry I'm late. I've just had seven cognacs and said goodbye to my wife. Deems, you know what that's like. You're my only friend, do you know that? The only one."

"There's some dinner in there, if you like," Deems said, gesturing toward the kitchen.

"No dinner. I've had dinner. I'll just have something to drink. Deems, you're my friend, but I'll tell you something, you'll become my enemy. You know what Oscar Wilde said— my favorite writer, my favorite in all the world. Anyone can choose his friends, but only the wise man can choose his enemies."

He was staring intently at Deems. It was like the grip of a madman, a kind of fury. His mouth had an expression of determination. When he went into the kitchen they could hear him among the bottles. He returned with a dangerous glassful and looked around boldly.

"Where is Beatrice?" Deems asked.

"Who?"

"Beatrice, your wife."

"Gone," Brennan said.

He searched for a chair.

"To visit her father?" Irene asked.

"What makes you think that?" Brennan said menacingly. To Ardis's alarm he sat down next to her.

"He's been in the hospital, hasn't he?"

"Who knows where he's been," Brennan said darkly. "He's a swine. Lucre, gain. He's a slum owner, a criminal. I would hang him myself. In the fashion of Gomez, the dictator, whose daughters are probably wealthy women."

He discovered Ardis and said to her, as if imitating someone, perhaps someone he assumed her to be,

"'N 'at funny? 'N 'at wonderful?"

To her relief he turned away.

"I'm their only hope," he said to Irene. "I'm living on their money and it's ruinous, the end of me." He held out his glass and asked mildly, "Can I have just a tiny bit of ice? I adore my wife." To Ardis he confided, "Do you know how we met? Unimaginable. She was walking by on the beach. I was unprepared. I saw the ventral, then the dorsal, I imagined the rest. Bang! We came together like planets. Endless fornication. Sometimes I just lie silent and observe her. *The black panther lies under his rose-tree,*" he recited. "*J'ai eu pitié des autres . . .*"

He stared at her.

"What is that?" she asked tentatively.

"*. . . but that the child walk in peace in her basilica,*" he intoned.

"Is it Wilde?"

"You can't guess? Pound. The sole genius of the century. No, not the sole. I am another: a drunk, a failure, and a great genius. Who are you?" he said. "Another little housewife?"

She felt the blood leave her face and stood to busy herself clearing the table. His hand was on her arm.

"Don't go. I know who you are, another priceless woman meant to languish. Beautiful figure," he said as she managed to free herself, "pretty shoes."

As she carried some plates into the kitchen she could hear him saying,

"Don't go to many of these parties. Not invited."

"Can't imagine why," someone murmured.

"But Deems is my friend, my very closest friend."

"Who is he? Ardis asked Irene in the kitchen.

"Oh, he's a poet. He's married to a Venezuelan woman and she runs off. He's not always this bad."

They had quieted him down in the other room. Ardis

could see her husband nervously pushing his glasses up on his nose with one finger. Deems, in a polo shirt and with rumpled hair, was trying to guide Brennan toward the back door. Brennan kept stopping to talk. For a moment he would seem reformed.

"I want to tell you something," he said. "I went past the school, the one on the street there. There was a poster. The First Annual Miss Fuck Contest. I'm serious. This is a fact."

"No, no," Deems said.

"It's been held, I don't know when. Question is, are they coming to their senses finally or losing them? A tiny bit more," he begged, his glass was empty. His mind doubled back, "Seriously, what do you think of that?"

In the light of the kitchen he seemed merely disheveled, like a journalist who has been working hard all night. The unsettling thing was the absence of reason in him, his glare. One nostril was smaller than the other. He was used to being ungovernable. Ardis hoped he would not notice her again. His forehead had two gleaming places, like nascent horns. Were men drawn to you when they knew they were frightening you?

She could feel his eyes. There was silence. She could feel him standing there like a menacing beggar.

"What are you, another bourgeois?" he said to her. "I know I've been drinking. Come and have dinner," he said. "I've ordered something wonderful for us. Vichyssoise. Lobster. S. G. Always on the menu like that, *selon grosseur*."

He was talking in an easy way, as if they were in the casino together, chips piled high before them, as if it were a shrewd discussion of what to bet on and her breasts in the dark T-shirt were a thing of indifference to him. He calmly reached out and touched one.

"I have money," he said. His hand remained where it was, cupping her. She was too stunned to move. "Do you want me to do more of that?"

"No," she managed to say.

His hand slipped down to her hip. Deems had taken an arm and was drawing him away.

"Ssh," Brennan whispered to her, "don't say anything. The two of us. Like an oar going into the water, gliding."

"We have to go," Deems insisted.

"What are you doing? Is this another of your ruses?" Brennan cried. "Deems, I shall end up destroying you yet!"

As he was herded to the door, he continued. Deems was the only man he didn't loathe, he said. He wanted them all to come to his house, he had everything. He had a phonograph, whisky! He had a gold watch!

At last he was outside. He walked unsteadily across the finely cut grass and got into his car, the side of which was dented in. He backed away in great lurches.

"He's headed for Cato's," Deems guessed. "I ought to call and warn them."

"They won't serve him. He owes them money," Irene said.

"Who told you that?"

"The bartender. Are you all right?" she asked Ardis.

"Yes. Is he actually married?"

"He's been married three or four times," Deems said.

Later they started dancing, some of the women together. Irene pulled Deems onto the floor. He came unresisting. He danced quite well. She was moving her arms sinuously and singing.

"Very nice," he said. "Have you ever entertained?"

She smiled at him.

"I do my best," she said.

At the end she put her hand on Ardis's arm and said again,

"I'm so embarrassed at what happened."

"It was nothing. I'm all right."

"I should have taken him and thrown him out," her husband said on the way home. "Ezra Pound. Do you know about Ezra Pound?"

"No."

"He was a traitor. He broadcast for the enemy during the war. They should have shot him."

"What happened to him?"

"They gave him a poetry prize."

They were going down a long empty stretch where on a corner, half hidden in trees, a small house stood, the gypsy house, Ardis thought of it as, a simple house with a water pump in the yard and occasionally in the daytime a girl in blue shorts, very brief, and high heels, hanging clothes on a line. Tonight there was a light on in the window. One light near the sea. She was driving with Warren and he was talking.

"The best thing is to just forget about tonight."

"Yes," she said. "It was nothing."

Brennan went through a fence on Hull Lane and up on to somebody's lawn at about two that morning. He had missed the curve where the road bent left, probably because his head-lights weren't on, the police thought.

She took the book and went over to a window that looked out on the garden behind the library. She read a bit of one thing or another and came to a poem some lines of which had been underlined, with penciled notes in the margin. It was "The River-Merchant's Wife"; she had never heard of it. Outside, the summer burned, white as chalk.

> *At fourteen I married My Lord you,* she read.
> *I never laughed, being bashful . . .*

There were three old men, one of them almost blind, it appeared, reading newspapers in the cold room. The thick glasses of the nearly blind man cast white moons onto his cheeks.

> *The leaves fall early this autumn, in wind.*
> *The paired butterflies are already yellow with August*
> *Over the grass in the West garden;*
> *They hurt me. I grow older.*

She had read poems and perhaps marked them like this, but that was in school. Of the things she had been taught she remembered only a few. There had been one My Lord though she did not marry him. She'd been twenty-one, her first year in the city. She remembered the building of dark brown brick on Fifty-eighth Street, the afternoons with their slitted light, her clothes in a chair or fallen to the floor, and the damp, mindless repetition, to it, or him, or who knew what: oh,

God, oh, God, oh, God. The traffic outside so faint, so far away . . .

She'd called him several times over the years, believing that love never died, dreaming foolishly of seeing him again, of his returning, in the way of old songs. To hurry, to almost run down the noontime street again, the sound of her heels on the sidewalk. To see the door of the apartment open . . .

> *If you are coming down the narrows of the river Kiang,*
> *Please let me know beforehand,*
> *And I will come out to meet you.*
> *As far as Chô-fu-Sa*

There she sat by the window with her young face that had a weariness in it, a slight distaste for things, even, one might imagine for oneself. After a while she went to the desk.

"Do you happen to have anything by Michael Brennan?" she asked.

"Michael Brennan," the woman said. "We've had them, but he takes them away because unworthy people read them, he says. I don't think there're any now. Perhaps when he comes back from the city."

"He lives in the city?"

"He lives just down the road. We had all of his books at one time. Do you know him?"

She would have liked to ask more but she shook her head.

"No," she said. "I've just heard the name."

"He's a poet," the woman said.

*

On the beach she sat by herself. There was almost no one. In her bathing suit she lay back with the sun on her face and knees. It was hot and the sea calm. She preferred to lie up by the dunes with the waves bursting, to listen while they crashed like the final chords of a symphony except they went on and on. There was nothing as fine as that.

She came out of the ocean and dried herself like the gypsy girl, ankles caked with sand. She could feel the sun burnishing her shoulders. Hair wet, deep in the emptiness of days, she walked her bicycle up to the road, the dirt velvety beneath her feet.

She did not go home the usual way. There was little traffic. The noon was bottle-green, large houses among the trees and wide farmland, like a memory, behind.

She knew the house and saw it far off, her heart beating strangely. When she stopped, it was casually, with the bike tilting to one side and she half-seated on it as if taking a rest. How beautiful a lone woman is, in a white summer shirt and bare legs. Pretending to adjust the bicycle's chain she looked at the house, its tall windows, water stains high on the roof. There was a gardener's shed, abandoned, saplings growing in the path that led to it. The long driveway, the sea porch, everything was empty.

Walking slowly, aware of how brazen she was, she went toward the house. Her urge was to look in the windows, no more than that. Still, despite the silence, the complete stillness, that was forbidden.

She walked farther. Suddenly someone rose from the side porch. She was unable to utter a sound or move.

It was a dog, a huge dog higher than her waist, coming

toward her, yellow-eyed. She had always been afraid of dogs, the Alsatian that had unexpectedly turned on her college roommate and torn off a piece of her scalp. The size of this one, its lowered head and slow, deliberate stride.

Do not show fear, she knew that. Carefully she moved the bicycle so that it was between them. The dog stopped a few feet away, its eyes directly on her, the sun along its back. She did not know what to expect, a sudden short rush.

"Good boy," she said. It was all she could think of. "Good boy."

Moving cautiously, she began wheeling the bicycle toward the road, turning her head away slightly so as to appear unworried. Her legs felt naked, the bare calves. They would be ripped open as if by a scythe. The dog was following her, its shoulders moving smoothly, like a kind of machine. Somehow finding the courage, she tried to ride. The front wheel wavered. The dog, high as the handlebars, came nearer.

"No," she cried. "No!"

After a moment or two, obediently, he slowed or veered off. He was gone.

She rode as if freed, as if flying through blocks of sunlight and high, solemn tunnels of trees. And then she saw him again. He was following—not exactly following, since he was some distance ahead. He seemed to float along in the fields, which were burning in the midday sun, on fire. She turned onto her own road. There he came. He fell in behind her. She could hear the clatter of his nails like falling stones. She looked back. He was trotting awkwardly, like a big man running in the rain. A line of spittle trailed from his jaw. When she reached her house he had disappeared.

That night in a cotton robe she was preparing for bed, cleaning her face, the bathroom door ajar. She brushed her hair with many rapid strokes.

"Tired?" her husband asked as she emerged.

It was his way of introducing the subject.

"No," she said.

So there they were in the summer night with the far-off sound of the sea. Among the things her husband admired that Ardis possessed was extraordinary skin, luminous and smooth, a skin so pure that to touch it would make one tremble.

"Wait," she whispered, "not so fast."

Afterward he lay back without a word, already falling into deepest sleep, much too soon. She touched his shoulder. She heard something outside the window.

"Did you hear that?"

"No, what?" he said drowsily.

She waited. There was nothing. It had seemed faint, like a sigh.

The next morning she said,

"Oh!" There, just beneath the trees, the dog lay. She could see his ears—they were small ears dashed with white.

"What is it?" her husband asked.

"Nothing," she said. "A dog. It followed me yesterday."

"From where?" he said, coming to see.

"Down the road. I think it might be that man's. Brennan's."

"Brennan?"

"I passed his house," she said, "and afterward it was following me."

"What were you doing at Brennan's?"

"Nothing. I was passing. He's not even there."

"What do you mean, he's not there?"

"I don't know. Somebody said that."

He went to the door and opened it. The dog—it was a deerhound—had been lying with its forelegs stretched out in front like a sphinx, its haunches round and high. Awkwardly it rose and after a moment moved, reluctantly it seemed, wandering slowly across the fields, never looking back.

In the evening they went to a party on Mecox Road. Far out toward Montauk, winds were sweeping the coast. The waves exploded in clouds of spray. Ardis was talking to a woman not much older than herself, whose husband had just died of a brain tumor at the age of forty. He had diagnosed it himself, the woman said. He'd been sitting in a theater when he suddenly realized he couldn't see the wall just to his right. At the funeral, she said, there had been two women she did not recognize and who did not come to the reception afterward.

"Of course, he was a surgeon," she said, "and they're drawn to surgeons like flies. But I never suspected. I suppose I'm the world's greatest fool."

The trees streamed past in the dark as they drove home. Their house rose in the brilliant headlights. She thought she had caught sight of something and found herself hoping her husband had not. She was nervous as they walked across the grass. The stars were numberless. They would open the door and go inside, where all was familiar, even serene.

After a while they would prepare for bed while the wind seized the corners of the house and the dark leaves thrashed each other. They would turn out the lights. All that was outside would be left in wildness, in the glory of the wind.

It was true. He was there. He was lying on his side, his whitish coat ruffled. In the morning light she approached slowly. When he raised his head his eyes were hazel and gold. He was not that young, she saw, but his power was that he was unbowed. She spoke in a natural voice.

"Come," she said.

She took a few steps. At first he did not move. She glanced back again. He was following.

It was still early. As they reached the road a car passed, drab and sun-faded. A girl was in the back seat, head fallen wearily, being driven home, Ardis thought, after the exhausting night. She felt an inexplicable envy.

It was warm but the true heat had not risen. Several times she waited while he drank from puddles at the edge of the road, standing in them as he did, his large, wet toenails gleaming like ivory.

Suddenly from a porch rushed another dog, barking fiercely. The great hound turned, teeth bared. She held her breath, afraid of the sight of one of them limp and bleeding, but violent as it sounded they kept a distance between them. After a few snaps it was over. He came along less steadily, strands of wet hair near his mouth.

At the house he went to the porch and stood waiting. It was plain he wanted to go inside. He had returned. He must be starving, she thought. She looked around to see if there was anyone in sight. A chair she had not noticed before was out on the grass, but the house was as still as ever, not even the curtains breathing. With a hand that seemed not even hers she tried the door. It was unlocked.

The hallway was dim. Beyond it was a living room in disorder, couch cushions rumpled, glasses on the tables, papers, shoes. In the dining room there were piles of books. It was the house of an artist, abundance, disregard.

There was a large desk in the bedroom, in the middle of which, among paper clips and letters, a space had been cleared. Here were sheets of paper written in an almost illegible hand, incomplete lines and words that omitted certain vowels. *Deth of fathr*, she read, then indecipherable things and something that seemed to be *carrges sent empty*, and at the bottom, set apart, two words, *anew, anew*. In a different hand was the page of a letter, *I deeply love you. I admire you. I love you and admire you.* She could not read anymore. She was too uneasy. There were things she did not want to know. In a hammered silver frame was the photograph of a woman, face darkened by shadow, leaning against a wall, the unseen white of a villa somewhere behind. Through the slatted blinds one could hear the soft clack of palm fronds, the birds high above, in the villa where he had found her, where her youth had been bold as a declaration of war. No, that was not it. He had met her on a beach, they had gone to the villa. What is powerful is a glimpse of a truer life. She read the slanting inscription in Spanish, *Tus besos me destierran.* She put the picture down. A photograph was sacrosanct, you were excluded from it, always. So that was the wife. *Tus besos*, your kisses.

She wandered, nearly dreaming, into a large bathroom that looked out on the garden. As she entered, her heart almost stopped—she caught sight of somebody in the mirror. It took a second before she realized it was herself and, as she looked more closely, a not wholly recognizable, even an illicit self, in soft, grainy light. She understood suddenly, she accepted the fate that meant she was to be found here, that Brennan would be returning and discover her, having stopped for the mail or bread. Out of nowhere she would hear the paralyzing sound of footsteps or a car. Still, she continued to look at herself. She was in the house of the poet, the demon. She had entered forbidden rooms. *Tus besos* . . . the words had not died. At that moment the dog came to the door, stood there, and then fell to the floor, his knowing eyes on her, like an intimate friend. She turned to him. All she had never done seemed at hand.

Deliberately, without thinking, she began to remove her clothes. She went no further than the waist. She was dazzled by what she was doing. There in the silence with the sunlight outside she stood slender and half-naked, the missing image of herself, of all women. The dog's eyes were raised to her as if in reverence. He was unbetraying, a companion like no other. She remembered certain figures ahead of her at school. Kit Vining, Nan Boudreau. Legendary faces and reputations. She had longed to be like them but never seemed to have the chance. She leaned forward to stroke the beautiful head.

"You're a big fellow." The words seemed authentic, more authentic than anything she had said for a long time. "A very big fellow."

His long tail stirred and with faint sound brushed the floor. She kneeled and stroked his head again and again.

There was the crackling of gravel beneath the tires of a car. It brought her abruptly to her senses. Hurriedly, almost in panic, she threw on her clothes and made her way to the kitchen. She would run along the porch if necessary and then from tree to tree.

She opened the door and listened. Nothing. As she was going quickly down the back steps, by the side of the house she saw her husband. Thank God, she thought helplessly.

They approached each other slowly. He glanced at the house.

"I brought the car. Is anyone here?"

There was a moment's pause.

"No, no one." She felt her face stiffen, as if she were telling a lie.

"What were you doing?" he asked.

"I was in the kitchen," she said. "I was trying to find something to feed him."

"Did you find it?"

"Yes. No," she said.

He stood looking at her and finally said,

"Let's go."

As they backed out, she caught sight of the dog just lying down in the shade, sprawled, disconsolate. She felt the nakedness beneath her clothes, the satisfaction. They turned onto the road.

"Somebody's got to feed him," she said as they drove. She was looking out at the houses and fields. Warren said nothing. He was driving faster. She turned back to look. For a moment she thought she saw him following, far behind.

Late that day she went shopping and came home about five. The wind, which had arisen anew, blew the door shut with a bang.

"Warren?"

"Did you see him?" her husband said.

"Yes."

He had come back. He was out there where the land went up slightly.

"I'm going to call the animal shelter," she said.

"They won't do anything. He's not a stray."

"I can't stand it. I'm calling someone," she said.

"Why don't you call the police? Maybe they'll shoot him."

"Why don't you do it?" she said coldly. "Borrow someone's gun. He's driving me crazy."

It remained light until past nine, and in the last of it, with the clouds a deeper blue than the sky, she went out quietly, far across the grass. Her husband watched from the window. She was carrying a white bowl.

She could see him very clearly, the gray of his muzzle there in the muted grass and when she was close the clear, tan eyes. In an almost ceremonial way she knelt down. The wind was blowing her hair. She seemed almost a mad person there in the fading light.

"Here. Drink something," she said.

His gaze, somehow reproachful, drifted away. He was like a fugitive sleeping on his coat. His eyes were nearly closed.

My life has meant nothing, she thought. She wanted above all else not to confess that.

They ate dinner in silence. Her husband did not look at her. Her face annoyed him, he did not know why. She could be good-looking but there were times when she was not. Her face was like a series of photographs, some of which ought to have been thrown away. Tonight it was like that.

"The sea broke through into Sag Pond today," she said dully.

"Did it?"

"They thought some little girl had drowned. The fire trucks were there. It turned out she had just strayed off." After a pause, "We have to do something," she said.

"Whatever happens is going to happen," he told her.

"This is different," she said. She suddenly left the room. She felt close to tears.

Her husband's business was essentially one of giving advice. He had a life that served other lives, helped them come to agreements, end marriages, defend themselves against former friends. He was accomplished at it. Its language and techniques were part of him. He lived amid disturbance and self-interest but always protected from it. In his files were letters, memorandums, secrets of careers. One thing he had seen: how near men could be to disaster no matter how secure they seemed. He had seen events turn, one ruinous thing following another. It could happen without warning. Sometimes they were able to save themselves, but there was a point at which they could not. He sometimes wondered about himself—when the blow came and the beams began to give and come apart, what would happen? She was calling Brennan's house again. There was never an answer.

During the night the wind blew itself out. In the morning at first light, Warren could feel the stillness. He lay in bed without moving. His wife's back was turned toward him. He could feel her denial.

He rose and went to the window. The dog was still there, he could see its shape. He knew little of animals and nothing of nature but he could tell what had happened. It was lying in a different way.

"What is it?" she asked. She had come up beside him. It seemed she stood there for a long time. "He's dead."

She started for the door. He held her by the arm.

"Let me go," she said.

"Ardis . . ."

She began to weep,

"Let me go."

"Leave him alone!" he called after her. "Let him be!"

She ran quickly across the grass in her nightgown. The ground was wet. As she came closer she paused to calm herself, to find courage. She regretted only one thing—she had not said good-bye.

She took a step or two forward. She could sense the heavy, limp weight of him, a weight that would disperse, become something else, the sinews fading, the bones becoming light. She longed to do what she had never done, embrace him. At that moment he raised his head.

"Warren!" she cried, turning toward the house. "Warren!"

As if the shouts distressed him, the dog was rising to his feet. He moved wearily off. Hands pressed to her mouth, she stared at the place where he had been, where the grass was flattened slightly. All night again. Again all night. When she looked, he was some distance off.

She ran after him. Warren could see her. She seemed free. She seemed like another woman, a younger woman, the kind one saw in the dusty fields by the sea, in a bikini, stealing potatoes in bare feet.

She did not see him again. She went many times past the house, occasionally seeing Brennan's car there, but never a sign of the dog, or along the road or off in the fields.

One night in Cato's at the end of August, she saw Brennan himself at the bar. His arm was in a sling, from what sort of accident she could not guess. He was talking intently to the bartender, the same fierce eloquence, and though the restaurant was crowded, the stools next to him were empty. He was alone. The dog was not outside, nor in his car, nor part of his life anymore—gone, lost, living else-where, his name perhaps to be written in a line someday though most probably he was forgotten, but not by her.

TWENTY MINUTES

This happened near Carbondale to a woman named Jane Vare. I met her once at a party. She was sitting on a couch with her arms stretched out on either side and a drink in one hand. We talked about dogs.

She had an old greyhound. She'd bought him to save his life, she said. At the tracks they put them down rather than feed them when they stopped winning, sometimes three or four together, threw them in the back of a truck and drove to the dump. This dog was named Phil. He was stiff and nearly blind, but she admired his dignity. He sometimes lifted his leg against the wall, almost as high as the door handle, but he had a fine face.

Tack on the kitchen table, mud on the wide-board floor. In she strode like a young groom in a worn jacket and boots. She had what they called a good seat and ribbons layered like feathers on the wall. Her father had lived in Ireland where they rode into the dining room on Sunday morning and the host died fallen on the bed in full attire. Her own life had become like that. Money and dents in the side of her nearly new Swedish car. Her husband had been gone for a year.

Around Carbondale the river drops down and widens.

There's a spidery trestle bridge, many times repainted, and they used to mine coal.

It was late in the afternoon and a shower had passed. The light was silvery and strange. Cars emerging from the rain drove with their headlights on and the windshield wipers going. The yellow road machinery parked along the shoulder seemed unnaturally bright.

It was the hour after work when irrigation water glistens high in the air, the hills have begun to darken and the meadows are like ponds.

She was riding alone up along the ridge. She was on a horse named Fiume, big, well formed, but not very smart. He didn't hear things and sometimes stumbled when he walked. They had gone as far as the reservoir and then come back, riding to the west where the sun was going down. He could run, this horse. His hooves were pounding. The back of her shirt was filled with wind, the saddle was creaking, his huge neck was dark with sweat. They came along the ditch and toward a gate—they jumped it all the time.

At the last moment something happened. It took just an instant. He may have crossed his legs or hit a hole but he suddenly gave way. She went over his head and as if in slow motion he came after. He was upside down—she lay there watching him float toward her. He landed on her open lap.

It was as if she'd been hit by a car. She was stunned but felt unhurt. For a minute she imagined she might stand up and brush herself off.

The horse had gotten up. His legs were dirty and there

was dirt on his back. In the silence she could hear the clink of the bridle and even the water flowing in the ditch. All around her were meadows and stillness. She felt sick to her stomach. It was all broken down there—she knew it although she could feel nothing. She knew she had some time. Twenty minutes, they always said.

The horse was pulling at some grass. She rose to her elbows and was immediately dizzy. "God damn you!" she called. She was nearly crying. "Git! Go home!" Someone might see the empty saddle. She closed her eyes and tried to think. Somehow she could not believe it—nothing that had happened was true.

It was that way the morning they came and told her Privet had been hurt. The foreman was waiting in the pasture. "Her leg's broken," he said.

"How did it happen?"

He didn't know. "It looks like she got kicked," he guessed.

The horse was lying under a tree. She knelt and stroked its boardlike nose. The large eyes seemed to be looking elsewhere. The vet would be driving up from Catherine Store trailing a plume of dust, but it turned out to be a long time before he came. He parked a little way off and walked over. Afterward he said what she had known he would say, they were going to have to put her down.

She lay remembering that. The day had ended. Lights were appearing in parts of distant houses. The six o'clock news was on. Far below she could see the hayfield of Piñones and much closer, a hundred yards off, a truck. It belonged to someone trying to build a house down there. It was up on blocks, it didn't run. There were other houses within a mile or so. On the other side of the ridge the metal roof, hidden in trees, of old man Vaughn who had once owned all of this and now could hardly walk. Further west the beautiful tan adobe Bill Millinger built before he went broke or whatever it was. He had wonderful taste. The house had the peeled log ceilings of the Southwest, Navajo rugs, and fireplaces in every room. Wide views of the mountains through windows of tinted glass. Anyone who knew enough to build a house like that knew everything.

She had given the famous dinner for him, unforgettable night. The clouds had been blowing off the top of Sopris all day, then came the snow. They talked in front of the fire. There were wine bottles crowded on the mantle and everyone in good clothes. Outside the snow poured down. She was wearing silk pants and her hair was loose. In the end she stood with him near the doorway to her kitchen. She was filled with warmth and a little drunk, was he?

He was watching her finger on the edge of his jacket lapel. Her heart thudded. "You're not going to make me spend the night alone?" she asked.

He had blond hair and small ears close to his head. "Oh . . ." he began.

"What?"

"Don't you know? I'm the other way."

Which way, she insisted. It was such a waste. The roads were almost closed, the house lost in snow. She began to plead—she couldn't help it—and then became angry. The silk pants, the furniture, she hated it all.

In the morning his car was outside. She found him in the kitchen making breakfast. He'd slept on the couch, combed his longish hair with his fingers. On his cheeks was a blond stubble. "Sleep well, darling?" he asked.

Sometimes it was the other way around—in Saratoga in the bar where the idol was the tall Englishman who had made so much money at the sales. Did she live there? he asked. When you were close his eyes looked watery but in that English voice which was so pure, "It's marvelous to come to a place and see someone like you," he said.

She hadn't really decided whether to stay or leave and she had a drink with him. He smoked a cigarette.

"You haven't heard about those?" she said.

"No, what about them?"

"They'll give thee cancer."

"Thee?"

"It's what the Quakers say."

"Are you really a Quaker?"

"Oh, back a ways."

He had her by the elbow. "Do you know what I'd like? I'd like to fuck thee," he said.

She bent her arm to remove it.

"I mean it," he said. "Tonight."

"Some other time," she told him.

"I don't have another time. My wife's coming tomorrow, I only have tonight."

"That's too bad. I have every night."

She hadn't forgotten him, though she'd forgotten his name. His shirt had elegant blue stripes. "Oh, damn you," she suddenly cried. It was the horse. He hadn't gone. He was over by the fence. She began to call him, "Here, boy. Come here," she begged. He wouldn't move.

She didn't know what to do. Five minutes had passed, perhaps longer. Oh, God, she said, oh, Lord, oh God our Father. She could see the long stretch of road that came up from the highway, the unpaved surface very pale. Someone would come up that road and not turn off. The disastrous road. She had been driving it that day with her husband. There was something he had been meaning to tell her, Henry said, his head tilted back at a funny angle. He was making a change in his life. Her heart took a skip. He was breaking off with Mara, he said.

There was a silence.

Finally she said, "With who?"

He realized his mistake. "The girl who . . . in the architect's office. She's the draftsman."

"What do you mean, breaking it off?" It was hard for her to speak. She was looking at him as one would look at a fugitive.

"You knew about that, didn't you? I was sure you knew. Anyway it's over. I wanted to tell you. I wanted to put it all behind us."

"Stop the car," she said. "Don't say any more, stop here."

He drove alongside her trying to explain but she was picking up the biggest stones she could find and throwing them at the car. Then she cut unsteadily across the fields, the sage bushes scratching her legs.

When she heard him drive up after midnight she jumped from bed and shouted from the window, "No, no! Go away!"

"What I never understood is why no one told me," she used to say. "They were supposed to be my friends."

Some failed, some divorced, some got shot in trailers like

Doug Portis who had the excavation business and was seeing the policeman's wife. Some like her husband moved to Santa Barbara and became the extra man at dinner parties.

It was growing dark. Help me, someone, help me, she kept repeating. Someone would come, they had to. She tried not to be afraid. She thought of her father who could explain life in one sentence, "They knock you down and you get up. That's what it's all about." He recognized only one virtue. He would hear what had happened, that she merely lay there. She had to try to get home, even if she went only a little way, even a few yards.

Pushing with her palms she managed to drag herself, calling the horse as she did. Perhaps she could grab a stirrup if he came. She tried to find him. In the last of the light she saw the fading cottonwoods but the rest had disappeared. The fence posts were gone. The meadows had drifted away.

She tried to play a game, she wasn't lying near the ditch, she was in another place, in all the places, on Eleventh Street in that first apartment above the big skylight of the restaurant, the morning in Sausalito with the maid knocking on the door and Henry trying to call in Spanish, not now, not now! And postcards on the marble of the dresser and things they'd bought. Outside the hotel in Haiti the cabdrivers were leaning on their cars and calling out in soft voices, Hey, *blanc*, you like to go to a nice beach? Ibo beach? They wanted thirty dollars for the day, they said, which meant the price was probably about five. Go ahead, give it to him, she said. She could be there so easily, or in her own bed reading on a stormy day with the rain gusting against the window and the dogs near her feet. On the desk were photographs: horses, and her

45

jumping, and one of her father at lunch outside when he was thirty, at Burning Tree. She had called him one day—she was getting married, she said. Married, he said, to whom? A man named Henry Vare, she said, who is wearing a beautiful suit, she wanted to add, and has wonderful wide hands. Tomorrow, she said.

"Tomorrow?" He sounded farther away. "Are you sure you're doing the right thing?"

"Absolutely."

"God bless you," he said.

That summer was the one they came here—it was where Henry had been living—and bought the place past the Macraes'. All year they fixed up the house and Henry started his landscaping business. They had their own world. Up through the fields in nothing but shorts, the earth warm under their feet, skin flecked with dirt from swimming in the ditch where the water was chilly and deep, like two sun-bleached children but far better, the screen door slamming, things on the kitchen table, catalogues, knives, new everything. Autumn with its brilliant blue skies and the first storms coming up from the west.

It was dark now, everywhere except up by the ridge. There were all the things she had meant to do, to go East again, to visit certain friends, to live a year by the sea. She could not believe it was over, that she was going to be left here on the ground.

Suddenly she started to call for help, wildly, the cords standing out in her neck. In the darkness the horse raised his head. She kept shouting. She already knew it was a thing she would pay for, she was loosing the demonic. At last she stopped. She could hear the pounding of her heart and beyond that something else. Oh, God, she began to beg. Lying there she heard the first solemn drumbeats, terrible and slow.

Whatever it was, however bad, I'm going to do it as my father would, she thought. Hurriedly she tried to imagine him and as she was doing it a length of something went through her, something iron. In one unbelievable instant she realized the power of it, where it would take her, what it meant.

Her face was wet and she was shivering. Now it was here. Now you must do it, she realized. She knew there was a God, she hoped it. She shut her eyes. When she opened them it had begun, so utterly unforeseen and with such speed. She saw something dark moving along the fence line. It was her pony, the one her father had given her long ago, her black pony going home, across the broad fields, across the grassland. Wait, wait for me!

She began to scream.

Lights were jerking up and down along the ditch. It was a pickup coming over the uneven ground, the man who was sometimes building the lone house and a high school girl named Fern who worked at the golf course. They had the windows up and, turning, their lights swept close to the horse but they didn't see him. They saw him later, coming back in silence, the big handsome face in the darkness looking at them dumbly.

"He's saddled," Fern said in surprise.

He was standing calmly. That was how they found her. They put her in the back—she was limp, there was dirt in her ears—and drove into Glenwood at eighty miles an hour, not even stopping to call ahead.

That wasn't the right thing, as someone said later. It would have been better if they had gone the other way, about three miles up the road to Bob Lamb's. He was the vet but he might have done something. Whatever you said, he was the best doctor around.

They would have pulled in with the headlights blooming on the white farmhouse as happened so many nights. Everyone knew Bob Lamb. There were a hundred dogs, his own among them, buried in back of the barn.

PLATINUM

The Brule apartment had a magnificent view of the park, bare and vast in winter and in the summer a rich sea of green. The apartment was in a fine building, narrow but tall, and it was in a way comforting to think of how many others there were, dignified and calm, building upon fine building, all with their unsmiling doormen and solemn entrances. Rare carpets, servants, expensive furniture. Brule had paid more than nine hundred thousand for it at a time when prices were high, but the apartment was worth far more now, priceless, in fact. It had high ceilings, afternoon sunlight, and wide doors with curved brass handles. There were deep armchairs, flowers, tables dense with photographs, and many pictures on the walls, including Vollard prints in the hallway that led to the bedrooms and a ravishing dark painting by Camille Bombois.

Brule was one of those men about whom more is rumored than known. He was in his fifties and successful. He had defended some notorious clients and, less publicized, was said to have done unpaid work for those with no resources or hope. Details were vague. He had a soft voice that nevertheless carried authority and iron beneath a calm smile. He walked to work, perhaps a mile down the avenue, in a cashmere overcoat and scarf during the winter, and the doormen, who murmured good morning, received five hundred dollars apiece at Christmas. He was a figure of decency and honor, and like the old men described by Cicero who planted orchards they would not live to see the fruit from, but who did it out of a sense of responsibility and respect for the gods, he had a desire to bequeath the best of what he had known to his descendants.

His wife, Pascale, who was French, was warm and understanding. She was his second wife and had herself been married before, to a famous Parisian jeweler. She had no children of her own and her only fault, Brule felt, was she didn't like to cook. She couldn't cook and talk at the same time, she said. She was not beautiful but had an intelligent, faintly Asiatic face. Her generosity and good instincts were inborn.

"Look," she had said to his daughters when she and Brule were married, "I'm not your mother and I can never be, but I hope that we'll be friends. If we are, good, and if not, you can still count on me for anything."

The daughters were young girls at the time. As it turned out, they loved her. The three of them and their husbands and children came on all the holidays and often, though not all at once, of course, for dinner. They were an intimate and devoted family, a matter of great pride to Brule, the more so since his first marriage had failed.

You belonged to the family, not as someone who happened to be married to a daughter, but entirely. You were one of them, one for all and all for one. The oldest daughter, Grace, had told her husband,

"You have to really get used to the plural of things now."

Brian Woodra had married Sally, the youngest, on a glorious summer day on a lawn set with countless white chairs, the women in clinging dresses. Sally was in a gown of white, stiffened silk, sleeveless, with wide shoulder straps and her dark hair gleaming on her slender back. Her ears had fluted silvery earrings and her face was filled with joy and the occasional concern that things go right, a lovely face with only the barest hint of smallness behind it and you instantly saw the expense of her upbringing. A New York girl, smart and assured. She'd gone to Skidmore, where she roomed with two nymphomaniacs, she liked to say, wanting to shock.

The groom was no taller than she was and slightly bow-legged with a wide jaw and winning smile. He was lively and well liked. His friends from college and even prep school came to the wedding and rose to give their fond recollections of him and predict the worst. At the moment of vow he found himself overcome by his wife-to-be's purity and beauty, as if it were for the first time fully revealed.

The great tent in which the wedding dinner was held had long tables with large arrangements of flowers. As evening came, the tent slowly bloomed with light from within like an immense, ethereal ship, destined for voyage on the sea or in the heavens, one could not tell. Brule told his new son-in-law that he, Brian, was now to know the greatest happiness that one could experience on earth, referring to matrimony, of course.

For a wedding present they were given a cruise in the wake of Odysseus along the Anatolian coast, and in not much more than a year their first child came, a little girl they named Lily, loving and good-natured. Sally was a mother who, though completely involved in her child, still found time for all the rest, entertaining, seeing films, dinners with her husband, equality, friends. The apartment was a little on the dark side, but she did not expect to be in it forever. Grace lived just ten blocks away with her husband and two children, and Eva, the middle sister, was married to a sculptor and lived downtown.

Lily was delicious. From the beginning she loved to be in bed with her mother and father, especially her father, and when she was three whispered to him in adoration,

"I want to be yours."

Two years later, as a reward, to make up for all the attention given to her new little brother, Brian took her to Paris for five days, just the two of them. In retrospect it was the moment of her childhood he cherished most. She behaved like a woman, a companion. It was impossible to love her more. They ate breakfast in the room and wrote postcards together, took the long, arrowy boat up and down the Seine, beneath the bridges, went to the bird market and the museums, Versailles, and in the giant Ferris wheel near the Concorde one afternoon rose high above the city, alarmingly high; Brian himself was frightened.

"Do you like it?" he asked.

"I'm trying to," she said.

No one is braver than you, he thought.

At day's end—the light was just fading—he felt spent. At the hotel, near the reception, there was a Canadian couple waiting for a taxi. Lily was watching the indicator light for the elevator, which had remained for a long time at the fifth floor.

"Is it broken, Daddy?"

"It's just someone taking their time."

He could hear the couple talking. The woman, blond and

smooth-browed, was in a glittering silver top. They were going out for the evening, into the stream of lights, boulevards, restaurants brimming with talk. He had only a glimpse of them setting forth, the light on her hair, the cab door held open for her, and for a moment forgot that he had everything.

"Here it comes," he heard his daughter call, "Daddy, here it comes."

In late April was Michael Brule's fifty-eighth birthday. For gifts he had asked only for things to eat or drink, but Del, Eva's husband, had carved a beautiful wooden seabird for him, unpainted and on legs thin as straws. Brule was deeply touched.

Brian was in the kitchen cooking. It was noisy. The children were playing some kind of game, to the annoyance of the dog, an old Scottie.

"Don't frighten her! Don't frighten her!" they cried.

It was risotto Brian was making, adding warm broth in small amounts and stirring slowly, to the rapt attention of one of the girls hired to help serve.

"It's almost ready," he called. He could hear the family voices, the dog barking, the laughter.

The girl, in a white shirt and velvety pants, was watching in fascination. He held out the wooden spoon on which there was a sample.

"Want to taste it?" he asked.

"Yes, darling," she said.

Ssh, he gestured playfully. Not looking at him, she took the portion of rice between her lips. Pamela was her name. She wasn't really a caterer; she worked at the U.N. She and the other girl were hired by the hour.

Her legs Brian saw when she came into the bar at the U.N. Hotel and sat down beside him with a smile, completely at ease. He had been nervous, but it left him immediately. From the first moment he felt a thrilling, natural complicity. His heart filled with excitement, like a sail.

"So," he began, "Pamela . . ."

"Pam."

"Would you like a drink?"

"Is that white wine?"

"Yes."

"Good. White wine."

She was twenty-two, from Pennsylvania, but with some kind of rare, natural polish.

"I must say, you are . . ." he said, then felt suddenly cautious.

"What?"

"Definitely good-looking."

"Oh, I don't know."

"It's unarguable. I'm just curious," he said, "how much do you weigh?"

"A hundred and sixteen."

"That's what I would have thought."

"Really?"

"No, but anything you would have said."

She had told them she had a doctor's appointment and needed extra time for lunch. She told him that. As she entered the hotel elevator he could not help but notice her fine hips. Then, incredibly, they were in the room. His heart was uncontrollable and everything was prepared for them, the sleek furnishings, the chairs, the thick fresh towels in the bath. There had been four murders in Brooklyn the night before. The brokers were going wild on Wall Street. On Fourteenth, men stood in the cold beside tables of watches and socks. The madman on Fifty-seventh was singing arias at the top of his voice, buildings were being torn down, new towers rising. She rose to draw the drapes and for a moment stood in the space between them, in the light and looking down. The splendor and newness of her! He had known nothing like it.

Her apartment was borrowed, from someone on assignment. Even at that, it was sparsely furnished. He wanted to give her something every time he saw her, a gift, something unexpected, a chrome and leather chair that he showed her in the window before he ordered it delivered, a ring, a rosewood box, but he was careful to keep nothing that came from her—note, email, photograph—that might betray him. There was one exception, a picture he had taken as she half sat up in bed, from over her bare shoulder, breasts, smooth stomach, thighs, you would not know who it was. He kept it at work between the pages of a book. He liked to turn to it and remember.

In those days of desire so deep that it left him empty-legged, he did not behave unnaturally at home—if anything he was more loving and devoted although Lily, especially, was beyond increased devotion. He came home filled with forbidden happiness, forbidden but unrivalled, and embraced his wife and played with or read to his children. The prohibited feeds the appetite for all the rest. He went from one to the other with a heart that was pure. On Park Avenue he stood on the island in the middle, waiting to cross. The traffic lights were turning red as far as he could see. The distant buildings stood majestic in the monied haze. Beside him were people in coats and hats, with packages, briefcases, none of them as fortunate as he. The city was a paradise. The glory of it was that it sheltered his singular life.

"Am I your mistress?" she asked one day.

"Mistress?" No, he thought, that was something older, even old-fashioned. He knew of no word to truly describe her other than probable downfall or perhaps fate.

"What's your wife like?" she said.

"My wife?"

"You'd rather not talk about her."

"No, you'd like her."

"That would be just my luck."

"She doesn't have quite your ideas of how to live."

"I don't know how to live."

"Yes, you do."

"I don't think so."

"You have something not a lot of people have."

"What's that?"

"Real nerve."

When he came home that evening, his wife said,

"Brian, there's something I want to talk to you about, something I have to ask you."

He felt his heart skip. His children were running toward him.

"Daddy!"

"Daddy and I have to talk for a minute," Sally told them. She led him into the living room.

"What's up?" he said as calmly as he could.

Grace and Harry, it turned out, wanted to come with their children and share the gardener's cottage during the two weeks in August that Lily would be off at sleepaway camp and some arrangement could be made for Ian so that Sally and Brian could have some time to themselves. Now that would be impossible.

She went on talking, but Brian barely listened. He was still hearing her first words that had been so frightening. He was rehearsing replies to a far more serious question. He would tell her the truth, could he do that? The truth was essential, yet it was the thing least wanted.

"We should do this over a drink," he would say. "We should do it when we're calmer."

"I'm not going to be calmer."

He had to somehow put it off until she was the way she often was, clever and understanding. He would say something about perspective.

"Just speak in plain English."

"You can't say it in plain English."

"Try," she said.

"You know these things happen. You're a smart woman. You know something about the world."

"Yes, tell me about it."

Her mouth was turned down, a corner of it trembling.

"There's been someone, but it's not important. Can't you see that it's not important?"

"Get out of here," she said, "and don't come back. Don't try to see the children, I won't let you. I'm going to change the locks."

"Sally, you can't do that. I could never live like that. Don't be melodramatic, please. That's not our kind of life." The words were beginning to jam up in his mouth. "This is nothing unsolvable. You know very well that Pascale was your father's mistress, I won't guess for how long."

"They got married."

"That isn't the point."

He was beginning to stutter.

"What *is* the point?"

"The point is there's a superior way of living we should be intelligent enough to understand."

"Which means you having some other woman?"

"You're making this caustic. Don't, please. It's beneath us just to play roles. We're above that. You know that."

"All I know is that you're a cheat."

"I'm not a cheat."

"Daddy's going to kill you."

He couldn't find the words. Whatever he thought of was torn apart by her single-mindedness. But it would never come to this.

On the other hand, Pamela had a life of her own; that was the only flaw. She went out at night, there were parties. Some Tunisians from the delegation were very nice.

"Is that right?" he said.

She'd gone to a party at the Four Seasons, she told him, and walked to work the next morning with a thousand dollars in her shoe, although she didn't say that. One of the Tunisians was particularly nice.

"They like to have fun," she said.

"You're turning into a playgirl," Brian said, a little sourly. "How do I know you're not playing around with this guy?"

"You'd know it."

"Maybe I would. Would you tell me? The truth? What's his name?"

"Tahar."

"I wish you wouldn't."

"I'm not," she said.

In June, Sally and the children went to the country for the summer. For most of the week, Brian was in the city by himself.

"How was I lucky enough to meet you?" he said.

They were having dinner amid the liveliness of the crowd, the intimacy within it, the voices all around. He had seen most of them. She was by far the prize of the room.

"We're going to be friends for a long time," she promised.

Summer mornings with their first, soft light. Amorous mornings, the red numbers flicking silently on the clock, the first sunlight in the trees. Her stunning naked back. The most sacred hours, he realized, of his life.

Dressing one morning, she asked,

"Whose are these?"

In a folded packet on the night table had been a pair of shining earrings.

"Are they your wife's?"

She was trying one on, fastening it to her ear. She turned her head one way and the other, looking at herself in the mirror.

"What are they, silver?"

"They're platinum. Better than silver."

"They're your wife's."

"They were being repaired. I had to pick them up."

It was hard not to admire her, her bare neck, her aplomb.

"Can I borrow them?" she asked.

"I can't. She knows I was supposed to pick them up."

"Just say they weren't ready."

"Darling . . ."

"I'll give them back. Is that what you're afraid of? I'd just like to wear them once, something that's hers but at the moment mine."

"That's very Bette Davis."

"Who?"

"Just be careful and don't lose them," he managed to say.

That was a Tuesday. Two nights later a terrible event occurred. It was at a reception given by a group dedicated to the Impressionists; Pascale was a supporter but was away that evening and couldn't attend. Sally had insisted that Brian go, and in the crowd coming up the stairway he had seen, with a stab of jealousy, more fierce because it was a complete surprise, Pamela. He began to push his way forward to see who she might be with.

"Hey, where are you going in such a hurry?"

It was Del, his brother-in-law.

"Where have you been hiding?"

"Hiding?"

"We haven't seen you for weeks."

Brian liked him, but not at this moment.

"Why don't you come to dinner with us tonight, afterward?"

"I can't," Brian said unthinkingly.

"Come on, we're going to Elio's," Del insisted. "Look at all these women. Where do they come from? They weren't around when I was single."

Brian hardly heard him. Past his brother-in-law, near the windows not fifteen feet away, he could see Pamela talking to Michael Brule, not just exchanging a greeting but in some sort of conversation. She was wearing a pale blue dress, one he liked, cut low in back. Her dark hair was tied and he could see quite clearly, she was wearing the earrings. They were unmistakable. He moved a bit so as not to be observed, his heart beating furiously. Finally Brule was gone.

"Darling, you must be crazy," he said in a furious, low voice when he reached her.

"Hello," she said cheerfully.

There was always such life in that voice.

"What are you doing?" he insisted.

"What do you mean?"

"The earrings!"

"I'm wearing them," she said.

"You can't wear them. That was my father-in-law. He bought them! He gave them to Sally! Why did you wear them here?"

His voice was still low but people close by could hear the anxiety.

"How was I to know?" Pamela said.

"Jesus, I knew I shouldn't have lent them to you."

"Oh, take the damned earrings," she said, suddenly annoyed.

"Don't do that."

She was taking them off. It was the first time he had seen

her angry and suddenly he was frightened, afraid to be in her disfavor.

"Don't, please. I'm the one who should be angry," he said.

She pushed them into his hand.

"And yes," she said, "he saw them." Then, with astounding confidence, "Don't worry, he won't say anything."

"What do you mean? What makes you so sure?" The answer suddenly struck him like an illness.

"Don't worry, he won't," she said.

Somebody was handing her a glass of wine.

"Thank you," she said calmly. "This is Brian, a friend of mine. Brian, this is Tahar."

She did not answer the phone that night. The next day, his father-in-law called and asked to meet for lunch, it was important.

They met at a restaurant Brule favored, with formal service and a European-looking clientele. It was near his office. Brule was reading the menu when Brian arrived. He looked up. His glasses, which were rimless, caught the light in a way that made his eyes almost invisible.

"I'm glad you were able to come," he said, returning to the menu.

Brian made an effort to read the menu himself. He made some remark about not having had a chance to say hello the night before.

"I was extremely disturbed by what I learned last night," Brule said, as if not having heard.

The waiter stood reciting some dishes that were not on the menu. Brian was preparing his reply, but after they had ordered, it was Brule who continued.

"Your behavior isn't worthy of the husband of my daughter," he said.

"I don't know if you're in a position to say that," Brian managed.

"Please don't interrupt me. Let me finish. You'll have your chance afterward. I discover that you've been having an affair with a young woman—I'm aware of the details, believe me— and if you place any value at all on your wife and family, I would say you have put that in grave jeopardy. If Sally were to learn of it, I'm certain she would leave you and, under the circumstances, probably retain custody, and I would support her in that. Fortunately, she doesn't know, so there is still the possibility of this not being disastrous, providing you do the necessary thing."

There was a pause. It was as if Brian had been asked a bewildering question, the answer to which he should know. His thoughts were fluttering, however, ungraspable.

"What thing is that?" he said, though knowing.

"You give up this girl and never see her again."

This wonderful girl, this smooth-shouldered girl.

"And what about you?" Brian said as evenly as he could.

Brule ignored it.

"Otherwise," Brule continued, "I'm loath to think of it, Sally will have to know."

Brian's jaw, despite his effort, was trembling. It was not only humiliation, there was a burning jealousy. His father-in-law seemed to hold every advantage. The manicured hands had touched her, the aging body had been imposed on hers. Some plates were served but Brian did not pick up his fork.

"She wouldn't be the only one to know, would she? Pascale would know everything, too," he said.

"If you mean you would try to implicate me, I can only say that would be futile and foolish."

"But you wouldn't be able to deny it," Brian said stubbornly.

"I'd most certainly deny it. It would just be seen as a frantic attempt to deflect your guilt and blacken others. No one would believe it, I assure you. Most important, Pamela would back me up."

"What an incredible, what a pompous statement. No, she won't."

"Yes, she will. I've taken care of that."

He was not to see or speak to her again, without explanation or any farewell.

"I don't believe it," Brian said.

He did not stay. He pushed back his chair, dropped his napkin on the table, and, excusing himself, left. Brule continued with lunch. He told the waiter to cancel the other order.

The earrings were still in his pocket. He set them in front of him and tried to call. She was away from her desk, her voice said. Please leave a message. He hung up. He felt a terrifying urgency; every minute was unbearable. He thought of going to her office but it would be difficult to talk to her there. She was away from her desk, in someone else's office. Even that caused him unhappiness and envy. He thought of the hotel bar. In she had come in a short black skirt and high heels, on her white neck an opaque, blue necklace. With Brule it could not have been anything but sordid, some suggestion in that low voice, some clumsy act on a couch. What could it have been on her part except resignation, finally? He called again, and three or four more times during the afternoon, leaving the message to please call back, it was important.

At six, he somehow made his way home. It was one of those evenings like the beginning of a marvelous performance in which everyone somehow had a role. Lights had come on in the windows, the sidewalk restaurants were filling, children were running home late from playing in the park, the promise of fulfillment was everywhere. In the elevator a pretty woman he did not recognize was carrying a large bunch of flowers somewhere upstairs. She avoided looking at him.

He let himself into his apartment and immediately felt its emptiness. The furniture stood silently. The kitchen seemed cold, as if it had never known use. He walked around aimlessly and dropped into a chair. It was six-thirty. She would be home by now, he decided. She wasn't. He made a drink and sat with it, sipping and thinking or rather letting the same helpless thoughts eat deeper, unalterable, as evening slowly filled the room. He turned on some lights and called her again.

The anguish was unbearable. She had been annoyed, but surely that was only at the moment. It could not be that. She had been frightened by Brule somehow. She was not the sort of person to be easily frightened. He made another drink and continued to call. Sometime after ten—his heart leapt—she answered.

"Oh, God," he said, "I've been calling you all day. Where have you been? I've been frantic to talk to you. I had to have lunch with Brule; it was disgusting. I walked out. Has he talked to you?"

"Yes," she said.

"I was afraid so. What did he say?"

"It's not that."

"Of course it's that. He made some threats. Look, I'm coming over."

"No, don't."

"Then you come here."

"I can't," she said.

"Of course you can. You can do anything you want. I feel so terrible. He wanted to prevent me from talking to you. Listen, darling. This may take a little time to work out. We'll have to lie a little low. You know I'm crazy about you. You know no one in the world has ever meant more to me. Whatever he said, nothing can affect that."

"I suppose."

He felt something then, a crack, a fissure. He had the sense of something impending and unbearable.

"It's not you suppose. You know it. Tell me something, tell me the truth. When did it happen between you and him? I just want to know. Before?"

"I don't want to talk about it now," she said.

"Just tell me."

Suddenly something he hadn't thought of came to him. He suddenly understood why she was so hesitant.

"Tell me one thing," he said. "Does he want to keep seeing you?"

"No."

"Is that the truth? You're telling me the truth?"

Sitting in a chair near her, legs sprawled like a lord, was Tahar with a bored look of patience.

"Yes, it's the truth," she said.

"I don't know what the solution is, but I know there is one," Brian assured her.

Tahar could hear only her end of the conversation and did not know who it was with, but he made a slight motion with his chin that said, finish with that. Pam nodded a little in agreement. Tahar did not drink but he offered a powerful intoxicant: darkened skin, white teeth, and a kind of strange perfume that clung even to his clothes. He offered rooms above the souk with a view of the city one could not even imagine, nights of an intense blueness, mornings when you had drifted far from the familiar world. Brian was someone she would remember, perhaps someone she could always call.

Tahar made another gesture of slight annoyance. For him, it was only the beginning.

SUCH FUN

When they left the restaurant, Leslie wanted to go and have a drink at her place, it was only a few blocks away, a large old apartment building with leaded windows on the ground floor and a view over Washington Square. Kathrin said fine, but Jane claimed she was tired.

"Just one drink," Leslie said. "Come on."

"It's too early to go home," Kathrin added.

In the restaurant they had talked about movies, ones they'd seen and ones they hadn't. They talked about movies and Rudy, the headwaiter.

"I always get one of the good tables," said Leslie.

"Is that right?"

"Always."

"And what does he get?"

"It's what he hopes he'll get," Leslie said.

"He's really looking at Jane."

"No, he's not," Jane protested.

"He's got half your clothes off already."

"Don't, please," Jane said.

Leslie and Kathrin had been roommates in college and friends ever since. They had hitchhiked through Europe together, getting as far as Turkey, sleeping in the same bed a lot of the nights and, except once, not fooling around with men or, as it happened that time, boys. Kathrin had long hair combed back dark from a handsome brow and a brilliant smile. She could easily have been a model. There was not much more to her than met the eye, but that had always been enough. Leslie had majored in music but hadn't done anything with it. She had a wonderful way on the telephone, as if she'd known you for years.

In the elevator, Kathrin said,

"God, he's cute."

"Who?"

"Your doorman. What's his name?"

"Santos. He's from Colombia someplace."

"What time does he get off is what I want to know."

"For God's sake."

"That's what they always asked. When I was tending."

"Here we are."

"No, really. Do you ever ask him to change a lightbulb or something?"

Leslie was searching for the key to her door.

"That's the super," Leslie said. "He's another story."

As they went in, she said,

"I don't think there's anything here but scotch. That's OK, isn't it? Bunning drank up everything else."

She went to the kitchen to get glasses and ice. Kathrin sat on the couch with Jane.

"Are you still seeing Andrew?" she said.

"Off and on," Jane said.

"Off and on, that's what I'm looking for. On and off is more like it."

Leslie came back with the glasses and ice. She began to make drinks.

"Well, here's to you," she said. "Here's to me. It's going to be hard moving out of here."

"You're not going to get to keep the apartment?" Kathrin said.

"Twenty-six hundred a month? I couldn't afford it."

"Aren't you going to get something from Bunning?"

"I'm not going to ask for anything. Some of the furniture—I can probably use that—and maybe a little something to get me by the first three or four months. I can stay with my mother if I have to. I hope I don't have to. Or I could stay with you, couldn't I?" she asked Kathrin.

Kathrin had a walk-up on Lexington, one room painted black with mirrors on one wall.

"Of course. Until one of us killed the other," Kathrin said.

"If I had a boyfriend, it would be no problem," Leslie said, "but I was too busy taking care of Bunning to have a boyfriend."

"You're lucky," she said to Jane, "you've got Andy."

"Not really."

"What happened?"

"Nothing, really. He wasn't serious."

"About you."

"That was part of it."

"So, what happened?" Leslie said.

"I don't know. I just wasn't interested in the things he was interested in."

"Such as?" Kathrin said.

"Everything."

"Give us an idea."

"The usual stuff."

"What?"

"Anal sex," Jane said. She'd made it up, on an impulse. She wanted to break through somehow.

"Oh, God," Kathrin said. "Makes me think of my ex."

"Malcolm," said Leslie, "so, where is Malcolm? Are you still in touch?"

"He's over in Europe. No, I never hear from him."

Malcolm wrote for a business magazine. He was short, but a very careful dresser—beautiful, striped suits and shined shoes.

"I wonder how I ever married him," Kathrin said. "I wasn't very foresighted."

"Oh, I can see how it happened," Leslie said. "In fact, I *saw* how it happened. He's very sexy."

"For one thing, it was because of his sister. She was great. We were friends from the first minute. God, this is strong," Kathrin said.

"You want a little more water?"

"Yes. She gave me my first oyster. 'Am I supposed to *eat* that?' I said. 'I'll show you how,' she said, 'just throw them back and swallow.' It was at the bar in Grand Central. Once I had them I couldn't stop. She was so completely up front. 'Are you sleeping with Malcolm?' she asked me. We'd hardly met. She wanted to know what it was like, if he was as good as he looked."

Kathrin had drunk a lot of wine in the restaurant and a cocktail before that. Her lips glistened.

"What was her name?" Jane asked.

"Enid."

"Oh, beautiful name."

"So, anyway, he and I went off—this was before we were married. We had this room with nothing in it but a window and a bed. That's when I was introduced to it."

"To what?" Leslie said.

"In the ass."

"And?"

"I liked it."

Jane was suddenly filled with admiration for her, admiration and embarrassment. This was not like the thing she had made up, it was actual. Why couldn't I ever admit something like that? she thought.

"But you got divorced," she said.

"Well, there's a lot beside that in life. We got divorced because I got tired of him chasing around. He was always covering stories in one place or another, but one time in London the phone rang at two in the morning and he went into the next room to talk. That's when I found out. Of course, she was just one of them."

"You're not drinking," Leslie said to Jane.

"Yes, I am."

"Anyway, we got divorced," Kathrin went on. "So, now it'll be both of us," she said to Leslie. "Join the club."

"Are you really getting divorced?" Jane asked.

"It'll be a relief."

"How long has it been? Six years?"

"Seven."

"That's a long time."

"A very long time."

"How did you meet?" Jane said.

"How did we meet? Through bad luck," Leslie said—she was pouring more scotch into her glass. "Actually, we met when he fell off a boat. I was going out with his cousin at the time. We were sailing, and Bunning claimed he had to do it to get my attention."

"That's so funny."

"Later, he changed his story and said he fell and it had to be *some*where."

Bunning's first name was actually Arthur, Arthur Bunning Hasset, but he hated the Arthur. Everyone liked him. His family owned a button factory and a big house in Bedford called Ha Ha, where he was brought up. In theory he wrote plays, at least one of which was close to being a success and had an off-Broadway run, but after that things became difficult. He had a secretary named Robin—she was called his assistant—who found him incredible and unpredictable, not to mention hilarious, and Leslie herself had always been amused by him, at least for several years, but then the drinking started.

The end had come a week or so before. They were invited to an opening night by a theatrical lawyer and his wife. First there was dinner, and at the restaurant, Bunning, who had started drinking at the apartment, ordered a martini.

"Don't," Leslie said.

He ignored her and was entertaining for a while but then sat silent and drinking while Leslie and the couple went on with the conversation. Suddenly Bunning said in a clear voice,

"Who are these people?"

There was a silence.

"Really, who are they?" Bunning asked again.

The lawyer coughed a little.

"We're their guests," Leslie said coldly.

Bunning's thoughts seemed to pass to something else and a few moments later he got up to go to the men's room. Half an hour passed. Finally Leslie saw him at the bar. He was drinking another martini. His expression was unfocused and childlike.

"Where've you been?" he asked. "I've been looking all over for you."

She was infuriated.

"This is the end," she said.

"No, really, where have you been?" he insisted.

She began to cry.

"I'm going home," he decided.

Still, she remembered the summer mornings in New England when they were first married. Outside the window the squirrels were running down the trunk of a great tree, headfirst, curling to the unseen side of it, their wonderful bushy tails. She remembered driving to little summer theaters, the old iron bridges, cows lying in the wide doorway of a barn, cut cornfields, the smooth slow look of nameless rivers, the beautiful, calm countryside—how happy one is.

"You know," she said, "Marge is crazy about him." Marge was her mother. "That should have been the tip-off."

She went to get more ice and in the hallway caught sight of herself in a mirror.

"Have you ever decided this is as far as you can go?" she said, coming back in.

"What do you mean?" said Kathrin.

Leslie sat down beside her. They were really two of a kind, she decided. They'd been bridesmaids at one another's wedding. They were truly close.

"I mean, have you ever looked at yourself in the mirror and said, I can't . . . this is it."

"What do you mean?"

"With men."

"You're just sore at Bunning."

"Who really needs them?"

"Are you kidding?"

"You want me to tell you something I've found out?"

"What?"

"I don't know . . ." Leslie said helplessly.

"What were you going to say?"

"Oh. My theory . . . My theory is, they remember you longer if you don't do it."

"Maybe," Kathrin said, "but then, what's the point?"

"It's just my theory. They want to divide and conquer."

"Divide?"

"Something like that."

Jane had had less to drink. She wasn't feeling well. She had spent the afternoon waiting to talk to the doctor and emerging onto the unreal street.

She was wandering around the room and picked up a photograph of Leslie and Bunning taken around the time they got married.

"So, what's going to happen to Bunning?" she asked.

"Who knows?" Leslie said. "He's going to go on like he's

going. Some woman will decide she can straighten him out. Let's dance. I feel like dancing."

She made for the CD player and began looking through the CDs until she found one she liked and put it on. There was a moment's pause and then an uneven, shrieking wail began, much too loud. It was bagpipes.

"Oh, God," she cried, stopping it. "It was in the wrong . . . it's one of his."

She found another and a low, insistent drumbeat started slowly, filling the room. She began dancing to it. Kathrin began, too. Then a singer or several of them became part of it, repeating the same words over and over. Kathrin paused to take a drink.

"Don't," Leslie said. "Don't drink too much."

"Why?"

"You won't be able to perform."

"Perform what?"

Leslie turned to Jane and motioned.

"Come on."

"No, I don't really . . ."

"Come on."

The three of them were dancing to the hypnotic, rhythmic singing. It went on and on. Finally Jane sat down, her face moist, and watched. Women often danced together or even alone, at parties. Did Bunning dance? she wondered. No, he wasn't the sort, nor was he embarrassed by it. He drank too much to dance, but really why did he drink? He didn't seem to care about things, but he probably cared very much, beneath.

Leslie sat down beside her.

"I hate to think about moving," she said, her head lolled back carelessly. "I'm going to have to find some other place. That's the worst part."

She raised her head.

"In two years, Bunning's not even going to remember me. Maybe he'll say 'my ex-wife' sometimes. I wanted to have a baby. He didn't like the idea. I said to him, I'm ovulating, and he said, that's wonderful. Well, that's how it is. I'll have one next time. If there is a next time. You have beautiful breasts," she said to Jane.

Jane was struck silent. She would never have had the courage to say something like that.

"Mine are saggy already," Leslie said.

"That's all right," Jane replied foolishly.

"I suppose I could have something done if I had the money. You can fix anything if you have the money."

It was not true, but Jane said,

"I guess you're right."

She had more than sixty thousand dollars she had saved or made from an oil company one of her colleagues had told her about. If she wanted to, she could buy a car, a Porsche Boxster came to mind. She wouldn't even have to sell the oil stock, she could get a loan and pay it off over three or four years and on weekends drive out to the country, to Connecticut, the little coastal towns, Madison, Old Lyme, Niantic, stopping somewhere to have lunch in a place that, in her imagination, was painted white outside. Perhaps there would be a man there, by himself, or even with some other men. He wouldn't have to fall off a boat. It wouldn't be Bunning, of course, but someone like him, wry, a little shy, the man she had somehow failed to meet until then. They'd have dinner, talk. They'd go to Venice, a thing she'd always wanted to do, in the winter, when no one else was there. They'd have a room above the canal and his shirts and shoes, a half-full bottle of she didn't bother to think of exactly what, some Italian wine, and perhaps some books. The sea air from the Adriatic would come in the window at night and she would wake early, before it was really light, to see him sleeping beside her, sleeping and breathing softly.

Beautiful breasts. That was like saying, I love you. She was warmed by it. She wanted to tell Leslie something but it wasn't the time, or maybe it was. She hadn't quite told herself yet.

Another number began and they were dancing again, coming together occasionally, arms flowing, exchanging smiles. Kathrin was like someone at one of the clubs, glamorous, uncaring. She had passion, daring. If you said something, she wouldn't even hear you. She was a kind of cheap goddess and would go on like that for a long time, spending too much for something that caught her fancy, a silk dress or pants, black and clinging, that widened at the bottom, the kind Jane would have with her in Venice. She hadn't had a love affair in college—she was the only one she knew who hadn't. Now she was sorry, she wished she'd had. And gone to the room with only a window and a bed.

"I have to go," she said.

"What?" Leslie said over the music.

"I have to go."

"This has been fun," Leslie said, coming over to her.

They embraced in the doorway, awkwardly, Leslie almost falling down.

"Talk to you in the morning," she said.

Outside, Jane caught a cab, a clean one as it happened, and gave the driver her address near Cornelia Street. They started off, moving fast through the traffic. In the rearview mirror the driver, who was young, saw that Jane, a nice-looking girl about his age, was crying. At a red light next to a drugstore where it was well lit, he could see the tears streaming down her face.

"Excuse me, is something wrong?" he asked.

She shook her head. It seemed she nearly answered.

"What is it?" he said.

"Nothing," she said, shaking her head. "I'm dying."

"You're sick?"

"No, not sick. I'm dying of cancer," she said.

She had said it for the first time, listening to herself. There were four levels and she had the fourth, Stage Four.

"Ah," he said, "are you sure?"

The city was filled with so many strange people he could not tell if she was telling the truth or just imagining something.

"You want to go to the hospital?" he asked.

"No," she said, unable to stop crying. "I'm all right," she told him.

Her face was appealing though streaked with tears. He raised his head a little to see the rest of her. Appealing, too. But what if she is speaking the truth? he wondered. What if God, for whatever reason, has decided to end the life of someone like this? You cannot know. That much he understood.

DUSK

Mrs. Chandler stood alone near the window in a tailored suit, almost in front of the neon sign that said in small red letters PRIME MEATS. She seemed to be looking at onions, she had one in her hand. There was no one else in the store. Vera Pini sat by the cash register in her white smock, staring at the passing cars. Outside it was cloudy and the wind was blowing. Traffic was going by in an almost continuous flow. "We have some good Brie today," Vera remarked without moving. "We just got it in."

"Is it really good?"

"Very good."

"All right, I'll take some." Mrs. Chandler was a steady customer. She didn't go to the supermarket at the edge of town. She was one of the best customers. Had been. She didn't buy that much anymore.

On the plate glass the first drops of rain appeared. "Look at that. It's started," Vera said.

Mrs. Chandler turned her head. She watched the cars go by. It seemed as if it were years ago. For some reason she found herself thinking of the many times she had driven out herself or taken the train, coming into the country, stepping down onto the long, bare platform in the darkness, her husband or a child there to meet her. It was warm. The trees were huge and black. Hello, darling. Hello, Mummy, was it a nice trip?

The small neon sign was very bright in the greyness, there was the cemetery across the street and her own car, a foreign one, kept very clean, parked near the door, facing in the wrong direction. She always did that. She was a woman who lived a certain life. She knew how to give dinner parties, take care of dogs, enter restaurants. She had her way of answering invitations, of dressing, of being herself. Incomparable habits, you might call them. She was a woman who had read books, played golf, gone to weddings, whose legs were good, who had weathered storms, a fine woman whom no one now wanted.

The door opened and one of the farmers came in. He was wearing rubber boots. "Hi, Vera," he said.

She glanced at him. "Why aren't you out shooting?"

"Too wet," he said. He was old and didn't waste words. "The water's a foot high in a lot of places."

"My husband's out."

"Wish you'd told me sooner," the old man said slyly. He had a face that had almost been obliterated by the weather. It had faded like an old stamp.

It was shooting weather, rainy and blurred. The season had started. All day there had been the infrequent sound of guns and about noon a flight of six geese, in disorder, passed over the house. She had been sitting in the kitchen and heard their foolish, loud cries. She saw them through the window. They were very low, just above the trees.

The house was amid fields. From the upstairs, distant barns and fences could be seen. It was a beautiful house, for years she had felt it was unique. The garden was tended, the wood stacked, the screens in good repair. It was the same inside, everything well selected, the soft white sofas, the rugs and chairs, the Swedish glasses that were so pleasant to hold, the lamps. The house is my soul, she used to say.

She remembered the morning the goose was on the lawn, a big one with his long black neck and white chinstrap, standing there not fifteen feet away. She had hurried to the stairs. "Brookie," she whispered.

"What?"

"Come down here. Be quiet."

They went to the window and then on to another, looking out breathlessly.

"What's he doing so near the house?"

"I don't know."

"He's big, isn't he?"

"Very."

"But not as big as Dancer."

"Dancer can't fly."

All gone now, pony, goose, boy. She remembered that night they came home from dinner at the Werners' where there had been a young woman, very pure featured, who had abandoned her marriage to study architecture. Rob Chandler had said nothing, he had merely listened, distracted, as if to a familiar kind of news. At midnight in the kitchen, hardly having closed the door, he simply announced it. He had turned away from her and was facing the table.

"What?" she said.

He started to repeat it but she interrupted.

"What are you saying?" she said numbly.

He had met someone else.

"You've what?"

She kept the house. She went just one last time to the apartment on Eighty-second Street with its large windows from which, cheek pressed to glass, you could see the entrance steps of the Met. A year later he remarried. For a while she veered off course. She sat at night in the empty living room, almost helpless, not bothering to eat, not bothering to do anything, stroking her dog's head and talking to him, curled on the couch at two in the morning still in her clothes. A fatal weariness had set in, but then she pulled herself together, began going to church and putting on lipstick again.

Now as she returned to her house from the market, there were great, leaden clouds marbled with light, moving above the trees. The wind was gusting. There was a car in the driveway as she turned in. For just a moment she was alarmed and then she recognized it. A figure came toward her.

"Hi, Bill," she said.

"I'll give you a hand." He took the biggest bag of groceries from the car and followed her into the kitchen.

"Just put it down on the table," she said. "That's it. Thanks. How've you been?"

He was wearing a white shirt and a sport coat, expensive at one time. The kitchen seemed cold. Far off was the faint pop of guns.

"Come in," she said. "It's chilly out here."

"I just came by to see if you had anything that needed to be taken care of before the cold weather set in."

"Oh, I see. Well," she said, "there's the upstairs bathroom. Is that going to be trouble again?"

"The pipes?"

"They're not going to break again this year?"

"Didn't we stuff some insulation in there?" he said. There was a slight, elegant slur in his speech, back along the edge of his tongue. He had always had it. "It's on the north side, is the trouble."

"Yes," she said. She was searching vaguely for a cigarette. "Why do you suppose they put it there?"

"Well, that's where it's always been," he said.

He was forty but looked younger. There was something hard and hopeless about him, something that was preserving his youth. All summer on the golf course, sometimes into December. Even there he seemed indifferent, dark hair blowing—even among companions, as if he were killing time. There were a lot of stories about him. He was a fallen idol. His father had a real-estate agency in a cottage on the highway. Lots, farms, acreage. They were an old family in these parts. There was a lane named after them.

"There's a bad faucet. Do you want to take a look at that?"

"What's wrong with it?"

"It drips," she said. "I'll show you."

She led the way upstairs. "There," she said, pointing toward the bathroom. "You can hear it."

He casually turned the water on and off a few times and felt under the tap. He was doing it at arm's length with a slight, careless movement of the wrist. She could see him from the bedroom. He seemed to be examining other things on the counter.

She turned on a light and sat down. It was nearly dusk and the room immediately became cozy. The walls were papered in a blue pattern and the rug was a soft white. The polished stone of the hearth gave a sense of order. Outside, the fields were disappearing. It was a serene hour, one she shrank from. Sometimes, looking toward the ocean, she thought of her son, although that had happened in the sound and long ago. She no longer found she returned to it every day. They said it got better after a time but that it never really went away. As with so many other things, they were right. He had been the youngest and very spirited though a little frail. She prayed for him every Sunday in church. She prayed just a simple thing: O Lord, don't overlook him, he's very small. . . . Only a little boy, she would sometimes add. The sight of anything dead, a bird scattered in the road, the stiff legs of a rabbit, even a dead snake, upset her.

"I think it's a washer," he said. "I'll try and bring one over sometime."

"Good," she said. "Will it be another month?"

"You know Marian and I are back together again. Did you know that?"

"Oh, I see." She gave a slight, involuntary sigh. She felt strange. "I, uh . . ." What weakness, she thought later. "When did it happen?"

"A few weeks ago."

After a bit she stood up. "Shall we go downstairs?"

She could see their reflections passing the stairway window. She could see her apricot-colored shirt go by. The wind was still blowing. A bare branch was scraping the side of the house. She often heard that at night.

"Do you have time for a drink?" she asked.

"I'd better not."

She poured some Scotch and went into the kitchen to get some ice from the refrigerator and add a little water. "I suppose I won't see you for a while."

It hadn't been that much. Some dinners at the Lanai, some improbable nights. It was just the feeling of being with someone you liked, someone easy and incongruous. "I . . ." She tried to find something to say.

"You wish it hadn't happened."

"Something like that."

He nodded. He was standing there. His face had become a little pale, the pale of winter.

"And you?" she said.

"Oh, hell." She had never heard him complain. Only about certain people. "I'm just a caretaker. She's my wife. What are you going to do, come up to her sometime and tell her everything?"

"I wouldn't do that."

"I hope not," he said.

When the door closed she did not turn. She heard the car start outside and saw the reflection of the headlights. She stood in front of the mirror and looked at her face coldly. Forty-six. It was there in her neck and beneath her eyes. She would never be any younger. She should have pleaded, she thought. She should have told him all she was feeling, all that suddenly choked her heart. The summer with its hope and long days was gone. She had the urge to follow him, to drive past his house. The lights would be on. She would see someone through the windows.

That night she heard the branches tapping against the house and the window frames rattle. She sat alone and thought of the geese, she could hear them out there. It had gotten cold. The wind was blowing their feathers. They lived a long time, ten or fifteen years, they said. The one they had seen on the lawn might still be alive, settled back into the fields with the others, in from the ocean where they went to be safe, the survivors of bloody ambushes. Somewhere in the wet grass, she imagined, lay one of them, dark sodden breast, graceful neck still extended, great wings striving to beat, bloody sounds coming from the holes in its beak. She went around and turned on lights. The rain was coming down, the sea was crashing, a comrade lay dead in the whirling darkness.

THE CINEMA

I.

At ten-thirty then, she arrived. They were waiting. The door at the far end opened and somewhat shyly, trying to see in the dimness if anyone was there, her long hair hanging like a schoolgirl's, everyone watching, she slowly, almost reluctantly approached. . . . Behind her came the young woman who was her secretary.

Great faces cannot be explained. She had a long nose, a mouth, a curious distance between the eyes. It was a face open and unknowable. It pronounced itself somehow indifferent to life.

When he was introduced to her, Guivi, the leading man, smiled. His teeth were large and there existed a space between the incisors. On his chin was a mole. These defects at that time were revered. He'd had only four or five roles, his discovery was sudden, the shot in which he appeared for the first time was often called one of the most memorable introductions in all of film. It was true. There is sometimes one image which outlasts everything, even the names are forgotten. He held her chair. She acknowledged the introductions faintly, one could hardly hear her voice.

The director leaned forward and began to talk. They would

rehearse for ten days in this bare hall. Anna's face was buried in her collar as he spoke. The director was new to her. He was a small man known as a hard worker. The saliva flew from his mouth as he talked. She had never rehearsed a film before, not for Fellini, not for Chabrol. She was trying to listen to what he said. She felt strongly the presence of others around her. Guivi sat calmly, smoking a cigarette. She glanced at him unseen.

They began to read, sitting at the table together. Make no attempt to find meaning, Iles told them, not so soon, this was only the first step. There were no windows. There was neither day nor night. Their words seemed to rise, to vanish like smoke above them. Guivi read his lines as if laying down cards of no particular importance. Bridge was his passion. He gave it all his nights. Halfway through, he touched her shoulder lightly as he was doing an intimate part. She seemed not to notice. She was like a lizard, only her throat was beating. The next time he touched her hair. That single gesture, so natural as to be almost unintended, made her quiet, stilled her fears.

She fled afterward. She went directly back to the Hotel de Ville. Her room was filled with objects. On the desk were books still wrapped in brown paper, magazines in various languages, letters hastily read. There was a small anteroom, not regularly shaped, and a bedroom beyond. The bed was large. In the manner of a sequence when the camera carefully, increasing our apprehension, moves from detail to detail, the bathroom door, half-open, revealed a vast array of bottles, of dark perfumes, medicines, things unknown. Far below on Via Sistina was the sound of traffic.

The next day she was better, she was like a woman ready to work. She brushed her hair back with her hand as she read. She was attentive, once she even laughed.

They were brought small cups of coffee from across the courtyard.

"How does it sound to you?" she asked the writer.

"Well . . ." he hesitated.

He was a wavering man named Peter Lang, at one time Lengsner. He had seen her in all her sacred life, a figure of lights, he had read the article, the love letter written to her in *Bazaar*. It described her perfect modesty, her instinct, the shape of her face. On the opposite page was the photograph he cut out and placed in his journal. This film he had written, this important work of the newest of the arts, already existed complete in his mind. Its power came from its chasteness, the discipline of its images. It was a film of indirection, the surface was calm with the calm of daily life. That was not to say still. Beneath the visible were emotions more potent for their concealment. Only occasionally, like the head of an iceberg ominously rising from nowhere and then dropping from sight did the terror come into view.

When she turned to him then, he was overwhelmed, he couldn't think of what to say. It didn't matter. Guivi gave an answer.

"I think we're still a little afraid of some of the lines," he said. "You know, you've written some difficult things."

"Ah, well . . ."

"Almost impossible. Don't misunderstand, they're good, except they have to be perfectly done."

She had already turned away and was talking to the director.

"Shakespeare is filled with lines like this," Guivi continued. He began to quote Othello.

It was now Iles' turn, the time to expose his ideas. He
plunged in. He was like a kind of crazy schoolmaster as he
described the work, part Freud, part lovelorn columnist,
tracing interior lines and motives deep as rivers. Members of
the crew had sneaked in to stand near the door. Guivi jotted
something in his script.

"Yes, notes, make notes," Iles told him, "I am saying some
brilliant things."

A performance was built up in layers, like a painting, that
was his method, to start with this, add this, then this, and so
forth. It expanded, became rich, developed depths and under-
currents. Then in the end they would cut it back, reduce it to
half its size. That was what he meant by good acting.

He confided to Lang, "I never tell them everything. I'll
give you an example: the scene in the clinic. I tell Guivi he's
going to pieces, he thinks he's going to scream, actually
scream. He has to stuff a towel in his mouth to prevent it.
Then, just before we shoot, I tell him: Do it without the towel.
Do you see?"

His energy began to infect the performers. A mood of
excitement, even fever came over them. He was thrilling
them, it was their world he was describing and then taking to
pieces to reveal its marvelous intricacies.

If he was a genius, he would be crowned in the end
because, like Balzac, his work was so vast. He, too, was filling
page after page, unending, crowded with the sublime and the

ordinary, fantastic characters, insights, human frailty, trash. If I make two films a year for thirty years, he said . . . The project was his life.

At six the limousines were waiting. The sky still had light, the cold of autumn was in the air. They stood near the door and talked. They parted reluctantly. He had converted them, he was their master. They drove off separately with a little wave. Lang was left standing in the dusk.

There were dinners. Guivi sat with Anna beside him. It was the fourth day. She leaned her head against his shoulder. He was discussing the foolishness of women. They were not genuinely intelligent, he said, that was a myth of Western society.

"I'm going to surprise you," Iles said, "do you know what I believe? I believe they're not as intelligent as men. They are *more* intelligent."

Anna shook her head very slightly.

"They're not logical," Guivi said. "It's not their way. A woman's whole essence is here." He indicated down near his stomach. "The womb," he said. "Nowhere else. Do you realize there are no great women bridge players?"

It was as if she had submitted to all his ideas. She ate without speaking. She barely touched dessert. She was content to be what he admired in a woman. She was aware of her power, he knelt to it nightly, his mind wandering. He was already becoming indifferent to her. He performed the act as one plays a losing hand, he did the best he could with it. The cloud of white leapt from him. She moaned.

"I am really a romantic and a classicist," he said. "I have *almost* been in love twice."

Her glance fell, he told her something in a whisper.

"But never really," he said, "never deeply. No, I long for that. I am ready for it."

Beneath the table her hand discovered this. The waiters were brushing away the crumbs.

Lang was staying at the Inghilterra in a small room on the side. Long after the evening was over he still swam in thoughts of it. He washed his underwear distractedly. Somewhere in the shuttered city, the river black with fall, he knew they were together, he did not resent it. He lay in bed like a poor student—how little life changes from the first to the last—and fell asleep clutching his dreams. The windows were open. The cold air poured over him like sea on a blind sailor, drenching him, filling the room. He lay with his legs crossed at the ankle like a martyr, his face turned to God.

Iles was at the Grand in a suite with tall doors and floors that creaked. He could hear chambermaids pass in the hall. He had a cold and could not sleep. He called his wife in America, it was just evening there, and they talked for a long time. He was depressed: Guivi was no actor.

"What's wrong with him?"

"Oh, he has nothing, no depth, no emotion."

"Can't you get someone else?"

"It's too late."

They would have to work around it, he said. He had the telephone propped on the pillow, his eyes were drifting aimlessly around the room. They would have to change the character somehow, make the falseness a part of it. Anna was all right. He was pleased with Anna. Well, they would do something, pump life into it somehow, make dead birds fly.

By the end of the week they were rehearsing on their feet. It was cold. They wore their coats as they moved from one place to another. Anna stood near Guivi. She took the cigarette from his fingers and smoked it. Sometimes they laughed.

Iles was alive with work. His hair fell in his face, he was explaining actions, details. He didn't rely on their knowledge, he arranged it all. Often he tied a line to an action, that is to say the words were keyed by it: Guivi touched Anna's elbow, without looking she said, "Go away."

Lang sat and watched. Sometimes they were working very close to him, just in front of where he was. He couldn't really pay attention. She was speaking *his* lines, things he had invented. They were like shoes. She tried them on, they were nice, she never thought who had made them.

"Anna has a limited range," Guivi confided.

Lang said yes. He wanted to learn more about acting, this secret world.

"But what a face," Guivi said.

"Her eyes!"

"There is a little touch of the idiot in them, isn't there?" Guivi said.

She could see them talking. Afterward she sent someone to Lang. Whatever he had told Guivi, she wanted to know, too. Lang looked over at her. She was ignoring him.

He was confused, he did not know if it was serious. The minor actors with nothing to do were sitting on two old sofas. The floor was chalky, dust covered their shoes. Iles was following the scenes closely, nodding his approval, yes, yes, good, excellent. The script girl walked behind him, a stopwatch around her neck. She was forty-five, her legs ached at night. She went along noting everything, careful not to step on any of the half-driven nails.

"My love," Iles turned to her, he had forgotten her name. "How long was it?"

They always took too much time. He had to hurry them, force them to be economical.

At the end, like school, there was the final test. They seemed to do it all perfectly, the gestures, the cadences he had devised. He was timing them like runners. Two hours and twenty minutes.

"Marvelous," he told them.

That night Lang was drunk at the party the producer gave. It was in a small restaurant. The entry was filled with odors and displays of food, the cooks nodded from the kitchen. Fifty people were there, a hundred, crowded together and speaking different languages. Among them Anna shone like a queen. On her wrist was a new bracelet from Bulgari's, she had coolly demanded a discount, the clerk hadn't known what to say. She was in a slim gold suit that showed her breasts. Her strange, flat face seemed to float without expression among the others, sometimes she wore a faint, a drifting smile.

Lang felt depressed. He did not understand what they had been doing, the exaggerations dismayed him, he didn't believe in Iles, his energies, his insight, he didn't believe in any of it. He tried to calm himself. He saw them at the biggest table, the producer at Anna's elbow. They were talking, why was she so animated? They always come alive when the lights are on, someone said.

He watched Guivi. He could see Anna leaning across to him, her long hair, her throat.

"It's stupid to be making it in color," Lang said to the man beside him.

"What?" He was a film company executive. He had a face like a fish, a bass, that had gone bad. "What do you mean, not in color?"

"Black and white," Lang told him.

"What are you talking about? You can't sell a black and white film. Life is in color."

"Life?"

"Color is real," the man said. He was from New York. The ten greatest films of all time, the twenty greatest, were in color, he said.

"What about . . ." Lang tried to concentrate, his elbow slipped, "*The Bicycle Thief*?"

"I'm talking about modern films."

II.

Today was sunny. He was writing in brief, disconsolate phrases. *Yesterday it rained, it was dark until late afternoon, the day before was the same.* The corridors of the Inghilterra were vaulted like a convent, the doors set deep in the walls. Still, he thought, it was comfortable. He gave his shirts to the maid in the morning, they were back the next day. She did them at home. He had seen her bending over to take linen from a cabinet. The tops of her stockings showed—it was classic Buñuel—the mysterious white of a leg.

The girl from publicity called. They needed information for his biography.

"What information?"

"We'll send a car for you," she said.

It never came. He went the next day by taxi and waited thirty minutes in her office, she was in seeing the producer. Finally she returned, a thin girl with damp spots under the arms of her dress.

"You called me?" Lang said.

She did not know who he was.

"You were going to send a car for me."

"Mr. Lang," she suddenly cried. "Oh, I'm sorry."

The desk was covered with photos, the chairs with newspapers and magazines. She was an assistant, she had worked on *Cleopatra, The Bible, The Longest Day.* There was money to be earned in American films.

"They've put me in this little room," she apologized.

Her name was Eva. She lived at home. Her family ate without speaking, four of them in the sadness of bourgeois surroundings, the radio which didn't work, thin rugs on the floor. When he was finished, her father cleared his throat. The meat was better the last time, he said. The *last* time? her mother asked.

"Yes, it was better," he said.

"The last time it was tasteless."

"Ah, well, two times ago," he said.

They fell into silence again. There was only the sound of forks, an occasional glass. Suddenly her brother rose from the table and left the room. No one looked up.

He was crazy, this brother, well, perhaps not crazy but

enough to make them weep. He would remain for days in his room, the door locked. He was a writer. There was one difficulty, everything worthwhile had already been written. He had gone through a period when he devoured books, three and four a day, and could quote vast sections of them afterward, but the fever had passed. He lay on his bed now and looked at the ceiling.

Eva was nervous, people said. Of course, she was nervous. She was thirty. She had black hair, small teeth, and a life in which she had already given up hope. They had nothing for his biography, she told Lang. They had to have a biography for everybody. She suggested finally he write it himself. Yes, of course, he imagined it would be something like that.

Her closest friend—like all Italians she was alert to friends and enemies—her most useful friend was an hysterical woman named Mirella Ricci who had a large apartment and aristocratic longings, also the fears and illnesses of women who live alone. Mirella's friends were homosexuals and women who were separated. She had dinner with them in the evening, she telephoned them several times a day. She was a woman with large nostrils and white skin, pale as paper, but she was still able to see white spots on it. Her doctor said they were a circulatory condition.

She was working on the film, like Eva. They talked of everyone, Iles: he knew actors, Mirella said. Whichever ones were brought in, he chose the best, well, he had made one or two mistakes. They were eating at Otello's, tortoises crawled on the floor. The script was interesting, Mirella said, but she didn't like the writer, he was cold. He was also a *frocio*, she knew the signs. As for the producer . . . she made a disgusted sound. He dyed his hair, she said. He looked thirty-nine but he was really fifty. He had already tried to seduce her.

"When?" Eva said.

They knew everything. They were like nurses whose tenderness was dead. It was they who ran the sickhouse. They knew how much money everyone was getting, who was not to be trusted.

The producer: first of all he was impotent, Mirella said. When he wasn't impotent, he was unwilling, the rest of the time he didn't know how to go about it and when he did, it was unsatisfactory. On top of that, he was a man who was always without a girl.

Her nostrils had darkness in them. She expected waiters to treat her well.

"How is your brother?" she said.

"Oh, the same."

"He still isn't working?"

"He has a job in a record shop but he won't be there long. They'll fire him."

"What is wrong with men?" she said.

"I'm exhausted," Eva sighed. She was haggard from late hours. She had to type letters for the producer because one of his secretaries was sick.

"He tried to make love to me, too," she admitted.

"Tell me," Mirella said.

"At his hotel . . ."

Mirella waited.

"I brought him some letters. He insisted I stay and talk. He wanted to give me a drink. Finally he tried to kiss me. He fell on his knees—I was cowering on the divan—and said, Eva, you smell so sweet. I tried to pretend it was all a joke."

The joys of rectitude. They drove around in little Fiats. They paid attention to their clothes.

The film was going well, a day ahead of schedule. Iles was working with a kind of vast assurance. He roamed around the great, black Mitchell in tennis shoes, he ate no lunch. The rushes were said to be extraordinary. Guivi never went to see them. Anna asked Lang about them, what did he think? He tried to decide. She was beautiful in them, he told her—it was true—there was a quality in her face which illuminated the entire film . . . he never finished. As usual, she was disinterested. She had already turned to someone else, the cameraman.

"Did you see them?" she said.

Iles wore an old sweater, the hair hung in his face. Two films a year, he repeated . . . that was the keystone of all his belief. Eisenstein only made six altogether, but he didn't work under the American system. Anyway, Iles had no confidence when he was at rest.

Whatever his weaknesses, his act of grandeur was in concealing the knowledge that the film was already wreckage: Guivi was simply not good enough, he worked without thinking, he worked as one eats a meal. Iles knew actors.

Farewell, Guivi. It was the announcement of death. He was already beginning to enter the past. He signed autographs, the space showing between his teeth. He charmed journalists. The perfect victim, he suspected nothing. The glory of his life had blinded him. He dined at the best tables, a bottle of fine Bordeaux before him. He mimicked the foolishness of Iles.

"Guivi, my love," he imitated, "the trouble is you are Russian, you are moody and violent. He's telling me what it is to be Russian. Next he'll start describing life under communism."

Anna was eating with very slow bites.

"Do you know something?" she said calmly.

He waited.

"I've never been so happy."

"Really?"

"Not in my whole life," she said.

He smiled. His smile was opera.

"With you I am the woman everyone believes I am," she said.

He looked at her long and deeply. His eyes were dark, the pupils invisible. Love scenes during the day, he thought wearily, love scenes at night. People were watching them from all around the room. When they rose to go, the waiters crowded near the door.

Within three years his career would be over. He would see himself in the flickering television as if it were some curious dream. He invested in apartment houses, he owned land in Spain. He would become like a woman, jealous, unforgiving, and perhaps one day in a restaurant even see Iles with a young actor, explaining with the heat of a fanatic some very ordinary idea. Guivi was thirty-seven. He had a moment on the screen that would never be forgotten. Tinted posters of him would peel from the sides of buildings more and more remote, the resemblance fading, his name becoming stale.

He would smile across alleys, into the sour darkness. Far-off dogs were barking. The streets smelled of the poor.

III.

There was a party for Anna's birthday at a restaurant in the outskirts, the restaurant in which Farouk, falling backward from the table, had died. Not everyone was invited. It was meant to be a surprise.

She arrived with Guivi. She was not a woman, she was a minor deity, she was some beautiful animal innocent of its grace. It was February, the night was cold. The chauffeurs waited inside the cars. Later they gathered quietly in the cloakroom.

"My love," Iles said to her, "you are going to be very, very happy."

"Really?"

He put his arm around her without replying; he nodded. The shooting was almost over. The rushes, he said, were the best he had ever seen. Ever.

"As for this fellow . . ." he said, reaching for Guivi.

The producer joined them.

"I want you for my next picture, both of you," he announced. He was wearing a suit a size too small, a velvet suit bought on Via Borgognona.

"Where did you get it?" Guivi said. "It's fantastic. Who is supposed to be the star here anyway?"

Posener looked down at himself. He smiled like a guilty boy.

"Do you like it?" he said. "Really?"

"No, where did you get it?"

"I'll send you one tomorrow."

"No, no . . ."

"Guivi, please," he begged, "I want to."

He was filled with goodwill, the worst was past. The actors had not run away or refused to work, he was overcome with love for them, as for a bad child who unexpectedly does something good. He felt he must do something in return.

"Waiter!" he cried. He looked around, his gestures always seemed wasted, vanished in empty air.

"Waiter," he called, "champagne!"

There were twenty or so people in the room, other actors, the American wife of a count. At the table Guivi told stories. He drank like a Georgian prince, he had plans for Geneva, Gstaad. There was the Italian producer, he said, who had an actress under contract, she was a second Sophia Loren. He had made a fortune with her. Her films were only shown in Italy, but everyone went to them, the money was pouring in. He always kept the journalists away, however, he never let them talk to her alone.

"Sellerio," someone guessed.

"Yes," said Guivi, "that's right. Do you know the rest of the story?"

"He sold her."

But half the contract only, Guivi said. Her popularity was fading, he wanted to get everything he could. There was a big ceremony, they invited all the press. She was going to sign. She picked up the pen and leaned forward a little for the photographers, you know, she had these enormous, eh . . . well, anyway, on the paper she wrote: with his finger Guivi made a large X. The newsmen all looked at each other. Then Sellerio took the pen and very grandly, just below her name: Guivi made one X and next to it, carefully, another. Illiterate. That's the truth. They asked him, look, what is the second X for? You know what he told them? *Dottore.*

They laughed. He told them about shooting in Naples with a producer so cheap he threw a cable across the trolley wires to steal power. He was clever, Guivi, he was a storyteller in the tradition of the east, he could speak three languages. Later, when she finally understood what had happened, Anna remembered how happy he seemed this night.

"Shall we go on to the Hostaria?" the producer said.

"What?" Guivi asked.

"The Hostaria . . ." As with the waiters, it seemed no one heard him. "The Blue Bar. Come on, we're going to the Blue Bar," he announced.

Outside the Botanical Gardens, parked in the cold, the small windows of the car frosted, Lang sat. His clothing was open. His flesh was pale in the refracted light. He had eaten dinner with Eva. She had talked for hours in a low, uncertain voice, it was a night for stories, she had told him everything, about Coleman the head of publicity, Mirella, her brother, Sicily, life. On the road to the mountains which overlooked Palermo there were cars parked at five in the afternoon. In each one was a couple, the man with a handkerchief spread in his lap.

"I am so lonely," she said suddenly.

She had only three friends, she saw them all the time.

They went to the theater together, the ballet. One was an actress. One was married. She was silent, she seemed to wait. The cold was everywhere, it covered the glass. Her breath was in crystals, visible in the dark.

"Can I kiss it?" she said.

She began to moan then, as if it were holy. She touched it with her forehead. She was murmuring. The nape of her neck was bare.

She called the next morning. It was eight o'clock.

"I want to read something to you," she said.

He was half-asleep, the racket was already drifting up from the street. The room was chill and unlighted. Within it, distant as an old record, her voice was playing. It entered his body, it commanded his blood.

"I found this," she said. "Are you there?"

"Yes."

"I thought you would like it."

It was from an article. She began to read.

In February of 1868, in Milan, Prince Umberto had given a splendid ball. *In a room which blazed with light the young bride who was one day to be Queen of Italy was introduced. It was the event of the year, crowded and gay, and while the world of fashion amused itself thus, at the same hour and in the same city a lone astronomer was discovering a new planet, the ninety-seventh on Chacornac's chart. . . .*

Silence. A *new planet.*

In his mind, still warmed by the pillow, it seemed a sacred calm had descended. He lay like a saint. He was naked, his ankles, his hipbones, his throat.

He heard her call his name. He said nothing. He lay there

becoming small, smaller, vanishing. The room became a window, a facade, a group of buildings, squares and sections, in the end all of Rome. His ecstasy was beyond knowing. The roofs of the great cathedrals shone in the winter air.

AKHNILO

It was late August. In the harbor the boats lay still, not the slightest stirring of their masts, not the softest clink of a sheave. The restaurants had long since closed. An occasional car, headlights glaring, came over the bridge from North Haven or turned down Main Street, past the lighted telephone booths with their smashed receivers. On the highway the discotheques were emptying. It was after three.

In the darkness Fenn awakened. He thought he had heard something, a slight sound, like the creak of a spring, the one on the screen door in the kitchen. He lay there in the heat. His wife was sleeping quietly. He waited. The house was unlocked though there had been many robberies and worse nearer the city. He heard a faint thump. He did not move. Several minutes passed. Without making a sound he got up and went carefully to the narrow doorway where some stairs descended to the kitchen. He stood there. Silence. Another thump and a moan. It was Birdman falling to a different place on the floor.

Outside, the trees were like black reflections. The stars were hidden. The only galaxies were the insect voices that filled the night. He stared from the open window. He was still not sure if he had heard anything. The leaves of the immense beech that overhung the rear porch were close enough to touch. For what seemed a long time he examined the shadowy area around the trunk. The stillness of everything made him feel visible but also strangely receptive. His eyes drifted from one thing to another behind the house, the pale Corinthian columns of the arbor next door, the mysterious hedge, the garage with its rotting sills. Nothing.

Eddie Fenn was a carpenter though he'd gone to Dartmouth and majored in history. Most of the time he worked alone. He was thirty-four. He had thinning hair and a shy smile. Not much to say. There was something quenched in him. When he was younger it was believed to be some sort of talent, but he had never really set out in life, he had stayed close to shore. His wife, who was tall and nearsighted, was from Connecticut. Her father had been a banker. *Of Greenwich and Havana* the announcement in the papers had said—he'd managed the branch of a New York bank there when she was a child. That was in the days when Havana was a legend and millionaires committed suicide after smoking a last cigar.

Years had passed. Fenn gazed out at the night. It seemed he was the only listener to an infinite sea of cries. Its vastness awed him. He thought of all that lay concealed behind it, the desperate acts, the desires, the fatal surprises. That afternoon he had seen a robin picking at something near the edge of the grass, seizing it, throwing it in the air, seizing it again: a toad, its small, stunned legs fanned out. The bird threw it again. In ravenous burrows the blind shrews hunted ceaselessly, the pointed tongues of reptiles were testing the air, there was the crunch of abdomens, the passivity of the trapped, the soft throes of mating. His daughters were asleep down the hall. Nothing is safe except for an hour.

As he stood there the sound seemed to change, he did not know how. It seemed to separate as if permitting something to come forth from it, something glittering and remote. He tried to identify what he was hearing as gradually the cricket, cicada, no, it was something else, something feverish and strange, became more clear. The more intently he listened, the more elusive it was. He was afraid to move for fear of losing it. He heard the soft call of an owl. The darkness of the trees which was absolute seemed to loosen, and through it that single, shrill note.

Unseen the night had opened. The sky was revealing itself, the stars shining faintly. The town was sleeping, abandoned sidewalks, silent lawns. Far off among some pines was the gable of a barn. It was coming from there. He still could not identify it. He needed to be closer, to go downstairs and out the door, but that way he might lose it, it might become silent, aware.

He had a disturbing thought, he was unable to dislodge it: it *was* aware. Quivering there, repeating and repeating itself above the rest, it seemed to be coming only to him. The rhythm was not constant. It hurried, hesitated, went on. It was less and less an instinctive cry and more a kind of signal, a code, not anything he had heard before, not a collection of long and short impulses but something more intricate, in a way almost like speech. The idea frightened him. The words, if that was what they were, were piercing and thin but the awareness of them made him tremble as if they were the combination to a vault.

Beneath the window lay the roof of the porch. It sloped gently. He stood there, perfectly still, as if lost in thought. His heart was rattling. The roof seemed wide as a street. He would have to go out on it hoping he was unseen, moving silently, without abruptness, pausing to see if there was a change in the sound to which he was now acutely sensitive. The darkness would not protect him. He would be entering a night of countless networks, shifting eyes. He was not sure if he should do it, if he dared. A drop of sweat broke free and ran quickly down his bare side. Tirelessly the call continued. His hands were trembling.

Unfastening the screen, he lowered it carefully and leaned it against the house. He was moving quietly, like a serpent, across the faded green roofing. He looked down. The ground seemed distant. He would have to hang from the roof and drop, light as a spider. The peak of the barn was still visible. He was moving toward the lodestar, he could feel it. It was almost as if he were falling. The act was dizzying, irreversible. It was taking him where nothing he possessed would protect him, taking him barefoot, alone.

As he dropped to the ground, Fenn felt a thrill go through him. He was going to be redeemed. His life had not turned out as he expected but he still thought of himself as special, as belonging to no one. In fact he thought of failure as romantic. It had almost been his goal. He carved birds, or he had. The tools and partially shaped blocks of wood were on a table in the basement. He had, at one time, almost become a naturalist. Something in him, his silence, his willingness to be apart, was adapted to that. Instead he began to build furniture with a friend who had some money, but the business failed. He was drinking. One morning he woke up lying by the car in the worn ruts of the driveway, the old woman who lived across the street warning away her dog. He went inside before his children saw him. He was very close, the doctor told him frankly, to being an alcoholic. The words astonished him. That was long ago. His family had saved him, but not without cost.

He paused. The earth was firm and dry. He went toward the hedge and across the neighbor's driveway. The tone that was transfixing him was clearer. Following it he passed behind houses he hardly recognized from the back, through neglected yards where cans and rubbish were hidden in dark grass, past empty sheds he had never seen. The ground began to slope gently down, he was nearing the barn. He could hear the voice, *his* voice, pouring overhead. It was coming from somewhere in the ghostly wooden triangle rising like the face of a distant mountain brought unexpectedly close by a turn of the road. He moved toward it slowly, with the fear of an explorer. Above him he could hear the thin stream trilling. Terrified by its closeness he stood still.

At first, he later remembered, it meant nothing, it was too glistening, too pure. It kept pouring out, more and more insane. He could not identify, he could never repeat, he could not even describe the sound. It had enlarged, it was pushing everything else aside. He stopped trying to comprehend it and instead allowed it to run through him, to invade him like a chant. Slowly, like a pattern that changes its appearance as one stares at it and begins to shift into another dimension, inexplicably the sound altered and exposed its real core. He began to recognize it. It *was* words. They had no meaning, no antecedents, but they were unmistakably a language, the first ever heard from an order vaster and more dense than our own. Above, in the whitish surface, desperate, calling, was the nameless pioneer.

In a kind of ecstasy he moved closer. Instantly he realized it was wrong. The sound hesitated. He closed his eyes in anguish but too late, it faltered and then stopped. He felt stupid, shamed. He stepped back a little, helplessly. All about him the voices clattered. The night was filled with them. He turned this way and that hoping to find it, but the thing he had heard was gone.

It was late. The first pale cast had come to the sky. He was standing near the barn with the fragments of a dream one must struggle to remember: four words, distinct and inimitable, that he had made out. Protecting them, concentrating on them with all his strength, he began to carry them back. The cries of the insects seemed louder. He was afraid something would happen, a dog would bark, a light go on in a bedroom and he would be distracted, he would lose his hold. He had to get back without seeing anything, without hearing anything, without thinking. He was repeating the words to himself as he went, his lips moving steadily. He hardly dared breathe. He could see the house. It had turned grey. The windows were dark. He had to get to it. The sound of the night creatures seemed to swell in torment and rage, but he was beyond that. He was escaping. He had gone an immense distance, he was coming to the hedge. The porch was not far away. He stood on the railing, the eave of the roof within reach. The rain gutter was firm, he pulled himself up. The crumbling green asphalt was warm beneath his feet. One leg over the sill, then the other. He was safe. He stepped back from the window instinctively. He had done it. Outside, the light seemed faint and historic. A spectral dawn began to come through the trees.

Suddenly he heard the floor creak. Someone was there, a figure in the soft light drained of color. It was his wife, he was stunned by the image of her holding a cotton robe about her, her face made plain by sleep. He made a gesture as if to warn her off.

"What is it? What's wrong?" she whispered.

He backed away making vague movements with his hands. His head was sideways, like a horse. He was moving backward. One eye was on her.

"What is it?" she said, alarmed. "What happened?"

No, he pleaded, shaking his head. A word had dropped away. No, no. It was fluttering apart like something in the sea. He was reaching blindly for it.

Her arm went around him. He pulled away abruptly. He closed his eyes.

"Darling, what is it?" He was troubled, she knew. He had never really gotten over his difficulty. He often woke at night, she would find him sitting in the kitchen, his face looking tired and old. "Come to bed," she invited.

His eyes were closed tightly. His hands were over his ears.

"Are you all right?" she said.

Beneath her devotion it was dissolving, the words were spilling away. He began to turn around frantically.

"What is it, what is it?" she cried.

The light was coming everywhere, pouring across the lawn. The sacred whispers were vanishing. He could not spare a moment. Hands clapped to his head he ran into the hall searching for a pencil while she ran after, begging him to tell her what was wrong. They were fading, there was just one left, worthless without the others and yet of infinite value. As he scribbled the table shook. A picture quivered on the wall. His wife, her hair held back with one hand, was peering at what he had written. Her face was close to it.

"What is that?"

Dena, in her nightgown, had appeared in a doorway awakened by the noise.

"What is it?" she asked.

"Help me," her mother cried.

"Daddy, what happened?"

Their hands were reaching for him. In the glass of the picture a brilliant square of blue and green was trembling, the luminous foliage of the trees. The countless voices were receding, turning into silence.

"What is it, what is it?" his wife pleaded.

"Daddy, please!"

He shook his head. He was nearly weeping as he tried to pull away. Suddenly he slumped to the floor and sat there and for Dena they had begun again the phase she remembered from the years she was first in school when unhappiness filled the house and slamming doors and her father clumsy with affection came into their room at night to tell them stories and fell asleep at the foot of her bed.

EYES OF THE STARS

She was short with short legs and her body had lost its shape. It began at her neck and continued down, and her arms were like a cook's. In her sixties, Teddy had looked the same for a decade and would probably go on looking the same, there was not that much to change. She had pouches under her eyes and a chin, slightly receding when she was a girl, that was lost now in several others, but she dressed neatly and people liked her.

Myron, her late husband, had been an ophthalmologist and proud of the fact that he treated the eyes of many stars, although frequently it was a relative of a star, a nephew or mother-in-law, almost the same thing. He could recite the exact condition of all these eyes, retinitis, mild amblyopia . . .

"So, what is that?"

Silvery-haired, he would confide,

"Lazy-eyed."

But Myron was gone. He hadn't really been a very interesting man, Teddy would sometimes admit, apart from knowing exactly what was wrong with famous patients' eyes. They had married when she was past forty and resigned to the idea of being single, not that she wouldn't have made a good wife in every way, but she had only her personality and good nature by that time, the rest, as she herself would say, had turned into a size fourteen.

It had not always been that way. Though she did not state, like London's notorious Mrs. Wilson two hundred years earlier, that she would not reveal the circumstances that had made her the mistress of an older man at the age of fifteen, Teddy had had something of the same experience. The first great episode of her life had been with a writer, a detoured novelist more than twenty years older than she was. He had first seen her at a bus stop. She was not, even in those days, exactly beautiful, but there was a body that spoke, at the time, of much that youth could offer. He took her to get her first diaphragm and she was his mistress for three years until he left town and returned to literature and in the end a large house in New Jersey.

She had stayed in touch with him for a time, her real link to the grown-up world, and read his books, of course, but slowly his letters became less frequent until they simply stopped and along with them the foolish hope that he would come back someday.

Through the years she began to remember him less and less as he had been and more as one lone image: driving. The boulevards in those days were wide and very white and the car was weaving a little while he, half-drunk, was telling her stories about actors and parties he had not taken her to.

He had gotten her a job in the story department and she began a long career in the world of movies with its intimate acquaintances, fraudulence, and dreams. One could, though, as that world went, rely on her and she tried to be honest. In the end she became a producer. She had never actually produced anything, but she had suggested things and seen them on the way to realization or oblivion, sometimes both. The marriage to Dr. Hirsch had helped. One of his patients was a rich man who owned a game-show company, and through him she met figures in television. It was after she was widowed that the long-awaited opportunity came. She was invited to coproduce a show that turned out to be a success, and a year later she became the sole producer when her partner fell in love and left to marry a Venezuelan businessman. Easygoing in manner, sentimental but shrewd, she drove to work in an inexpensive car and was well liked by the crew. They wanted to please her, to see her laugh and smile.

You will probably recognize the outlines of the plot. A romantic and mysterious figure, cynical and well able to take care of himself, is, beneath all that, a lost idealist. In this version he is a lawyer, first in his class at law school, who throws it all in after several years in a large firm and proceeds on his own, as much investigator as anything else and not above fixing a DUI charge for a suitable fee. In short, the dark hero of dime novels. In one memorable episode he leaves the office in evening clothes to drive to a birthday party in Palm Springs where he sees the moral rot of his rich client and ends up seducing the wife.

The fortunate thing was how well the actor fit the role. Boothman Keck was in his forties but looked younger. He had come late to acting, taking his twelve-year-old son to an open call one afternoon and being asked if he had ever done any acting himself.

"No," he said.

"None? Never?"

"Well, not that I know of."

He had a quality they were seeking for a small part as an alcoholic who still had an essential manhood.

"So, what do you do for a living?"

"I'm a swimming coach," Keck said.

"Personal?"

"No, I coach a team. A high-school team," he explained.

They liked him. Luck followed. The movie got some attention and he with it. Teddy had hired him. He was not impressed with her at first, but over time he began to see her differently and even to like her looks, the fact that she was heavy, that she was short. For some reason she called him Bud. They got along. He had had an ordinary life but was now living one that was the complete opposite. He never lost his modesty.

"It's all a dream," he would admit.

Then Deborah Legley, who had not been in a movie for some years but whose name was still alive—the slender arrogance when she was younger, the marriage to an immortal —came from the east for a guest appearance. She was being paid a lot of money, too much, Teddy felt, and from the beginning she was difficult. She came off the plane in dark glasses and no makeup though expecting to be recognized. Teddy met her on arrival. They had to wait a little too long for the car. On the set she turned out to be a monster. She made everyone wait, snubbed the director, and barely acknowledged the presence of the crew.

Teddy had to invite her to dinner and invited Keck, too,

whose wife was out of town, to make the evening bearable. She bought caviar, Beluga, in the large round tin with the sturgeon on the label. She set the caviar in crushed ice with lemon halves around it. They would have caviar, a drink, and go on to the restaurant. Keck was picking up Deborah at the hotel. Teddy looked at her watch. It was past seven. They would arrive before long.

Parking beneath the tall black palms, Keck went into the hotel and up to the suite. A dog began to bark when he knocked. He waited and then knocked again. He stood looking at the carpet. Finally,

"Who is it?"

"It's Booth."

"Who?"

"Booth," he said loudly.

"Just a minute."

An equally long time passed. The dog had stopped barking. There was silence. He knocked again. At last, like the sweeping aside of a great curtain, the door opened.

"Come in," she said. "I'm sorry, were you waiting?"

She was wearing a tan silk jacket, casual in a way, and a smooth white T-shirt beneath.

"Something spilled in the bathroom," she explained, fastening an earring and preceding him into the room. "Anyway, this ghastly dinner. What are we going to do?"

The dog was sniffing his leg.

"The thought of spending the evening with that boring

woman," she went on, "is more than I can bear. I don't know how you put up with her. Here, sit."

She patted the couch beside her. The dog leapt onto it.

"Get down, Sammy," she said, pushing him with the back of her hand.

She patted the couch again.

"She's an idiot. That driver at the airport had a big sign with my name on it, can you imagine? Put that down, I told him."

Her nostrils flared in annoyance or anger, Keck could not tell. She had two distinct ways of doing it. One was in pride and anger, a thoroughbred flaring. The other was more intimate, like the raising of an eyebrow.

"The stupidity! He wanted to wave it around so people could see it, make himself important. Exactly what one needs, isn't it? If there'd been anything, the least little thing wrong here at the hotel, I'd have flown straight back to New York. Bye-bye. But of course, they know me here, I've been here so many times."

"I guess so."

"So, what are we going to do?" she said. "Let's have a drink and figure something out. There's white wine in the fridge. I only drink white wine now. Is that all right for you? We can order something."

"I don't think we have enough time," Keck said.

"We have plenty of time."

The dog had gripped Keck's leg with its own two front legs.

"Sammy," she said, "stop."

Keck tried to disengage himself.

"Later, Sammy," he said.

"He seems to like you," she said. "But then who wouldn't, hm? You have your car, don't you? Why don't we just drive down to Santa Monica and have dinner?"

"You mean, without Teddy?"

"Completely without her."

"We should call her."

"Darling, that's for you," she said in a warm voice.

Keck sat down by the phone, uncertain of what to say.

"Hello, Teddy? It's Booth. No, I'm at the hotel," he said. "Listen, Deborah's dog is sick. She isn't going to be able to come to dinner. We'll have to call it off."

"Her dog? What's wrong with it?" Teddy said.

"Oh, it's been throwing up and it can't . . . it's having trouble walking."

"She's probably looking for a vet. I have a good one. Hold on, I'll get the number."

"No that's all right," Keck said. "One is already coming. She got him through the hotel."

"Well, tell her I'm sorry. If you need the other number, call me."

When he hung up, Keck said,

"It's OK."

"You lie almost as well as I do."

She poured some wine.

"Or would you rather have something else?" she said again. "We can drink here or we can drink there."

"Where's that?"

"Do you know Rank's? It's down off Pacific. I haven't been there in ages."

It was not quite night. The sky was an intense, deep blue, vast and cloudless. She sat beside him as they headed for the beach, her graceful neck, her cheeks, her perfume. He felt like an imposter. She still represented beauty. Her body seemed youthful. How old was she? Fifty-five, at least, but with barely a wrinkle. A goddess still. It would have once been beyond imagination to think of driving down Wilshire with her toward the last of the light.

"You don't smoke, do you?" she said.

"No."

"Good. I hate cigarettes. Nick smoked day and night. Of course, it killed him. That's something you never want to see, when it spreads to the bone and nothing stops the pain. It's horrible. Here we are."

There was a blue neon sign from which the first letter—F—was gone; it had been gone for years. Inside it was noisy and dark.

"Is Frank here?" Deborah asked the waiter.

"Just a minute," he said. "I'll go and see."

Some heads had turned when she walked past the bar, her insolent walk and then seeing who she was. After a few minutes a young man in a shirt without a tie came back to where they were sitting.

"You were asking for Frank?" he said, recognizing them but politely not showing it. "Frank isn't here anymore."

"What happened?" Deborah said.

"He sold the place."

"When was that?"

"A year and a half ago."

Deborah nodded.

"You ought to change the name or something," she said, "so you don't fool people."

"Well, it's always been the name of the place. We have the same menu, the same chef," he explained cordially.

"Good for you," she said. Then to Keck, "Let's go."

"Did I say something wrong?" the new owner asked.

"Probably," she said.

Teddy had called and cancelled the reservation. She wondered about the dog. She hadn't bothered to remember its name. It had lain in its bed on the set, head on paws, watching. Teddy had had a dog for years, an English pug named Ava, all wrinkled velvet with bulging eyes and a comic nature. Deaf and nearly blind at the end, unable to walk, she was carried into the garden four or five times a day where she stood on trembling legs and looked up at Teddy helplessly with chalky, unseeing eyes. At last there was nothing that could be done and Teddy drove her to the vet for the last time. She carried her in, tears running down her cheeks. The vet pretended not to notice. He greeted the old dog instead.

"Hello, princess," he said gently.

With one of the small ivory spoons Teddy put some caviar on a piece of toast and ate it. She went into the kitchen for the chopped egg and brought it into the living room. She decided to have some vodka as well. There was a bottle of it in the freezer.

With the egg and a squeeze of lemon she served herself more caviar. There was far too much of it to even think of eating; she would bring it to the set the next day, she decided.

There were only two more weeks of shooting. Perhaps she would take a short vacation afterward. She might go down to Baja where some friends were going. She had been to Baja when she was sixteen. You were able to drink in Mexico and do anything, although by that time they were often in separate beds. They had twin beds in the apartment on Venice Boulevard and also that summer in Malibu in a house rented from an actor who had gone on location for six weeks. There was a leafy passageway that led to the beach. She didn't wear a bikini that summer, she was too embarrassed to, she remembered. She had a one-piece black bathing suit, the same one every day, and an abortion that fall.

There was a moth on the windshield as they headed back. They were going forty miles an hour; its wings were quivering in what must have been a titanic wind as it resisted being borne into the night. Still, stubbornly, it clung, like gray ash but thick and trembling.

"What are you doing?" she said.

Keck had pulled over and stopped. He reached out and pushed the moth a little. Abruptly it flew into the darkness.

"Are you a Buddhist or something?"

"No," he said. "I didn't know if it wanted to go where we're going, that's all."

At Jack's they were quickly given a good table. She had come here all the time when she lived out here and was making movies, she said.

"I've seen all of them," Keck said.

"Well, you should have. They were good. But you were a little kid. How old are you?"

"Forty-three."

"Forty-three. Not bad," she said.

"I won't ask you."

"Don't be crass," she warned.

"Whatever it is, you don't look it. You look about thirty."

"Thank you."

"I mean, it's astonishing."

"Don't let it be too astonishing."

What was her accent, was it English or just languid upper-class? It was different in those days, she was saying. That was when there were geniuses, great directors, Huston, Billy Wilder, Hitch. You learned a lot from them.

"You know why?" she said. "Because they had actually lived, they just didn't grow up on movies. They'd been in the war."

"Hitchcock?"

"Huston, Ford."

"How did you and Nick meet?" Keck asked.

"He saw a photo of me," she said.

"Is that the truth?"

"In a white bathing suit. No, somebody made that up. They make up all kinds of things. We met at a party at the Bistro. I was eighteen. He asked me to dance. Somehow I lost an earring and was looking for it. He'd find it, he said, call him the next day. Well, you can imagine, he was one of the god kings, it was pretty heady stuff. Anyway, I called. He said to come to his house."

Keck could see it, eighteen and more or less innocent,

everything still ahead of her. If she took off her clothes you would never forget it.

"So, you did."

"When I got there," she said, "he had a bottle of champagne and the bed turned down."

"So that was it?"

"Not quite," she said.

"What happened?"

"I told him, thanks, just the earring, please."

"That's the truth?"

"Look, he was forty-five, I was eighteen. I mean, let's see what's going on. Let's not raise the curtain so fast."

"The curtain?"

"You know what I mean. He'd been quite the ladies' man. I took care of that," she said.

She looked at him with knowing eyes.

"You men get all excited by young girls. You think they're some kind of erotic toy. You haven't met a real woman, that's the difference."

"The difference."

Her nostrils flared.

"With a real woman, the buck stops here," she said.

"I don't know what that means."

"You don't, eh? I think you do."

After a while, she said,

"So, where is your wife this evening?"

"Vancouver. She's visiting her sister."

"All the way up in Vancouver."

"Yeah."

"That's a long way from here. You know one of the things I've learned?" she said.

"No, what?"

"One never has the human company one longs for. Something else is always offered."

Perhaps it was a line from a play.

"Like me, you mean?"

"No, sweetheart, not like you. At least I don't think so."

He felt uneasy. *What's wrong, are you afraid of something?* she was going to say. *No, why? You're acting afraid.*

There was a knot in his stomach. *What is it, your wife?* she was going to ask. *Oh, yes, I forgot, the wife. There's always the wife.*

Deborah had gone to the ladies' room.

"Hello, Teddy?" Keck said. He was talking on his cell phone. "I just thought I'd call you."

"Where are you? What's happened? Is the dog all right?"

"Yeah, the dog's OK. We're at a restaurant."

"Well, it's a little late . . ."

"Don't you even budge. I'm taking care of it. I'll handle it."

"Is she behaving?"

"This woman? Let me tell you something: it's even worse if she likes you."

"What do you mean?"

"I can't talk anymore, I see her coming back. You're lucky you're not here."

Teddy, having hung up the phone, sat by herself. The vodka had left her with a pleasant feeling and the disinclination to wonder where the two of them were. The chair was comfortable. The garden, through the French doors, was dark. She was not thinking of anything in particular. She looked around at the familiar furniture, the flowers, the lamplight. She found herself, for some reason, thinking about her life, a thing she did not do often. She had a nice house, not large but perfect for her. You could even, from a place on the lawn, see a bit of the ocean. There was a maid's room and a guest room, the closet in the latter filled with her clothes. She had difficulty throwing things away and there were clothes for any occasion, though the occasion may have been long past. Still, she did not like to think of beautifully made things in the trash. But there was no one to give them to, the maid had no use for them, there was no one who would even wear them.

The years of her marriage, looking back, had been good ones. Myron Hirsch had left her with more than enough to take care of herself, and the success she had had was on top of that. For a woman of few talents—was that true? perhaps she was shortchanging herself—she had done pretty well. She was remembering how it had started. She remembered the beer bottles rolling around in the back of the car when she was fifteen and he was making love to her every morning and she did not know if she was beginning life or throwing it away, but she loved him and would never forget.

COMET

Philip married Adele on a day in June. It was cloudy and the wind was blowing. Later the sun came out. It had been a while since Adele had married and she wore white: white pumps with low heels, a long white skirt that clung to her hips, a filmy blouse with a white bra underneath, and around her neck a string of freshwater pearls. They were married in her house, the one she'd gotten in the divorce. All her friends were there. She believed strongly in friendship. The room was crowded.

"I, Adele," she said in a clear voice, "give myself to you, Phil, completely as your wife . . ." Behind her as best man, somewhat oblivious, her young son was standing, and pinned to her panties as something borrowed was a small silver disc, actually a St. Christopher's medal her father had worn in the war; she had several times rolled down the waistband of her skirt to show it to people. Near the door, under the impression that she was part of a garden tour, was an old woman who held a little dog by the handle of a cane hooked through his collar.

At the reception Adele smiled with happiness, drank too much, laughed, and scratched her bare arms with long showgirl nails. Her new husband admired her. He could have licked her palms like a calf does salt. She was still young enough to be good-looking, the final blaze of it, though she was too old for children, at least if she had anything to say about it. Summer was coming. Out of the afternoon haze she would appear, in her black bathing suit, limbs all tan, the brilliant sun behind her. She was the strong figure walking up the smooth sand from the sea, her legs, her wet swimmer's hair, the grace of her, all careless and unhurried.

They settled into life together, hers mostly. It was her furniture and her books, though they were largely unread. She liked to tell stories about DeLereo, her first husband—Frank, his name was—the heir to a garbage-hauling empire. She called him Delerium, but the stories were not unaffectionate. Loyalty—it came from her childhood as well as the years of marriage, eight exhausting years, as she said—was her code. The terms of marriage had been simple, she admitted. Her job was to be dressed, have dinner ready, and be fucked once a day. One time in Florida with another couple they chartered a boat to go bonefishing off Bimini.

"We'll have a good dinner," DeLereo had said happily, "get on board and turn in. When we get up we'll have passed the Gulf Stream."

It began that way but ended differently. The sea was very rough. They never did cross the Gulf Stream—the captain was from Long Island and got lost. DeLereo paid him fifty dollars to turn over the wheel and go below.

"Do you know anything about boats?" the captain asked.

"More than you do," DeLereo told him.

He was under an ultimatum from Adele, who was lying, deathly pale, in their cabin. "Get us into port somewhere or get ready to sleep by yourself," she'd said.

Philip Ardet had heard the story and many others often. He was mannerly and elegant, his head held back a bit as he talked, as though you were a menu. He and Adele had met on the golf course when she was learning to play. It was a wet day and the course was nearly empty. Adele and a friend were teeing off when a balding figure carrying a cloth bag with a few clubs in it asked if he could join them. Adele hit a passable drive. Her friend bounced his across the road and teed up another, which he topped. Phil, rather shyly, took out an old three wood and hit one two hundred yards straight down the fairway.

That was his persona, capable and calm. He'd gone to Princeton and been in the navy. He looked like someone who'd been in the navy, Adele said—his legs were strong. The first time she went out with him, he remarked it was a funny thing, some people liked him, some didn't.

"The ones that do, I tend to lose interest in."

She wasn't sure just what that meant but she liked his appearance, which was a bit worn, especially around the eyes. It made her feel he was a real man, though perhaps not the man he had been. Also he was smart, as she explained it, more or less the way professors were.

To be liked by her was worthwhile but to be liked by him seemed somehow of even greater value. There was something about him that discounted the world. He appeared in a way to care nothing for himself, to be above that.

He didn't make much money, as it turned out. He wrote for a business weekly. She earned nearly that much selling houses. She had begun to put on a little weight. This was a few years after they were married. She was still beautiful—

her face was—but she had adopted a more comfortable outline. She would get into bed with a drink, the way she had done when she was twenty-five. Phil, a sport jacket over his pajamas, sat reading. Sometimes he walked that way on their lawn in the morning. She sipped her drink and watched him.

"You know something?"

"What?"

"I've had good sex since I was fifteen," she said.

He looked up.

"I didn't start quite that young," he confessed.

"Maybe you should have."

"Good advice. Little late though."

"Do you remember when we first got started?"

"I remember."

"We could hardly stop," she said. "You remember?"

"It averages out."

"Oh, great," she said.

After he'd gone to sleep she watched a movie. The stars grew old, too, and had problems with love. It was different, though—they had already reaped huge rewards. She watched, thinking. She thought of what she had been, what she had had. She could have been a star.

What did Phil know—he was sleeping.

Autumn came. One evening they were at the Morrisseys'—Morrissey was a tall lawyer, the executor of many estates and trustee of others. Reading wills had been his true education, a look into the human heart, he said.

At the dinner table was a man from Chicago who'd made

a fortune in computers, a nitwit it soon became apparent, who during the meal gave a toast,

"To the end of privacy and the life of dignity," he said.

He was with a dampened woman who had recently found out that her husband had been having an affair with a black woman in Cleveland, an affair that had somehow been going on for seven years. There may even have been a child.

"You can see why coming here is like a breath of fresh air for me," she said.

The women were sympathetic. They knew what she had to do—she had to rethink completely the past seven years.

"That's right," her companion agreed.

"What is there to be rethought?" Phil wanted to know.

He was answered with impatience. The deception, they said, the deception—she had been deceived all that time. Adele meanwhile was pouring more wine for herself. Her napkin covered the place where she had already spilled a glass of it.

"But that time was spent in happiness, wasn't it?" Phil asked guilelessly. "That's been lived. It can't be changed. It can't be just turned into unhappiness."

"That woman stole my husband. She stole everything he had vowed."

"Forgive me," Phil said softly. "That happens every day."

There was an outcry as if from a chorus, heads thrust forward like the hissing, sacred geese. Only Adele sat silent.

"Every day," he repeated, his voice drowned out, the voice of reason or at least of fact.

"I'd never steal anyone's man," Adele said then. "Never." Her face had a tone of weariness when she drank, a weariness that knew the answer to everything. "And I'd never break a vow."

"I don't think you would," Phil said.

"I'd never fall for a twenty-year-old, either."

She was talking about the tutor, the girl who had come that time, youth burning through her clothes.

"No, you wouldn't."

"He left his wife," Adele told them.

There was silence.

Phil's bit of smile had gone but his face was still pleasant.

"I didn't leave my wife," he said quietly. "She threw me out."

"He left his wife and children," Adele said.

"I didn't leave them. Anyway it was over between us. It had been for more than a year. He said it evenly, almost as if it had happened to someone else. It was my son's tutor," he explained. "I fell in love with her."

"And you began something with her?" Morrissey suggested.

"Oh, yes."

There is love when you lose the power to speak, when you cannot even breathe.

"Within two or three days," he confessed.

"There in the house?"

Phil shook his head. He had a strange, helpless feeling. He was abandoning himself.

"I didn't do anything in the house."

"He left his wife and children," Adele repeated.

"You knew that," Phil said.

"Just walked out on them. They'd been married fifteen years, since he was nineteen."

"We hadn't been married fifteen years."

"They had three children," she said, "one of them retarded."

Something had happened—he was becoming speechless, he could feel it in his chest like a kind of nausea. As if he were giving up portions of an intimate past.

"He wasn't retarded," he managed to say. "He was . . . having trouble learning to read, that's all."

At that instant an aching image of himself and his son from years before came to him. They had rowed one afternoon to the middle of a friend's pond and jumped in, just the two of them. It was summer. His son was six or seven. There was a layer of warm water over deeper, cooler water, the faded green of frogs and weeds. They swam to the far side and then all the way back, the blond head and anxious face of his boy above the surface like a dog's. Year of joy.

"So tell them the rest of it," Adele said.

"There is no rest."

"It turned out this tutor was some kind of call girl. He found her in bed with some guy."

"Is that right?" Morrissey said.

He was leaning on the table, his chin in his hand. You think you know someone, you think because you have dinner with them or play cards, but you really don't. It's always a surprise. You know nothing.

"It didn't matter," Phil murmured.

"So stupid marries her anyway," Adele went on. "She comes to Mexico City where he's working and he marries her."

"You don't understand anything, Adele," he said.

He wanted to say more but couldn't. It was like being out of breath.

"Do you still talk to her?" Morrissey asked casually.

"Yes, over my dead body," Adele said.

None of them could know, none of them could visualize Mexico City and the first unbelievable year, driving down to the coast for the weekend, through Cuernavaca, her bare legs with the sun lying on them, her arms, the dizziness and submission he felt with her as before a forbidden photograph, as if before an overwhelming work of art. Two years in Mexico City oblivious to the wreckage. It was the sense of godliness that empowered him. He could see her neck bent forward with its slender nape. He could see the faint trace of bones like pearls that ran down her smooth back. He could see himself, his former self.

"I talk to her," he admitted.

"And your first wife?"

"I talk to her. We have three kids."

"He left her," Adele said. "Casanova here."

"Some women have minds like cops," Phil said to no one in particular. "This is right, that's wrong. Well, anyway . . ."

He stood up. He had done everything wrong, he realized, in the wrong order. He had scuttled his life.

"Anyway there's one thing I can say truthfully. I'd do it all over again if I had the chance."

After he had gone outside they went on talking. The woman whose husband had been unfaithful for seven years knew what it was like.

"He pretends he can't help it," she said. "I've had the

136

same thing happen. I was going by Bergdorf's one day and saw a green coat in the window that I liked and I went in and bought it. Then a little while later, someplace else, I saw one that was better than the first one, I thought, so I bought that. Anyway, by the time I was finished I had four green coats hanging in the closet—it was just because I couldn't control my desires."

Outside, the sky, the topmost dome of it, was brushed with clouds and the stars were dim. Adele finally made him out, standing far off in the darkness. She walked unsteadily toward him. His head, she saw, was raised. She stopped a few yards away and raised her head, too. The sky began to whirl. She took an unexpected step or two to steady herself.

"What are you looking at?" she finally said.

He did not answer. He had no intention of answering. Then,

"The comet," he said. "It's been in the papers. This is the night it's supposed to be most visible."

There was silence.

"I don't see any comet," she said.

"You don't?"

"Where is it?"

"It's right up there," he gestured. "It doesn't look like anything, just like another small star. It's that extra one, by the Pleiades." He knew all the constellations. He had seen them rise in darkness over heartbreaking coasts.

"Come on, you can look at it tomorrow," she said, almost consolingly, though she came no closer to him.

"It won't be there tomorrow. One time only."

"How do you know where it'll be?" she said. "Come on, it's late, let's get out of here."

He did not move. After a bit she walked toward the house where, extravagantly, every window upstairs and down was lit. He stood where he was, looking up at the sky and then at her as she became smaller and smaller going across the lawn, reaching first the aura, then the brightness, then tripping on the kitchen steps.

THE DESTRUCTION OF THE GOETHEANUM

In the garden, standing alone, he found the young woman who was a friend of the writer William Hedges, then unknown but even Kafka had lived in obscurity, she said, and so moreover had Mendel, perhaps she meant Mendeleyev. They were staying in a little hotel across the Rhine. No one could seem to find it, she said.

The river there flowed swiftly, the surface was alive. It carried things away, broken wood and branches. They spun around, went under, emerged. Sometimes pieces of furniture passed, ladders, windows. Once, in the rain, a chair.

They were living in the same room, but it was completely platonic. Her hand, he noticed, bore no ring or jewelry of any kind. Her wrists were bare.

"He doesn't like to be alone," she said. "He's struggling with his work." It was a novel, still far from finished though parts were extraordinary. A fragment had been published in Rome. "It's called *The Goetheanum*," she said. "Do you know what that is?"

He tried to remember the curious word already dissolving in his mind. The lights inside the house had begun to appear in the blue evening.

"It's the one great act of his life."

The hotel she had spoken of was small with small rooms and letters in yellow across the facade. There were many buildings like it. From the cool flank of the cathedral it was visible amid them, below and a little downstream. Also through the windows of antique shops and alleys.

Two days later he saw her from a distance. She was unmistakable. She moved with a kind of negligent grace, like a dancer whose career is ended. The crowd ignored her.

"Oh," she greeted him, "yes, hello."

Her voice seemed vague. He was sure she did not recognize him. He didn't know exactly what to say.

"I was thinking about some of the things you told me . . ." he began.

She stood with people pushing past, her arms filled with packages. The street was hot. She did not understand who he was, he was certain of it. She was performing simple errands, those of a remote and saintly couple.

"Forgive me," she said, "I'm really not myself."

"We met at Sarren's," he explained.

"Yes, I know."

A silence followed. He wanted to say something quite simple to her but she was preventing it.

She had been to the museum. When Hedges worked he had to be alone, sometimes she would find him asleep on the floor.

"He's crazy," she said. "Now he's sure there'll be a war. Everything's going to be destroyed."

Her own words seemed to disinterest her. The crowd was pulling her away.

"Can I walk with you for a minute?" he asked. "Are you going toward the bridge?"

She looked both ways.

"Yes," she decided.

They went down the narrow streets. She said nothing. She glanced in shop windows. She had a mouth which curved downward, a serving girl's mouth, a girl from small towns.

"Are you interested in painting?" he heard her say.

"Yes."

In the museum there were Holbeins and Hodlers, El Grecos, Max Ernst. The silence of long salons. In them one understood what it meant to be great.

"Do you want to go tomorrow?" she said. "No, tomorrow we're going somewhere. Perhaps the day after?"

That day he woke early, already nervous. The room seemed empty. The sky was yellow with light. The surface of the river, between stone banks, was incandescent. The water rushed in fragments white as fire, at their center one could not even look.

By nine the sky had faded, the river was broken into silver. At ten it was brown, the color of soup. Barges and old-fashioned steamers were working slowly upstream or going swiftly down. The piers of the bridges trailed small wakes.

A river is the soul of a city, only water and air can purify. At Basel, the Rhine lies between well-established stone banks. The trees are carefully trimmed, the old houses hidden behind them.

He looked for her everywhere. He crossed the Rheinbrucke and, watching faces, went to the open market through the crowds. He searched among the stalls. Women were buying flowers, they boarded streetcars and sat with the bunches in their laps. In the Borse restaurant fat men were eating, their small ears close to their heads.

She was nowhere to be found. He even entered the cathedral, expecting for a moment to find her waiting. There was no one. The city was turning to stone. The pure hour of sunlight had passed, there was nothing left now but a raging afternoon that burned his feet. The clocks struck three. He gave up and returned to the hotel. There was an edge of white paper in his box. It was a note, she would meet him at four.

In excitement he lay down to think. She had not forgotten. He read it again. Were they really meeting in secret? He was not certain what that meant. Hedges was forty, he had almost no friends, his wife was somewhere back in Connecticut, he had left her, he had renounced the past. If he was not great, he was following the path of greatness which is the same as disaster, and he had the power to make one devote oneself to his life. She was with him constantly. I'm never out of his sight, she complained. Nadine: it was a name she had chosen herself.

She was late. They ended up going to tea at five o'clock; Hedges was busy reading English newspapers. They sat at a table overlooking the river, the menus in their hands long and slim as airline tickets. She seemed very calm. He wanted to keep looking at her. *Hummersalat*, he was reading somehow, *rump steak*. She was very hungry, she announced. She had been at the museum, the paintings made her ravenous.

"Where were you?" she said.

Suddenly he realized she had expected him. There were young couples strolling the galleries, their legs washed in sunlight. She had wandered among them. She knew quite well what they were doing: they were preparing for love. His eyes slipped.

"I'm starving," she said.

She ate asparagus, then a goulash soup, and after that a cake she did not finish. The thought crossed his mind that perhaps they had no money, she and Hedges, that it was her only meal of the day.

"No," she said. "William has a sister who's married to a very rich man. He can get money there."

It seemed she had the faintest accent. Was it English?

"I was born in Genoa," she told him.

She quoted a few lines of Valéry which he later found out were incorrect. *Afternoons torn by wind, the stinging sea . . .* She adored Valéry. An anti-Semite, she said.

She described a trip to Dornach, it was forty minutes away by streetcar, then a long walk from the station where she had stood arguing with Hedges about which way to go, it always annoyed her that he had no sense of direction. It was uphill, he was soon out of breath.

Dornach had been chosen by the teacher Rudolf Steiner to be the center of his realm. There, not far from Basel, beyond the calm suburbs, he had dreamed of establishing a community with a great central building to be named after Goethe, whose ideas had inspired it, and in 1913 the cornerstone for it was finally laid. The design was Steiner's own, as were all the details, techniques, the paintings, the specially engraved glass. He invented its construction just as he had its shape.

It was to be built entirely of wood, two enormous domes

which intersected, the plot of that curve itself was a mathematical event. Steiner believed only in curves, there were no right angles anywhere. Small, tributary domes like helmets contained the windows and doors. Everything was wood, everything except the gleaming Norwegian slates that covered the roof. The earliest photographs showed it surrounded by scaffolding like some huge monument, in the foreground were groves of apple trees. The construction was carried on by people from all over the world, many of them abandoned professions and careers. By the spring of 1914 the roof timbers were in position, and while they were still laboring the war broke out. From the nearby provinces of France they could actually hear the rumble of cannon. It was the hottest month of summer.

She showed him a photograph of a vast, brooding structure.

"The Goetheanum," she said.

He was silent. The darkness of the picture, the resonance of the domes began to invade him. He submitted to it as to the mirror of a hypnotist. He could feel himself slipping from reality. He did not struggle. He longed to kiss the fingers which held the postcard, the lean arms, the skin which smelled like lemons. He felt himself trembling, he knew she could see it. They sat like that, her gaze was calm. He was entering the grey, the Wagnerian scene before him which she might close at any moment like a matchbox and replace in her bag. The windows resembled an old hotel somewhere in middle Europe. In Prague. The shapes sang to him. It was a fortification, a terminal, an observatory from which one could look into the soul.

"Who is Rudolf Steiner?" he asked.

He hardly heard her explanation. He was beginning to have ecstasies. Steiner was a great teacher, a savant who believed deep insights could be revealed in art. He believed in movements and mystery plays, rhythms, creation, the stars. Of course. And somehow from this she had learned a scenario. She had become the illusionist of Hedges' life.

It was Hedges, the convict Joyce scholar, the rumpled ghost at literary parties, who had found her. He was distant at first, he barely spoke a word to her the night they met. She had not been in New York long then. She was living on Twelfth Street in a room with no furniture. The next day the phone rang. It was Hedges. He asked her to lunch. He had known from the first exactly who she was, he said. He was calling from a phone booth, the traffic was roaring past.

"Can you meet me at Haroot's?" he said.

His hair was uncombed, his fingers unsteady. He was sitting by the wall, too nervous to look at anything except his hands. She became his companion.

They spent long days together wandering in the city. He wore shirts the color of blue ink, he bought her clothes. He was wildly generous, he seemed to care nothing for money, it was crumpled in his pockets like wastepaper, when he paid for things it would fall on the floor. He made her come to restaurants where he was dining with his wife and sit at the bar so he could watch her while they ate.

Slowly he began her introduction to another world, a world which scorned exposure, a world more rich than the one she knew, certain occult books, philosophies, even music. She discovered she had a talent for it, an instinct. She achieved a kind of power over herself. There were periods of deep affection, serenity. They sat in a friend's house and listened to Scriabin. They ate at the Russian Tea Room, the waiters knew his name. Hedges was performing an extraordinary act, he was fusing her life. He, too, had found a new existence: he was a criminal at last. At the end of a year they came to Europe.

"He's intelligent," she explained. "You feel it immediately. He has a mind that touches everything."

"How long have you been with him?"

"Forever," she said.

They walked back toward her hotel in that one, dying hour which ends the day. The trees by the river were black as stone. *Wozzeck* was playing at the theater to be followed by *The Magic Flute*. In the print shops were maps of the city and drawings of the famous bridge as it looked in Napoleon's time. The banks were filled with newly minted coins. She was strangely silent. They stopped once, before a restaurant with a tank of fish, great speckled trout larger than a shoe lazing in green water, their mouths working slowly. Her face was visible in the glass like a woman's on a train, indifferent, alone. Her beauty was directed toward no one. She seemed not to see him, she was lost in her thoughts. Then, coldly, without a word, her eyes met his. They did not waver. In that moment he realized she was worth everything.

They had not had an easy time. Reason is unequal to man's problems, Hedges said. His wife had somehow gotten hold of his bank account, not that it was much, but she had a nose like a ferret, she found other earnings that might have come his way. Further, he was sure his letters to his children were not being delivered. He had to write them at school and in care of friends.

The question above all and always, however, was money. It was crushing them. He wrote articles but they were hard to sell, he was no good at anything topical. He did a piece about Giacometti with many haunting quotations which were entirely invented. He tried everything. Meanwhile, on every side it seemed, young men were writing film scripts or selling things for enormous sums.

Hedges was alone. The men his age had made their reputations, everything was passing him by. Anyway he often felt it. He knew the lives of Cervantes, Stendhal, Italo Svevo but none of them was as improbable as his own. And wherever they went there were his notebooks and papers to carry. Nothing is heavier than paper.

In Grasse he had trouble with his teeth, something went bad in the roots of old repairs. He was in misery, they had to pay a French dentist almost every penny they had. In Venice he was bitten by a cat. A terrible infection developed, his arm swelled to twice its size, it seemed the skin would burst. The *cameriera* told them cats had venom in their mouth like snakes, the same thing had happened to her son. The bites were always deep, she said, the poison entered the blood. Hedges was in agony, he could not sleep. It would have been much worse fifty years ago, the doctor told them. He touched a point up near his shoulder. Hedges was too weak to ask what it meant. Twice a day a woman came with a hypodermic in a battered tin box and gave him shots. He was growing more feverish. He could no longer read. He wanted to dictate some final things, Nadine took them down. He insisted on being buried with her photograph over his heart, he had made her promise to tear it from her passport.

"How will I get home?" she had asked.

Beneath them in the sunlight the great river flowed, almost without a sound. The lives of artists seem beautiful at last, even the terrible arguments about money, the nights there is nothing to do. Besides, through it all, Hedges was never helpless. He lived one life and imagined ten others, he could always find refuge in one of them.

"But I'm tired of it," she confessed. "He's selfish. He's a child."

She did not look like a woman who had suffered. Her clothes were silky. Her teeth were white. On the far pathways couples were having lunch, the girls with their shoes off, their feet slanting down the bank. They were throwing bits of bread in the water.

The development of the individual had reached its apogee, Hedges believed, that was the essence of our time. A new direction must be found. He did not believe in collectivism, however. That was a blind road. He wasn't certain yet of what the path would be. His writing would reveal it, but he was working against time, against a tide of events, he was in exile, like Trotsky. Unfortunately, there was no one to kill him. It didn't matter, his teeth would do it in the end, he said.

Nadine was staring into the water.

"There are nothing but eels down there," she said.

He followed her gaze. The surface was impenetrable. He tried to find a single, black shadow betrayed by its grace.

"When the time comes to mate," she told him, "they go to the sea."

She watched the water. When the time came they heard somehow, they slithered across meadows in the morning, shining like dew. She was fourteen years old, she told him, when her mother took her favorite doll down to the river and threw it in, the days of being a young girl were over.

"What shall I throw in?" he asked.

She seemed not to hear. Then she looked up.

"Do you mean that?" she finally said.

She wanted them to have dinner together, would Hedges sense something or not? He tried not to think about it or allow himself to be alarmed. There were scenes in every literature of this moment, but still he could not imagine what it would be like. A great writer might say, I know I cannot keep her, but would he dare give her up? Hedges, his teeth filled with cavities and all the years lying on top of his unwritten works?

"I owe him so much," she had said.

Still, it was difficult to face the evening calmly. By five o'clock he was in a state of nerves, playing solitaire in his room, rereading articles in the paper. It seemed that he had forgotten how to speak about things, he was conscious of his facial expressions, nothing he did seemed natural. The person he had been had somehow vanished, it was impossible to create another. Everything was impossible, he imagined a dinner at which he would be humiliated, deceived.

At seven o'clock, afraid the telephone would ring at any moment, he went down in the elevator. The glimpse of himself in the mirror reassured him, he seemed ordinary, he seemed calm. He touched his hair. His heart was thundering. He looked at himself again. The door slid open. He stepped out, half expecting to find them there. There was no one. He turned the pages of the Zurich paper while keeping an eye on the door. Finally he managed to sit in one of the chairs. It was awkward. He moved. It was seven-ten. Twenty minutes later an old Citroën backed straight into the grill of a Mercedes parked in the street with a great smashing of glass. The concierge and desk clerk went running out. There were pieces everywhere. The driver of the Citroën was opening his door.

"Oh, Christ," he murmured, looking around.

It was William Hedges. Alone.

They all began to talk at once. The owner of the Mercedes, which was blinded, fortunately was not present. A policeman was making his way along the street.

"Well, it's not too serious," Hedges said. He was inspecting his own car. The taillights were shattered. There was a dent in the trunk.

After much discussion he was finally allowed to enter the hotel. He was wearing a striped cotton jacket and a shirt the color of ink. He had a white face, damp with sweat, the face of an unpopular schoolboy, high forehead, thinning hair, a soft beard touched with grey, the beard of an explorer, a man who washed his socks in the Amazon.

"Nadine will be along a little later," he said.

When he reached for a drink, his hand was trembling.

"My foot slipped off the brake," he explained. He quickly

lit a cigarette. "The insurance pays that, don't they? Probably not."

He seemed to have reached a stop, the first of many enormous pauses during which he looked in his lap. Then, as if it were the thing he had been struggling to think of, he inquired painfully, "What do you . . . think of Basel?"

The headwaiter had placed them on opposite sides of the table, the empty chair between them. Its presence seemed to weigh on Hedges. He asked for another drink. Turning, he knocked over a glass. That act, somehow, relieved him. The waiter dabbed at the wet tablecloth with a napkin. Hedges spoke around him.

"I don't know exactly what Nadine has told you," he said softly. A long pause. "She sometimes tells . . . fantastic lies."

"Oh, yes?"

"She's from a little town in Pennsylvania," Hedges muttered. "Julesberg. She's never been . . . she was just a . . . an ordinary girl when we met."

They had come to Basel to visit certain institutions, he explained. It was an . . . interesting city. History has certain sites upon which whole epochs turn, and the village of Dornach gave evidence of a very . . . The sentence was never finished. Rudolf Steiner had been a student of Goethe. . . .

"Yes, I know."

"Of course. Nadine's been telling you, hasn't she?"

"No."

"I see."

He finally began again, about Goethe. The range of that intellect, he said, had been so extraordinary that he was able, like Leonardo before him, to encompass all of what was then human knowledge. That, in itself, implied an overall . . . coherence, and the fact that no man had been capable of it since could easily mean the coherence no longer existed, it was dissolved. . . . The ocean of things known had burst its shores.

"We are on the verge," Hedges said, "of radical departures in the destiny of man. Those who reveal them . . ."

The words, coming with agonized slowness, seemed to take forever. They were a ruse, a feint. It was difficult to hear them out.

". . . will be torn to pieces like Galileo."

"Is that what you think?"

A long pause again.

"Oh, yes."

They had another drink.

"We are a little strange, I suppose, Nadine and I," Hedges said, as if to himself.

It was finally the time.

"I don't think she's a very happy woman."

There was a moment of silence.

"Happy?" Hedges said. "No, she isn't happy. She isn't capable of being happy. Ecstasies. She is ecstatic. She tells me so every day," he said. He put his hand to his forehead, half covering his eyes. "You see, you don't know her at all."

She was not coming, suddenly that was clear. There was going to be no dinner.

Something should have been said, it ended too vaguely. Ten minutes after Hedges had gone, leaving behind an embarrassing expanse of white and three places set, the thought came of what he should have demanded: I want to talk to her.

All doors had closed. He was miserable, he could not imagine someone with weaknesses, incapacities like his own. He had intended to mutilate a man and it turned into monologue—probably they were laughing about it at that very moment. It had all been humiliating. The river was moving beneath his window, even in darkness the current showed. He stood looking down upon it. He walked about trying to calm himself. He lay on the bed, it seemed his limbs were trembling. He detested himself. Finally he was still.

He had just closed his eyes when in the emptiness of the room the telephone rang. It rang again. A third time. Of course! He had expected it. His heart was jumping as he picked it up. He tried to say hello quite calmly. A man's voice answered. It was Hedges. He was humble.

"Is Nadine there?" he managed to say.

"Nadine?"

"Please, may I speak to her," Hedges said.

"She's not here."

There was a silence. He could hear Hedges' helpless breathing. It seemed to go on and on.

"Look," Hedges began, his voice was less brave, "I just want to talk to her for a moment, that's all. . . . I beg you . . ."

She was somewhere in the town then, he hurried out to find her. He didn't bother to decide where she might be. Somehow the night had turned in his direction, everything was changing. He walked, he ran through the streets, afraid to be late.

It was nearly midnight, people were coming out of the theaters, the café at the Casino was roaring. A sea of hidden and half-hidden faces with the waiters always standing so someone could be hidden behind them, he combed it slowly. Surely she was there. She was sitting at a table by herself, she expected to be found.

The same cars were turning through the streets, he stepped among them. People walked slowly, stopping at lighted windows. She would be looking at a display of expensive shoes, antique jewelry perhaps, gold necklaces. At the corners he had a feeling of loss. He passed down interior arcades. He was leaving the more familiar section. The newsstands were locked, the cinemas dark.

Suddenly, like the first truth of illness, the certainty left him. Had she gone back to her hotel? Perhaps she was even at his, or had been there and gone. He knew she was capable of aimless, original acts. Instead of drifting in the darkness of the city, her somewhat languid footsteps existing only to be devoured by his, instead of choosing a place in which to be found as cleverly as she had drawn him to follow, she might have become discouraged and returned to Hedges to say only, I felt like a walk.

There is always one moment, he thought, it never comes again. He began going back, as if lost, along streets he had already seen. The excitement was gone, he was searching, he was no longer sure of his instincts but wondering instead what she might have decided to do.

On the stairway near the Heuwaage, he stopped. The

square was empty. He was suddenly cold. A lone man was passing below. It was Hedges. He was wearing no tie, the collar of his jacket was turned up. He walked without direction, he was in search of his dreams. His pockets had bank notes crumpled in them, cigarettes bent in half. The whiteness of his skin was visible from afar. His hair was uncombed. He did not pretend to be young, he was past that, into the heart of his life, his failed work, a man who took commuter trains, who drank tea, hoping for something, some proof in the end that his talents had been as great as the others'. This world is giving birth to another, he said. We are nearing the galaxy's core. He was writing that, he was inventing it. His poems would become our history.

The streets were deserted, the restaurants had turned out their lights. Alone in a café in the repetition of empty tables, the chairs placed upon them upside down, his dark shirt, his doctor's beard, Hedges sat. He would never find her. He was like a man out of work, an invalid, there was no place to go. The cities of Europe were silent. He coughed a little in the chill.

The Goetheanum of the photograph, the one she had shown him, did not exist. It had burned on the night of December 31, 1922. There had been an evening lecture, the audience had gone home. The night watchman discovered smoke and soon afterward the fire became visible. It spread with astonishing rapidity and the firemen battled without effect. At last the situation seemed beyond hope. An inferno was rising within the great windows. Steiner called everyone out of the building. Exactly at midnight the main dome was breached, the flames burst through and roared upward. The windows with their special glass were glowing, they began to explode from the heat. A huge crowd had come from the nearby villages and even from Basel itself where, miles away, the fire was visible. Finally the dome collapsed, green and blue flames soaring from the metal organ pipes. The Goetheanum disappeared, its master, its priest, its lone creator walking slowly in the ashes at dawn.

A new structure made of concrete rose in its place. Of the old, only photos remained.

BANGKOK

Hollis was in the back at a table piled with books and a space among them where he was writing when Carol came in.

"Hello," she said.

"Well, look who's here," he said coolly. "Hello."

She was wearing a gray jersey sweater and a narrow skirt; as always, dressed well.

"Didn't you get my message?" she asked.

"Yes."

"You didn't call back."

"No."

"Weren't you going to?"

"Of course not," he said.

He looked wider than the last time and his hair, halfway to the shoulder, needed to be cut.

"I went by your apartment but you'd gone. I talked to Pam, that's her name, isn't it? Pam."

"Yes."

"We talked. Not that long. She didn't seem interested in talking. Is she shy?"

"No, she's not shy."

"I asked her a question. Want to know what it was?"

"Not especially," he said.

He leaned back. His jacket was draped over the back of the

chair and his sleeves rolled partway up. She noticed a round wristwatch with a brown leather strap.

"I asked her if you still liked to have your cock sucked."

"Get out of here," he ordered. "Go on, get out."

"She didn't answer," Carol said.

He had a moment of fear, of guilt almost, about consequences. On the other hand, he didn't believe her.

"So, do you?" she said.

"Leave, will you? Please," he said in a civilized tone. He made a dispersing motion with his hand. "I mean it."

"I'm not going to stay long, just a few minutes. I wanted to see you, that's all. Why didn't you call back?"

She was tall with a long, elegant nose like a thoroughbred's. What people look like isn't the same as what you remember. She had been coming out of a restaurant one time, down some steps long after lunch in a silk dress that clung around the hips and the wind pulled against her legs. The afternoons, he thought for a moment.

She sat down in the leather chair opposite and gave a slight, uncertain smile.

"You have a nice place."

It had the makings of one, two rooms on the garden floor with a little grass and the backs of discrete houses behind, though there was just one window and the floorboards were worn. He sold fine books and manuscripts, letters for the most part, and had too big an inventory for a dealer his size. After ten years in retail clothing he had found his true life. The rooms had high ceilings, the bookcases were filled and against them, on the floor, a few framed photographs leaned.

"Chris," she said, "tell me something. Whatever happened

to that picture of us taken at that lunch Diana Wald gave at her mother's house that day? Up there on that fake hill made from all the old cars? Do you still have that?"

"It must have gotten lost."

"I'd really like to have it. It was a wonderful picture. Those were the days," she said. "Do you remember the boat house we had?"

"Of course."

"I wonder if you remember it the way I remember it."

"That would be hard to say." He had a low, persuasive voice. There was confidence in it, perhaps a little too much.

"The pool table, do you remember that? And the bed by the windows."

He didn't answer. She picked up one of the books from the table and was looking through it; *e.e. cummings*, The Enormous Room, *dust jacket with some small chips at bottom, minor soil on title page, otherwise very good. First edition.* The price was marked in pencil on the corner of the flyleaf at the top. She turned the pages idly.

"This has that part in it you like so much. What is it, again?"

"Jean Le Nègre."

"That's it."

"Still unrivaled," he said.

"Makes me think of Alan Baron for some reason. Are you still in touch with him? Did he ever publish anything? Always telling me about Tantric yoga and how I should try it. He wanted to show it to me."

"So, did he?"

"You're kidding."

She was leafing through the pages with her long thumbs.

"They're always talking about Tantric yoga," she said, "or telling you about their big dicks. Not you, though. So, how is Pam, incidentally? I couldn't really tell. Is she happy?"

"She's very happy."

"That's nice. And you have a little girl now, how old is she again?"

"Her name is Chloe. She's six."

"Oh, she's big. They know a lot at that age, don't they? They know and they don't know," she said. She closed the book and put it down. "Their bodies are so pure. Does Chloe have a nice body?"

"You'd kill for it," he said casually.

"A perfect little body. I can picture it. Do you give her baths? I bet you do. You're a model father, the father every little girl ought to have. How will you be when she's bigger, I wonder? When the boys start coming around."

"There're not going to be a lot of boys coming around."

"Oh, for God's sake. Of course, there will. They'll be coming around just quivering. You know that. She'll have breasts and that first, soft pubic hair."

"You know, Carol, you're disgusting."

"You don't like to think of it, that's all. But she's going to be a woman, you know, a young woman. You remember how you felt about young women at that age. Well, it didn't all stop with you. It continues, and she'll be part of it, perfect body and all. How is Pam's, by the way?"

"How's yours?"

"Can't you tell?"

"I wasn't paying attention."

"Do you still have sex?" she asked unconcernedly.

"There are times."

"I don't. Rarely."

"That's a little hard to believe."

"It never measures up, that's the trouble. It's never what it should be or used to be. How old are you now? You look a little heavier. Do you exercise? Do you go to the steam room and look down at yourself?"

"I don't have the time."

"Well, if you *had* more time. If you were free you'd be able to steam, shower, put on fresh clothes, and, let's see, not too early to go down to, what, the Odeon and have a drink and see if anyone's there, any girls. You could have the bartender offer them a drink or simply talk to them yourself, ask if they were doing anything for dinner, if they had any plans. As easy as that. You always liked good teeth. You liked slim arms and, how to put it, great tits, not necessarily big—good-sized, that's all. And long legs. Do you still like to tie their hands? You used to like to, it's always exciting to find out if they'll let you do it or not. Tell me, Chris, did you love me?"

"Love you?" He was leaning back in the chair. For the first time she had the impression he might have been drinking a little more than usual these days. Just the look of his face. "I thought about you every minute of the day," he said. "I loved everything you did. What I liked was that you were absolutely new and everything you said and did was. You were incomparable. With you I felt I had everything in life, everything anyone ever dreamed of. I adored you."

"Like no other woman?"

"There was no one even close. I could have feasted on you forever. You were the intended."

"And Pam? You didn't feast on her?"

"A little. Pam is something different."

"In what way?"

"Pam doesn't take all that and offer it to someone else. I don't come back from a trip unexpectedly and find an unmade bed where you and some guy have been having a lovely time."

"It wasn't that lovely."

"That's too bad."

"It was far from lovely."

"So, why did you do it, then?"

"I don't know. I just had the foolish impulse to try something different. I didn't know that real happiness lies in having the same thing all the time."

She looked at her hands. He noticed again her long, flexible thumbs.

"Isn't that right?" she asked coolly.

"Don't be nasty. Anyway, what do you know about true happiness?"

"Oh, I've had it."

"Really?"

"Yes," she said. "With you."

He looked at her. She did not return his look, nor was she smiling.

"I'm going to Bangkok," she said. "Well, Hong Kong first. Have you ever stayed at the Peninsula Hotel?"

"I've never been to Hong Kong."

"They say it's the greatest hotel anywhere, Berlin, Paris, Tokyo."

"Well, I wouldn't know."

"You've been to hotels. Remember Venice and that little hotel by the theater? The water in the street up to your knees?"

"I have a lot of work to do, Carol."

"Oh, come on."

"I have a business."

"Then how much is this e.e. cummings?" she said. "I'll buy it and you can take a few minutes off."

"It's already sold," he said.

"Still has the price in it."

He shrugged a little.

"Answer me about Venice," she said.

"I remember the hotel. Now let's say good-bye."

"I'm going to Bangkok with a friend."

He felt a phantom skip of the heart, however slight.

"Good," he said.

"Molly. You'd like her."

"Molly."

"We're traveling together. You know Daddy died."

"I didn't know that."

"Yes, a year ago. He died. So my worries are over. It's a nice feeling."

"I suppose. I liked your father."

He'd been a man in the oil business, sociable, with certain freely admitted prejudices. He wore expensive suits and had been divorced twice but managed to avoid loneliness.

"We're going to stay in Bangkok for a couple of months,

perhaps come back through Europe, Carol said. Molly has a lot of style. She was a dancer. What was Pam, wasn't she a teacher or something? Well, you love Pam, you'd love Molly. You don't know her, but you would." She paused. "Why don't you come with us?" she said.

Hollis smiled slightly.

"Shareable, is she?" he said.

"You wouldn't have to share."

It was meant to torment him, he knew.

"Leave my family and business, just like that?"

"Gauguin did it."

"I'm a little more responsible than that. Maybe it's something you would do."

"If it were a choice," she said. "Between life and . . ."

"What?"

"Life and a kind of pretend life. Don't act as if you didn't understand. There's nobody that understands better than you."

He felt an unwanted resentment. That the hunt be over, he thought. That it be ended. He heard her continue.

"Travel. The Orient. The air of a different world. Bathe, drink, read . . ."

"You and me."

"And Molly. As a gift."

"Well, I don't know. What does she look like?"

"She's good-looking, what would you expect? I'll undress her for you."

"I'll tell you something funny," Hollis said, "something I heard. They say that everything in the universe, the planets, all the galaxies, everything—the entire universe—came originally from something the size of a grain of rice that exploded and formed what we have now, the sun, stars, earth, seas, everything there is, including what I felt for you. That morning on Hudson Street, sitting there in the sunlight, feet up, fulfilled and knowing it, talking, in love with one another—I knew I had everything life would ever offer."

"You felt that?"

"Of course. Anyone would. I remember it all, but I can't feel it now. It's passed."

"That's sad."

"I have something more than that now. I have a wife I love and a kid."

"It's such a cliché, isn't it? A wife I love."

"It's just the truth."

"And you're looking forward to the years together, the ecstasy."

"It's not ecstasy."

"You're right."

"You can't have ecstasy daily."

"No, but you can have something as good," she said. "You can have the anticipation of it."

"Good. Go ahead and have it. You and Molly."

"I'll think of you, Chris, in the house we'll have on the river in Bangkok."

"Oh, don't bother."

"I'll think of you lying in bed at night, bored to death with it all."

"Quit it, for God's sake. Leave it alone. Let me like you a little bit."

"I don't want you to like me." In a half-whisper she said, "I want you to curse me."

"Keep it up."

"It's so sweet," she said. "The little family, the lovely books. All right, then. You missed your chance. Bye-bye. Go back and give her a bath, your little girl. While you still can, anyway."

She looked at him a last time from the doorway. He could hear the sound of her heels as she went through the front room. He could hear them go past the display cases and toward the door where they seemed to hesitate, then the door closing.

The room was swimming, he could not hold on to his thoughts. The past, like a sudden tide, had swept back over him, not as it had been but as he could not help remembering it. The best thing was to resume work. He knew what her skin felt like, it was silky. He should not have listened.

On the soft, silent keys he began to write: *Jack Kerouac, typed letter signed ("Jack"), 1 page, to his girlfriend, the poet Lois Sorrells, single-spaced, signed in pencil, slight crease from folding.* It was not a pretend life.

DIRT

Billy was under the house. It was cool there, it smelled of the unturned earth of fifty years. A kind of rancid dust sifted down through the floorboards and fell on his face like a light rain. He spit it out. He turned his head and, reaching carefully up, wiped around his eyes with the sleeve of his shirt. He looked back toward the strip of daylight at the edge of the house. Harry's legs were in the sun—every so often, with a groan, he would kneel down and see how it was going.

They were leveling the floor of the old Bryant place. Like all of them it had no foundation, it sat on pieces of wood.

"Feller could start right there," Harry called.

"This one?"

"That's it."

Billy slowly wiped the dirt from his eyes again and began to set up the jack. The joists were a few inches above his face.

They ate lunch sitting outside. It was hot, mountain weather. The sun was dry, the air thin as paper. Harry ate slowly. He had a wrinkled neck and white stubble along his jowl line.

Death was coming for Harry Mies. He would lie emptied, his cheeks rouged, the fine, old man's ears unhearing. There was no telling the things he knew. He was alone in the far fields of his life. The rain fell on him, he did not move.

There are animals that finally, when the time comes, will not lie down. He was like that. When he kneeled he would get up again slowly. He would rise to one knee, pause, and finally sway to his feet like an old horse.

"Feller in town with all the hair . . ." he said.

Billy's fingers made black marks on the bread.

"The hair?"

"What's he supposed to be?"

"I think a drummer," Billy said.

"A drummer."

"He's with a band."

"Must be with something," Harry said.

He unscrewed the cap from a battered thermos and poured what looked like tea. They sat in the quiet of the tall cottonwoods, not even the highest leaves were moving.

They drove to the dump, the sun in the windshield was burning their knees. There was an old cattle gate salvaged from somewhere, some bankrupt ranch. It was open, Harry drove in. They were in a field of junk and garbage on the edge of the creek, a bare field forever smoldering. A black man in overalls appeared from a shack surrounded by bedsprings. He was round-shouldered, heavy as a bull. There was an old green Chrysler parked on the far side.

"Looking for some pipe, Al," Harry said.

The man said nothing. He gave a sort of halfhearted signal. Harry had already gone past and turned down an alley of old furniture, stoves, aluminum chairs. There was a sour smell in the air. A few refrigerators, indestructible, had fallen down the bank and were lying half-buried in the stream.

The pipe was all in one place. It was mostly rusted, Billy kicked aimlessly at some sections.

"We can use it," Harry commented.

They began carrying pieces back to the car and put them on the roof. They drove slowly, the old man's head tilted back a little. The car swayed in and out of holes. The pipe rolled in the rack.

"Pretty good feller, Al," Harry said. They were coming to the shack. He lifted his hand as they passed. No one was there.

Billy's mind was wandering. The ride to town seemed long.

"They give him a lot of trouble," Harry said. He was watching the road, the empty road which connects all these towns.

"There's none of that stuff much good out there," he said. "Sometimes he tries to charge a little for it. People feel like they ought to be able to carry it off for nothing."

"He didn't charge you."

"Me? No, I bring him a little something now and then," Harry said. "Old Al and me are friends."

After a while, "Claims to be a free country, I dunno . . ." he said.

The cowboys at Gerhart's called him the Swede, but he never went in there. They would see him go by outside, papery skin, dangling arms, the slowness of age as he walked. He may have looked a little Swedish, pale-eyed from those mornings of invincible white, mornings of the great Southwest, black coffee in his cup, the day ahead. The ashtrays on the bar were plastic, the clock had the name of a whiskey printed on its face.

It was five-thirty. Billy walked in.

"There he is."

He ignored them.

"What'll it be, then?" Gerhart said.

"Beer."

On the wall was the stuffed head of a bear with a pair of glasses on its nose and a red plaster tongue. Above it hung an American flag with a sign: NO DOGS ALLOWED. Around the middle of the day there were a few people like Wayne Garrich who had the insurance agency, they wore straw rancher's hats rolled at the sides. Later there were construction workers in T-shirts and sunglasses, gas company men. It was always crowded after five. The ranch hands sat together at the tables with their legs stretched out. They had belt buckles with a gold-plated steerhead on them.

"Be thirty cents," Gerhart said. "What're you up to? Still working for old Harry?"

"Yeah, well . . ." Billy's voice wandered.

"What's he paying you?"

He was too embarrassed to tell the truth.

"Two fifty an hour," Billy said.

"Jesus Christ," Gerhart said. "I pay that for sweeping floors."

Billy nodded. He had no reply.

Harry took three dollars an hour himself. There were probably people in town would take more, he said, but that was his rate. He'd pour a foundation for that, he said, take three weeks.

There was not one day of rain. The sun laid on their backs like boards.

Harry got the shovel and hoe from the trunk of his car. He was tall, he carried them in one hand. He turned the wheelbarrow right side up, the bags of cement were piled beneath on a piece of plywood. He flushed out the wheelbarrow with the hose. Then he began mixing the first load of concrete: five shovels of gravel, three of sand, one of cement. Occasionally he'd stop and pick out a twig or piece of grass. The sun beat down like flats of tin. Ten thousand days of it down in Texas and all around. He turned the dry mixture over upon itself again and again, finally he began adding water. He added more water, working it in. The color became a rich, river-grey, the smooth face broken by gravel. Billy stood watching.

"Don't want it too runny," the old man said. There was always the feeling he might be talking to himself. He laid down the hoe. "Okey-dokey," he said.

His shoulders were stooped, they had the set of labor in them. He took the handles of the barrow without straightening up.

"I'll get it," Billy said, reaching.

"That's all right," Harry muttered. His teeth whistled on the "s."

He wheeled it himself, the surface now smooth and shifting a little from side to side, and set it down with a jolt near the wooden forms he'd built—Billy had dug the trench. Checking them one last time, he tilted the wheelbarrow and the heavy liquid fell from its lip. He scraped it empty and then moved along the trench with his shovel, jabbing to fill the voids. On the second trip he let Billy push the barrow, naked to the waist, the sun roaring down on his shoulders and back, his muscles jumping as he lifted. The next day he let him shovel.

Billy lived near the Catholic church, in a room on the ground floor. It had a metal shower. He slept without sheets, in the morning he drank milk from the carton. He was going out with a girl named Alma who was a waitress at Daly's. She had legs with hard calves. She didn't say much, her complaisance drove him crazy, sometimes she was at Gerhart's with someone else in a haze of voices, the bark of laughter, famous heavyweights behind her tacked on the wall. There were water stains near the ceiling. The door to the men's room slammed.

They talked about her. They stood at the bar so they could see her by turning a little. She was a girl in a small town. The television had exhibition football coming from Grand Junction. They were thinking of her legs as they watched the game, she was like an animal they wanted. She smoked a lot, Alma, but her teeth were white. She was flat-faced, like a fighter. She would be living in the trailer park, Billy told her. Her kids would eat white bread in big soft packages from the Woody Creek Store.

"Oh, yeah?"

She didn't deny it. She looked away. Like an animal, it didn't matter how pure they were, how beautiful. They went down the highway in clattering steel trucks, wisps of straw blowing clear as they passed. They were watched by the cold eyes of cowboys. They entered the house of blood, its sudden bone-cleaving blows, its muffled cries. He didn't spend much money on her—he was saving up. She never mentioned it.

They poured the side of the house that faced Third Street and started along the front. He thought of her in the sunlight that was browning his arms. He lifted the heavy barrow and became strong everywhere, like a tightened cable. When they finished in the evening, Harry washed off everything with the hose, he put the shovel and hoe in the trunk of his car. He sat on the front seat with the door open. He smiled to himself. He lifted his cap and smoothed his hair.

"Say," he said. There was something he wanted to tell. He looked at the ground. "Ever been West?"

It was a story of California in the thirties. There was a whole bunch of them going from town to town, looking for work. One day they came to a place, he forgot the name, and went into some little restaurant. You could get a whole meal for thirty cents in those days, but when they came to pay the check, the owner told them it would cost a dollar fifty each. If they didn't like it, he said, there was the state police just down the street. Afterward Harry walked over to the barbershop— he looked like that musician, he had so much hair. The barber put the sheet around him. Haircut, Harry told him. Then, hey, wait a minute, how much will it be? The barber had the scissors in his hand. I see you been eating over to the Greek's, he said.

He laughed a little, almost shyly. He glanced at Billy, his long teeth showed. They were his own. Billy was buttoning his shirt.

It was hot in the evening. The hottest summer in years, everyone said, the hottest ever. At Gerhart's they stood around in big, dusty shoes.

"Shit, it's hot," they told each other.

"Can't get much hotter."

"What'll it be, then?" Gerhart would ask. His idiot son was rinsing glasses.

"Beer."

"Hot enough for you?" Gerhart said as he served it.

They stood at the bar, their arms covered with dust. Across the street was the movie house. Up toward the pass, the sand and gravel pit. There was ranching all around, a macadam plant, men like Wayne Garrich who hardly spoke at all, the bitterness had penetrated to the bone. They were deliberate, their habits were polished smooth. They looked out through the big storelike windows.

"There's Billy."

"Yeah, that's him."

"Well, what do you think?" They laid out phrases in low voices, like bets. Their arms were big as firewood on the bar. "Is he going to it or coming from it?"

The foundation was finished at the beginning of September. There was a little sand where the pile had been, a few specks of gravel. The nights were already cold, the first emptiness of winter, not a light on in town. The trees seemed silent, subdued. They would begin to turn suddenly, the big ones going last.

Harry died about three in the morning. He had been leaning on the cart in the supermarket, behind the stacks, struggling for breath. He tried to drink some tea. He sat in his chair. He was between sleep and waking, the kitchen light was on. Suddenly he felt a terrible, a bursting pain. His mouth fell open, his lips were dry.

He left very little, a few clothes, the Chevrolet filled with tools. Everything seemed lifeless and drab. The handle of his hammer was smooth. He had worked all over, built ships in Galveston during the war. There were photographs when he was twenty, the same hooked nose, the hard, country face. He looked like a pharaoh there in the funeral home. They had folded his hands. His cheeks were sunken, his eyelids like paper.

Billy Amstel went to Mexico in a car he and Alma bought for a hundred dollars. They agreed to share expenses. The sun polished the windshield in which they sat going southward. They told each other stories of their life.

AMERICAN EXPRESS

It's hard now to think of all the places and nights, Nicola's like a railway car, deep and gleaming, the crowd at the *Un, Deux, Trois*, Billy's. Unknown brilliant faces jammed at the bar. The dark, dramatic eye that blazes for a moment and disappears.

In those days they were living in apartments with funny furniture and on Sundays sleeping until noon. They were in the last rank of the armies of law. Clever junior partners were above them, partners, associates, men in fine suits who had lunch at the Four Seasons. Frank's father went there three or four times a week, or else to the Century Club or the Union where there were men even older than he. Half of the members can't urinate, he used to say, and the other half can't stop.

Alan, on the other hand, was from Cleveland where his father was well known, if not detested. No defendant was too guilty, no case too clear-cut. Once in another part of the state he was defending a murderer, a black man. He knew what the jury was thinking, he knew what he looked like to them. He stood up slowly. It could be they had heard certain things, he began. They may have heard, for instance, that he was a big-time lawyer from the city. They may have heard that he wore three-hundred-dollar suits, that he drove a Cadillac and smoked expensive cigars. He was walking along as if looking for something on the floor. They may have heard that he was Jewish.

He stopped and looked up. Well, he was from the city, he said. He wore three-hundred-dollar suits, he drove a Cadillac, smoked big cigars, and he was Jewish. "Now that we have that settled, let's talk about this case."

Lawyers and sons of lawyers. Days of youth. In the morning in stale darkness the subways shrieked.

"Have you noticed the new girl at the reception desk?"

"What about her?" Frank asked.

They were surrounded by noise like the launch of a rocket. "She's hot," Alan confided.

"How do you know?"

"I know."

"What do you mean, you know?"

"Intuition."

"Intuition?" Frank said.

"What's wrong?"

"That doesn't count."

Which was what made them inseparable, the hours of work, the lyric, the dreams. As it happened, they never knew the girl at the reception desk with her nearsightedness and wild, full hair. They knew various others, they knew Julie, they knew Catherine, they knew Ames. The best, for nearly two years, was Brenda who had somehow managed to graduate from Marymount and had a walk-through apartment on West Fourth. In a smooth, thin, silver frame was the photograph of her father with his two daughters at the Plaza, Brenda, thirteen, with an odd little smile.

"I wish I'd known you then," Frank told her.

Brenda said, "I bet you do."

It was her voice he liked, the city voice, scornful and warm. They were two of a kind, she liked to say, and in a way it was true. They drank in her favorite places where the owner played the piano and everyone seemed to know her. Still, she counted on him. The city has its incomparable moments—rolling along the wall of the apartment, kissing, bumping like stones. Five in the afternoon, the vanishing light. "No," she was commanding. "No, no, no."

He was kissing her throat. "What are you going to do with that beautiful struma of yours?"

"You won't take me to dinner," she said.

"Sure I will."

"Beautiful what?"

She was like a huge dog, leaping from his arms.

"Come here," he coaxed.

She went into the bathroom and began combing her hair. "Which restaurant are we going to?" she called.

She would give herself but it was mostly unpredictable. She would do anything her mother hadn't done and would live as her mother lived, in the same kind of apartment, in the same soft chairs. Christmas and the envelopes for the doormen, the snow sweeping past the awning, her children coming home from school. She adored her father. She went on a trip to Hawaii with him and sent back postcards, two or three scorching lines in a large, scrawled hand.

It was summer.

"Anybody here?" Frank called.

He rapped on the door which was ajar. He was carrying his jacket, it was hot.

"All right," he said in a loud voice, "come out with your hands over your head. Alan, cover the back."

The party, it seemed, was over. He pushed the door open. There was one lamp on, the room was dark.

"Hey, Bren, are we too late?" he called. She appeared mysteriously in the doorway, barelegged but in heels. "We'd have come earlier but we were working. We couldn't get out of the office. Where is everybody? Where's all the food? Hey, Alan, we're late. There's no food, nothing."

She was leaning against the doorway.

"We tried to get down here," Alan said. "We couldn't get a cab."

Frank had fallen onto the couch. "Bren, don't be mad," he said. "We were working, that's the truth. I should have called. Can you put some music on or something? Is there anything to drink?"

"There's about that much vodka," she finally said.

"Any ice?"

"About two cubes." She pushed off the wall without much enthusiasm. He watched her walk into the kitchen and heard the refrigerator door open.

"So, what do you think, Alan?" he said. "What are you going to do?"

"Me?"

"Where's Louise?" Frank called.

"Asleep," Brenda said.

"Did she really go home?"

"She goes to work in the morning."

"So does Alan."

Brenda came out of the kitchen with the drinks.

"I'm sorry we're late," he said. He was looking in the glass. "Was it a good party?" He stirred the contents with one finger. "This is the ice?"

"Jane Harrah got fired," Brenda said.

"That's too bad. Who is she?"

"She does big campaigns. Ross wants me to take her place."

"Great."

"I'm not sure if I want to," she said lazily.

"Why not?"

"She was sleeping with him."

"And she got fired?"

"Doesn't say much for him, does it?"

"It doesn't say much for her."

"That's just like a man. God."

"What does she look like? Does she look like Louise?"

The smile of the thirteen-year-old came across Brenda's face. "No one looks like Louise," she said. Her voice squeezed the name whose legs Alan dreamed of. "Jane has these thin lips."

"Is that all?"

"Thin-lipped women are always cold."

"Let me see yours," he said.

"Burn up."

"Yours aren't thin. Alan, these aren't thin, are they? Hey, Brenda, don't cover them up."

"Where were you? You weren't really working."

He'd pulled down her hand. "Come on, let them be

natural," he said. "They're not thin, they're nice. I just never noticed them before." He leaned back. "Alan, how're you doing? You getting sleepy?"

"I was thinking. How much the city has changed," Alan said.

"In five years?"

"I've been here almost six years."

"Sure, it's changing. They're coming down, we're going up."

Alan was thinking of the vanished Louise who had left him only a jolting ride home through the endless streets. "I know."

That year they sat in the steam room on limp towels, breathing the eucalyptus and talking about Hardmann Roe. They walked to the showers like champions. Their flesh still had firmness. Their haunches were solid and young.

Hardmann Roe was a small drug company in Connecticut that had strayed slightly outside of its field and found itself suing a large manufacturer for infringement of an obscure patent. The case was highly technical with little chance of success. The opposing lawyers had thrown up a barricade of motions and delays and the case had made its way downwards, to Frik and Frak whose offices were near the copying machines, who had time for such things, and who pondered it amid the hiss of steam. No one else wanted it and this also made it appealing.

So they worked. They were students again, sitting around in polo shirts with their feet on the desk, throwing off hopeless ideas, crumpling wads of paper, staying late in the library and having the words blur in books.

They stayed on through vacations and weekends some-times sleeping in the office and making coffee long before anyone came to work. After a late dinner they were still talking about it, its complexities, where elements somehow fit in, the sequence of letters, articles in journals, meetings, the limits of meaning. Brenda met a handsome Dutchman who worked for a bank. Alan met Hopie. Still there was this infinite forest, the trunks and vines blocking out the light, the roots of distant things joined. With every month that passed they were deeper into it, less certain of where they had been or if it could end. They had become like the old partners whose existence had been slowly sealed off, fewer calls, fewer consultations, lives that had become lunch. It was known they were swallowed up by the case with knowledge of little else. The opposite was true—no one else understood its details. Three years had passed. The length of time alone made it important. The reputation of the firm, at least in irony, was riding on them.

Two months before the case was to come to trial they quit Weyland, Braun. Frank sat down at the polished table for Sunday lunch. His father was one of the best men in the city. There is a kind of lawyer you trust and who becomes your friend. "What happened?" he wanted to know.

"We're starting our own firm," Frank said.

"What about the case you've been working on? You can't leave them with a litigation you've spent years preparing."

"We're not. We're taking it with us," Frank said.

There was a moment of dreadful silence.

"Taking it with you? You can't. You went to one of the best schools, Frank. They'll sue you. You'll ruin yourself."

"We thought of that."

"Listen to me," his father said.

Everyone said that, his mother, his Uncle Cook, friends. It was worse than ruin, it was dishonor. His father said that.

Hardmann Roe never went to trial, as it turned out. Six weeks later there was a settlement. It was for thirty-eight million, a third of it their fee.

His father had been wrong, which was something you could not hope for. They weren't sued either. That was settled, too. In place of ruin there were new offices overlooking Bryant Park which from above seemed like a garden behind a dark château, young clients, opera tickets, dinners in apartments with divorced hostesses, surrendered apartments with books and big, tiled kitchens.

The city was divided, as he had said, into those going up and those coming down, those in crowded restaurants and those on the street, those who waited and those who did not, those with three locks on the door and those rising in an elevator from a lobby with silver mirrors and walnut paneling.

And those like Mrs. Christie who was in the intermediate state though looking assured. She wanted to renegotiate the settlement with her ex-husband. Frank had leafed through the papers. "What do you think?" she asked candidly.

"I think it would be easier for you to get married again."

She was in her fur coat, the dark lining displayed. She gave a little puff of disbelief. "It's not that easy," she said.

He didn't know what it was like, she told him. Not long ago she'd been introduced to someone by a couple she knew very well. "We'll go to dinner," they said, "you'll love him, you're perfect for him, he likes to talk about books."

They arrived at the apartment and the two women immediately went into the kitchen and began cooking. What did she think of him? She'd only had a glimpse, she said, but she liked him very much, his beautiful bald head, his dressing gown. She had begun to plan what she would do with the apartment which had too much blue in it. The man—Warren was his name—was silent all evening. He'd lost his job, her friend explained in the kitchen. Money was no problem, but he was depressed. "He's had a shock," she said. "He likes you." And in fact he'd asked if he could see her again.

"Why don't you come for tea, tomorrow?" he said.

"I could do that," she said. "Of course. I'll be in the neighborhood," she added.

The next day she arrived at four with a bag filled with books, at least a hundred dollars' worth which she'd bought as a present. He was in pajamas. There was no tea. He hardly seemed to know who she was or why she was there. She said she remembered she had to meet someone and left the books. Going down in the elevator she felt suddenly sick to her stomach.

"Well," said Frank, "there might be a chance of getting the settlement overturned, Mrs. Christie, but it would mean a lot of expense."

"I see." Her voice was smaller. "Couldn't you do it as one of those things where you got a percentage?"

"Not on this kind of case," he said.

It was dusk. He offered her a drink. She worked her lips,

in contemplation, one against the other. "Well, then, what can I do?"

Her life had been made up of disappointments, she told him, looking into her glass, most of them the result of foolishly falling in love. Going out with an older man just because he was wearing a white suit in Nashville which was where she was from. Agreeing to marry George Christie while they were sailing off the coast of Maine. "I don't know where to get the money," she said, "or how."

She glanced up. She found him looking at her, without haste. The lights were coming on in buildings surrounding the park, in the streets, on homeward bound cars. They talked as evening fell. They went out to dinner.

At Christmas that year Alan and his wife broke up. "You're kidding," Frank said. He'd moved into a new place with thick towels and fine carpets. In the foyer was a Biedermeier desk, black, tan, and gold. Across the street was a private school.

Alan was staring out the window which was as cold as the side of a ship. "I don't know what to do," he said in despair. "I don't want to get divorced. I don't want to lose my daughter." Her name was Camille. She was two.

"I know how you feel," Frank said.

"If you had a kid, you'd know."

"Have you seen this?" Frank asked. He held up the alumni magazine. It was the fifteenth anniversary of their graduation. "Know any of these guys?"

Five members of the class had been cited for achievement. Alan recognized two or three of them. "Cummings," he said, "he was a zero—elected to Congress. Oh, God, I don't know what to do."

"Just don't let her take the apartment," Frank said.

Of course, it wasn't that easy. It was easy when it was someone else. Nan Christie had decided to get married. She brought it up one evening.

"I just don't think so," he finally said.

"You love me, don't you?"

"This isn't a good time to ask."

They lay silently. She was staring at something across the room. She was making him feel uncomfortable. "It wouldn't work. It's the attraction of opposites," he said.

"We're not opposites."

"I don't mean just you and me. Women fall in love when they get to know you. Men are just the opposite. When they finally know you they're ready to leave."

She got up without saying anything and began gathering her clothes. He watched her dress in silence. There was nothing interesting about it. The funny thing was that he had meant to go on with her.

"I'll get you a cab," he said.

"I used to think that you were intelligent," she said, half to herself. Exhausted, he was searching for a number. "I don't want a cab. I'm going to walk."

"Across the park?"

"Yes." She had an instant glimpse of herself in the next day's paper. She paused at the door for a moment. "Goodbye," she said coolly.

She wrote him a letter which he read several times. *Of all the loves I have known, none has touched me so. Of all the men, no one has given me more.* He showed it to Alan who did not comment.

"Let's go out and have a drink," Frank said.

They walked up Lexington. Frank looked carefree, the scarf around his neck, the open topcoat, the thinning hair. "Well, you know . . ." he managed to say.

They went into a place called Jack's. Light was gleaming from the dark wood and the lines of glasses on narrow shelves. The young bartender stood with his hands on the edge of the bar. "How are you this evening?" he said with a smile. "Nice to see you again."

"Do you know me?" Frank asked.

"You look familiar," the bartender smiled.

"Do I? What's the name of this place, anyway? Remind me not to come in here again."

There were several other people at the bar. The nearest of them carefully looked away. After a while the manager came over. He had emerged from the brown-curtained back. "Anything wrong, sir?" he asked politely.

Frank looked at him. "No," he said, "everything's fine."

"We've had a big day," Alan explained. "We're just unwinding."

"We have a dining room upstairs," the manager said. Behind him was an iron staircase winding past framed drawings of dogs—borzois they looked like. "We serve from six to eleven every night."

"I bet you do," Frank said. "Look, your bartender doesn't know me."

"He made a mistake," the manager said.

"He doesn't know me and he never will."

"It's nothing, it's nothing," Alan said, waving his hands.

They sat at a table by the window. "I can't stand these out-of-work actors who think they're everybody's friend," Frank commented.

At dinner they talked about Nan Christie. Alan thought of her silk dresses, her devotion. The trouble, he said after a while, was that he never seemed to meet that kind of woman, the ones who sometimes walked by outside Jack's. The women he met were too human, he complained. Ever since his separation he'd been trying to find the right one.

"You shouldn't have any trouble," Frank said. "They're all looking for someone like you."

"They're looking for you."

"They think they are."

Frank paid the check without looking at it. "Once you've been married," Alan was explaining, "you want to be married again."

"I don't trust anyone enough to marry them," Frank said.

"What do you want then?"

"This is all right," Frank said.

Something was missing in him and women had always done anything to find out what it was. They always would. Perhaps it was simpler, Alan thought. Perhaps nothing was missing.

The car, which was a big Renault, a tourer, slowed down and pulled off the *autostrada* with Brenda asleep in back, her mouth a bit open and the daylight gleaming off her cheekbones. It was near Como, they had just crossed, the border police had glanced in at her.

"Come on, Bren, wake up," they said, "we're stopping for coffee."

She came back from the ladies' room with her hair combed and fresh lipstick on. The boy in the white jacket behind the counter was rinsing spoons.

"Hey, Brenda, I forget. Is it *espresso* or *expresso*?" Frank asked her.

"*Espresso,*" she said.

"How do you know?"

"I'm from New York," she said.

"That's right," he remembered. "The Italians don't have an *x*, do they?"

"They don't have a *j* either," Alan said.

"Why is that?"

"They're such careless people," Brenda said. "They just lost them."

It was like old times. She was divorced from Doop or Boos or whoever. Her two little girls were with her mother. She had that quirky smile.

In Paris Frank had taken them to the Crazy Horse. In blackness like velvet the music struck up and six girls in unison kicked their legs in the brilliant light. They wore high heels and a little strapping. The nudity that is immortal. He was leaning on one elbow in the darkness. He glanced at Brenda. "Still studying, eh?" she said.

They were over for three weeks. Frank wasn't sure, maybe they would stay longer, take a house in the south of France or something. Their clients would have to struggle along without them. There comes a time, he said, when you have to get away for a while.

They had breakfast together in hotels with the sound of workmen chipping at the stone of the fountain outside. They listened to the angry woman shouting in the kitchen, drove to little towns, and drank every night. They had separate rooms, like staterooms, like passengers on a fading boat.

At noon the light shifted along the curve of buildings and people were walking far off. A wave of pigeons rose before a trotting dog. The man at the table in front of them had a pair of binoculars and was looking here and there. Two Swedish girls strolled past.

"Now they're turning dark," the man said.

"What is?" said his wife.

"The pigeons."

"Alan," Frank confided.

"What?"

"The pigeons are turning dark."

"That's too bad."

There was silence for a moment.

"Why don't you just take a photograph?" the woman said.

"A photograph?"

"Of those women. You're looking at them so much."

He put down the binoculars.

"You know, the curve is so graceful," she said. "It's what makes this square so perfect."

"Isn't the weather glorious?" Frank said in the same tone of voice.

"And the pigeons," Alan said.

"The pigeons, too."

After a while the couple got up and left. The pigeons leapt up for a running child and hissed overhead. "I see you're still playing games," Brenda said. Frank smiled.

"We ought to get together in New York," she said that evening. They were waiting for Alan to come down. She reached across the table to pick up a magazine. "You've never met my kids, have you?" she said.

"No."

"They're terrific kids." She leafed through the pages not paying attention to them. Her forearms were tanned. She was not wearing a wedding band. The first act was over or rather the first five minutes. Now came the plot. "Do you remember those nights at Goldie's?" she said.

"Things were different then, weren't they?"

"Not so different."

"What do you mean?"

She wiggled her bare third finger and glanced at him. Just then Alan appeared. He sat down and looked from one of them to the other. "What's wrong?" he asked. "Did I interrupt something?"

When the time came for her to leave she wanted them to drive to Rome. They could spend a couple of days and she would catch the plane. They weren't going that way, Frank said.

"It's only a three-hour drive."

"I know, but we're going the other way," he said.

"For God's sake. Why won't you drive me?"

"Let's do it," Alan said.

"Go ahead. I'll stay here."

"You should have gone into politics," Brenda said. "You have a real gift."

After she was gone the mood of things changed. They were by themselves. They drove through the sleepy country to the north. The green water slapped as darkness fell on Venice. The lights in some *palazzos* were on. On the curtained upper floors the legs of countesses uncoiled, slithering on the sheets like a serpent.

In Harry's, Frank held up a dense, icy glass and murmured his father's line, "Good night, nurse." He talked to some people at the next table, a German who was manager of a hotel in Düsseldorf and his girlfriend. She'd been looking at him. "Want a taste?" he asked her. It was his second. She drank looking directly at him. "Looks like you finished it," he said.

"Yes, I like to do that."

He smiled. When he was drinking he was strangely calm. In Lugano in the park that time a bird had sat on his shoe.

In the morning across the canal, wide as a river, the buildings of the Giudecca lay in their soft colors, a great sunken barge with roofs and the crowns of hidden trees. The first winds of autumn were blowing, ruffling the water.

Leaving Venice, Frank drove. He couldn't ride in a car unless he was driving. Alan sat back, looking out the window, sunlight falling on the hillsides of antiquity. European days, the silence, the needle floating at a hundred.

In Padua, Alan woke early. The stands were being set up in the market. It was before daylight and cool. A man was laying out boards on the pavement, eight of them like doors to set bags of grain on. He was wearing the jacket from a suit.

Searching in the truck he found some small pieces of wood and used them to shim the boards, testing with his foot.

The sky became violet. Under the colonnade the butchers had hung out chickens and roosters, spurred legs bound together. Two men sat trimming artichokes. The blue car of the *carabiniere* lazed past. The bags of rice and dry beans were set out now, the tops folded back like cuffs. A girl in a tailored coat with a scarf around her head called, "*Signore*," then arrogantly, "*dica!*"

He saw the world afresh, its pavements and architecture, the names that had lasted for a thousand years. It seemed that his life was being clarified, the sediment was drifting down. Across the street in a jeweler's shop a girl was laying things out in the window. She was wearing white gloves and arranging the pieces with great care. She glanced up as he stood watching. For a moment their eyes met, separated by the lighted glass. She was holding a lapis lazuli bracelet, the blue of the police car. Emboldened, he formed the silent words. *Quanto costa? Tre cento settante mille*, her lips said. It was eight in the morning when he got back to the hotel. A taxi pulled up and rattled the narrow street. A woman dressed for dinner got out and went inside.

The days passed. In Verona the points of the steeples and then its domes rose from the mist. The white-coated waiters appeared from the kitchen. *Primi, secondi, dolce.* They stopped in Arezzo. Frank came back to the table. He had some postcards. Alan was trying to write to his daughter once a week. He never knew what to say: where they were and what they'd seen. Giotto—what would that mean to her?

They sat in the car. Frank was wearing a soft tweed jacket.

It was like cashmere—he'd been shopping in Missoni and everywhere, windbreakers, shoes. Schoolgirls in dark skirts were coming through an arch across the street. After a while one came through alone. She stood as if waiting for someone. Alan was studying the map. He felt the engine start. Very slowly they moved forward. The window glided down.

"*Scusi, signorina,*" he heard Frank say.

She turned. She had pure features and her face was without expression, as if a bird had turned to look, a bird which might suddenly fly away.

Which way, Frank asked her, was the *centro*, the center of town? She looked one way and then the other. "There," she said.

"Are you sure?" he said. He turned his head unhurriedly to look more or less in the direction she was pointing.

"*Si,*" she said.

They were going to Siena, Frank said. There was silence. Did she know which road went to Siena?

She pointed the other way.

"Alan, you want to give her a ride?" he asked.

"What are you talking about?"

Two men in white smocks like doctors were working on the wooden doors of the church. They were up on top of some scaffolding. Frank reached back and opened the rear door.

"Do you want to go for a ride?" he asked. He made a little circular motion with his finger.

They drove through the streets in silence. The radio was playing. Nothing was said. Frank glanced at her in the rear-view mirror once or twice. It was at the time of a famous murder in Poland, the killing of a priest. Dusk was falling. The lights were coming on in shop windows and evening papers were in the kiosks. The body of the murdered man l ay in a long coffin in the upper right corner of the *Corriere Della Sera*. It was in clean clothes like a worker after a terrible accident.

"Would you like an *aperitivo*?" Frank asked over his shoulder.

"*No*," she said.

They drove back to the church. He got out for a few minutes with her. His hair was very thin, Alan noticed. Strangely, it made him look younger. They stood talking, then she turned and walked down the street.

"What did you say to her?" Alan asked. He was nervous.

"I asked if she wanted a taxi."

"We're headed for trouble."

"There's not going to be any trouble," Frank said.

His room was on the corner. It was large, with a sitting area near the windows. On the wooden floor there were two worn oriental carpets. On a glass cabinet in the bathroom were his hairbrush, lotions, cologne. The towels were a pale green with the name of the hotel in white. She didn't look at any of that. He had given the *portiere* forty thousand lire. In Italy the laws were very strict. It was nearly the same hour of the afternoon. He kneeled to take off her shoes.

He had drawn the curtains but light came in around them. At one point she seemed to tremble, her body shuddered. "Are you all right?" he said.

She had closed her eyes.

Later, standing, he saw himself in the mirror. He seemed

to have thickened around the waist. He turned so that it was less noticeable. He got into bed again but was too hasty. "*Basta*," she finally said.

They went down later and met Alan in a café. It was hard for him to look at them. He began to talk in a foolish way. What was she studying at school, he asked. For God's sake, Frank said. Well, what did her father do? She didn't understand.

"What work does he do?"

"Furniture," she said.

"He sells it?"

"*Restauro*."

"In our country, no *restauro*," Alan explained. He made a gesture. "Throw it away."

"I've got to start running again," Frank decided.

The next day was Saturday. He had the *portiere* call her number and hand him the phone.

"Hello, Eda? It's Frank."

"I know."

"What are you doing?"

He didn't understand her reply.

"We're going to Florence. You want to come to Florence?" he said. There was a silence. "Why don't you come and spend a few days?"

"No," she said.

"Why not?"

In a quieter voice she said, "How do I explain?"

"You can think of something."

At a table across the room children were playing cards while three well-dressed women, their mothers, sat and talked. There were cries of excitement as the cards were thrown down.

"Eda?"

She was still there. "*Si*," she said.

In the hills they were burning leaves. The smoke was invisible but they could smell it as they passed through, like the smell from a restaurant or paper mill. It made Frank suddenly remember childhood and country houses, raking the lawn with his father long ago. The green signs began to say Firenze. It started to rain. The wipers swept silently across the glass. Everything was beautiful and dim.

They had dinner in a restaurant of plain rooms, whitewashed, like vaults in a cellar. She looked very young. She looked like a young dog, the white of her eyes was that pure. She said very little and played with a strip of pink paper that had come off the menu.

In the morning they walked aimlessly. The windows displayed things for women who were older, in their thirties at least, silk dresses, bracelets, scarves. In Fendi's was a beautiful coat, the price beneath in small metal numbers.

"Do you like it?" he asked. "Come on, I'll buy it for you."

He wanted to see the coat in the window, he told them inside.

"For the *signorina*?"

"Yes."

She seemed uncomprehending. Her face was lost in the fur. He touched her cheek through it.

"You know how much that is?" Alan said. "Four million five hundred thousand."

"Do you like it?" Frank asked her.

She wore it continually. She watched the football matches on television in it, her legs curled beneath her. The room was in disorder, they hadn't been out all day.

"What do you say to leaving here?" Alan asked unexpectedly. The announcers were shouting in Italian. "I thought I'd like to see Spoleto."

"Sure. Where is it?" Frank said. He had his hand on her knee and was rubbing it with the barest movement, as one might a dozing cat.

The countryside was flat and misty. They were leaving the past behind them, unwashed glasses, towels on the bathroom floor. There was a stain on his lapel, Frank noticed in the dining room. He tried to get it off as the headwaiter grated fresh Parmesan over each plate. He dipped the corner of his napkin in water and rubbed the spot. The table was near the doorway, visible from the desk. Eda was fixing an earring.

"Cover it with your napkin," Alan told him.

"Here, get this off, will you?" he asked Eda.

She scratched at it quickly with her fingernail.

"What am I going to do without her?" Frank said.

"What do you mean, without her?"

"So this is Spoleto," he said. The spot was gone. "Let's have some more wine." He called the waiter. "*Senta.* Tell him," he said to Eda.

They laughed and talked about old times, the days when they were getting eight hundred dollars a week and working ten, twelve hours a day. They remembered Weyland and the veins in his nose. The word he always used was "vivid," testimony a bit too vivid, far too vivid, a rather vivid decor.

They left talking loudly. Eda was close between them in

her huge coat. "*Alla rovina*," the clerk at the front desk muttered as they reached the street, "*alle macerie*," he said, the girl at the switchboard looked over at him, "*alla polvere*." It was something about rubbish and dust.

The mornings grew cold. In the garden there were leaves piled against the table legs. Alan sat alone in the bar. A waitress, the one with the mole on her lip, came in and began to work the coffee machine. Frank came down. He had an overcoat across his shoulders. In his shirt without a tie he looked like a rich patient in some hospital. He looked like a man who owned a produce business and had been playing cards all night.

"So, what do you think?" Alan said.

Frank sat down. "Beautiful day," he commented. "Maybe we ought to go somewhere."

In the room, perhaps in the entire hotel, their voices were the only sound, irregular and low, like the soft strokes of someone sweeping. One muted sound, then another.

"Where's Eda?"

"She's taking a bath."

"I thought I'd say good-bye to her."

"Why? What's wrong?"

"I think I'm going home."

"What happened?" Frank said.

Alan could see himself in the mirror behind the bar, his sandy hair. He looked pale somehow, nonexistent. "Nothing happened," he said. She had come into the bar and was sitting at the other end of the room. He felt a tightness in his chest. "Europe depresses me."

Frank was looking at him. "Is it Eda?"

"No. I don't know." It seemed terribly quiet. Alan put his hands in his lap. They were trembling.

"Is that all it is? We can share her," Frank said.

"What do you mean?" He was too nervous to say it right. He stole a glance at Eda. She was looking at something outside in the garden.

"Eda," Frank called, "do you want something to drink? *Cosa vuoi?*" He made a motion of glass raised to the mouth. In college he had been a great favorite. Shuford had been shortened to Shuf and then Shoes. He had run in the Penn Relays. His mother could trace her family back for six generations.

"Orange juice," she said.

They sat there talking quietly. That was often the case, Eda had noticed. They talked about business or things in New York.

When they came back to the hotel that night, Frank explained it. She understood in an instant. No. She shook her head. Alan was sitting alone in the bar. He was drinking some kind of sweet liqueur. It wouldn't happen, he knew. It didn't matter anyway. Still, he felt shamed. The hotel above his head, its corridors and quiet rooms, what else were they for?

Frank and Eda came in. He managed to turn to them. She seemed impassive—he could not tell. What was this he was drinking, he finally asked? She didn't understand the question. He saw Frank nod once slightly, as if in agreement. They were like thieves.

In the morning the first light was blue on the window glass. There was the sound of rain. It was leaves blowing in the garden, shifting across the gravel. Alan slipped from the bed to fasten the loose shutter. Below, half hidden in the hedges, a statue gleamed white. The few parked cars shone faintly. She was asleep, the soft, heavy pillow beneath her head. He was afraid to wake her. "Eda," he whispered, "Eda."

Her eyes opened a bit and closed. She was young and could stay asleep. He was afraid to touch her. She was unhappy, he knew, her bare neck, her hair, things he could not see. It would be a while before they were used to it. He didn't know what to do. Apart from that, it was perfect. It was the most natural thing in the world. He would buy her something himself, something beautiful.

In the bathroom he lingered at the window. He was thinking of the first day they had come to work at Weyland, Braun—he and Frank. They would become inseparable. Autumn in the gardens of the Veneto. It was barely dawn. He would always remember meeting Frank. He couldn't have done these things himself. A young man in a cap suddenly came out of a doorway below. He crossed the driveway and jumped onto a motorbike. The engine started, a faint blur. The headlight appeared and off he went, delivery basket in back. He was going to get the rolls for breakfast. His life was simple. The air was pure and cool. He was part of that great, unchanging order of those who live by wages, whose world is unlit and who do not realize what is above.

PALM COURT

Late one afternoon, near the close, his assistant, Kenny, palm over the mouthpiece, said there was someone named Noreen on the phone.

"You know her, she says."

"Noreen? I'll take it," Arthur said. "Just a minute."

He got up and closed the door to his cubicle. He was still visible through the glass as he sat and turned toward the window, distancing himself from all that was going on, the dozens of customers' men, some of them women, which once would have been unthinkable, looking at their screens and talking on the phone. His heart was tripping faster when he spoke.

"Hello?"

"Arthur?"

The one word and a kind of shiver went through him, a frightened happiness, as when your name is called by the teacher.

"It's Noreen," she said.

"Noreen. How are you? God, it's been a long time. Where are you?"

"I'm here. I'm living back here now," she said.

"No kidding. What happened?"

"We broke up."

"That's too bad," he said. "I'm sorry to hear that."

He always seemed completely sincere, even in the most ordinary comments.

"It was a mistake," she said. "I never should have done it. I should have known."

The floor around the desk was strewn with paper, reports, annual statements with their many numbers. That was not his strength. He liked to talk to people, he could talk and tell stories all day. And he was known to be honest. He had taken as models the old-timers, men long gone such as Henry Braver, Patsy Millinger's father, who'd been a partner and had started before the war. Onassis had been one of his clients. Braver had an international reputation as well as a nose for the real thing. Arthur didn't have the nose, but he could talk and listen. There were all kinds of ways of making money in this business. His way was finding one or two big winners to go down and double on. And he talked to his clients every day.

"Mark, how are you, tootsula? You ought to be here. The numbers came in on Micronics. They're all crying. We were so smart not to get involved in that. Sweetheart, you want to know something? There are some very smart guys here who've taken a bath." He lowered his voice. "Morris, for one."

"Morris? They should give him an injection. Put him to sleep."

"He was a little too smart this time. Living through the Depression didn't help this time."

Morris had a desk near the copy machine, a courtesy desk. He had been a partner, but after he retired there was nothing to do—he hated Florida and didn't play golf—and so he came back to the firm and traded for himself. His age alone set him apart. He was a relic with perfect, false teeth and lived in some amberoid world with an aged wife. They all joked about him. The years had left him, as if marooned, alone at his desk and in an apartment on Park Avenue no one had ever been to.

Morris had lost a lot on Micronics. It was impossible to say how much. He kept his own shaky figures, but Arthur had gotten it out of Marie, the sexless woman who cleared trades.

"A hundred thousand," she said. "Don't say anything."

"Don't worry, darling," Arthur told her.

Arthur knew everything and was on the phone all day. It was one unending conversation: gossip, affection, news. He looked like Punch, with a curved nose, up-pointing chin, and innocent smile. He was filled with happiness, but the kind that knew its limits. He had been at Frackman, Wells from the time there were seven employees, and now there were nearly two hundred with three floors in the building. He himself had become rich, beyond anything he could have imagined, although his life had not changed and he still had the same apartment in London Terrace. He was living there the night he first met Noreen in Goldie's. She did something few girls had ever done with him, she laughed and sat close. From the first moment there was openness between them. Noreen. The piano rippling away, the old songs, the noise.

"I'm divorced," she said. "How about you?"

"Me? The same," he said.

The street below was filled with hurrying people, cars. The sound of it was faint.

"Really?" she said.

It had been years since he had talked to her. There was a time they had been inseparable. They were at Goldie's every night or at Clarke's, where he also went regularly. They always gave him a good table, in the middle section with the side door or in back with the crowd and the unchanging menu written neatly in chalk. Sometimes they stood in front at the long, scarred bar with the sign that said under no circumstances would women be served there. The manager, the bartenders, waiters, everybody knew him. Clarke's was his real home; he merely went elsewhere to sleep. He drank very little despite his appearance, but he always paid for drinks and stayed at the bar for hours, occasionally taking a few steps to the men's room, a pavilion of its own, long and old-fashioned, where you urinated like a grand duke on blocks of ice. To Clarke's came advertising men, models, men like himself, and off-duty cops late at night. He showed Noreen how to recognize them, black shoes and white socks. Noreen loved it. She was a favorite there, with her looks and wonderful laugh. The waiters called her by her first name.

Noreen was dark blond, though her mother was Greek, she said. There were a lot of blonds in the north of Greece where her family came from. The ranks of the Roman legions had become filled with Germanic tribesmen as time passed, and when Rome fell some of the scattered legions settled in the mountains of Greece; at least that was the way she had heard it.

"So I'm Greek but I'm German, too," she told Arthur.

"God, I hope not," he said. "I couldn't go with a German."

"What do you mean?"

"Be seen with."

"Arthur," she explained, "you have to accept the way things are, what I am and what you are and why it's so good."

There were things she wanted to tell him but didn't, things he wouldn't like to hear, or so she felt. About being a young girl and the night at the St. George Hotel when she was nineteen and went upstairs with a guy she thought was really nice. They went to his boss's suite. The boss was away and they were drinking his twelve-year-old scotch, and the next thing she knew she was lying facedown on the bed with her hands tied behind her. That was in a different world than Arthur's. His was decent, forgiving, warm.

They went together for nearly three years, the best years. They saw one another almost every night. She knew all about his work. He could make it seem so interesting, the avid individuals, the partners, Buddy Frackman, Warren Sender. And Morris; she had actually seen Morris once on the elevator.

"You're looking very well," she told him nervily.

"You, too," he said, smiling.

He didn't know who she was, but a few moments later he leaned toward her and silently formed the words,

"Eighty-seven."

"Really?"

"Yes," he said proudly.

"I'd never guess."

She knew how, one day coming back from lunch, Arthur and Buddy had seen Morris lying in the street, his white shirt covered with blood. He had accidentally fallen, and there were two or three people trying to help him up.

"Don't look. Keep going," Arthur had said.

"He's lucky, having friends like you," Noreen said.

She worked at Grey Advertising, which made it so conven-
ient to meet. Seeing her always filled him with pleasure, even
when it became completely familiar. She was twenty-five and
filled with life. That summer he saw her in a bathing suit, a
bikini. She was stunning, with a kind of glow to her skin. She
had a young girl's unself-conscious belly and ran into the
waves. He went in more cautiously, as befitted a man who
had been a typist in the army and salesman for a dress manufacturer before coming to what he called Wall Street, where
he had always dreamed of being and would have worked for
nothing.

The waves, the ocean, the white blinding sand. It was at
Westhampton, where they went for the weekend. On the
train every seat was taken. Young men in T-shirts and with
manly chests were joking in the aisles. Noreen sat beside
him, the happiness coming off her like heat. She had a small
gold cross, the size of a dime, on a thin gold necklace lying
on her shirt. He hadn't noticed it before. He was about to say
something when the train began bucking and slowed to a
stop.

"What is it? What's happened?"

They were not in a station but alongside a low embank-
ment, amid weedy-looking growth. After a while the word
came back, they had hit a bicyclist.

"Where? How?" Arthur said. "We're in a forest."

No one knew much more. People were speculating,
should they get off and try to find a taxi; where were they,
anyhow? There were guesses. A few individuals did get off
and were walking by the side of the train.

"God, I knew something like this would happen," Arthur said.

"Something like this?" Noreen said. "How could there be something like this?"

"When we hit the cow," a man sitting across from them offered.

"The cow? We also hit a cow?" Arthur exclaimed.

"A couple of weeks ago," the man explained.

That night Noreen showed him how to eat a lobster.

"My mother would die if she knew this," Arthur said.

"How will she know?"

"She'd disown me."

"You start with the claws," Noreen said.

She had tucked the napkin into his collar. They drank some Italian wine.

Westhampton, her tanned legs and pale heels. The feeling she gave him of being younger, even, God help him, debonair. He was playful. On the beach he wore a coconut hat. He had fallen in love, deeply, and without knowing it. He hadn't realized he had been living a shallow life. He only knew that he was happy, happier than he had ever been, in her company. This warmhearted girl with her legs, her fragrance, and perfect little ears that were tuned to him. And she took some kind of pleasure in him! They were guests of the Senders and he slept in a separate room in the basement while she was upstairs, but they were under the same roof and he would see her in the morning.

"When are you going to marry her?" everyone asked.

"She wouldn't have me," he equivocated.

Then, offhandedly, she admitted meeting someone else. It

was sort of a joke, Bobby Piro. He was stocky, he lived with his mother, had never married.

"He has black, shiny hair," Arthur guessed as if good-naturedly.

He had to treat it lightly, and Noreen did the same. She would make fun of Bobby when talking about him, his brothers, Dennis and Paul, his wanting to go to Vegas, his mother making chicken Vesuvio, Sinatra's favorite, for her.

"Chicken Vesuvio," Arthur said.

"It was pretty good."

"So you met his mother."

"I'm too skinny," she said.

"She sounds like my mother. Are you sure she's Italian?"

She liked Bobby, at least a little, he could see. Still it was difficult to think of him as being really significant. He was someone to talk about. He wanted her to go away on a weekend with him.

"To the Euripides," Arthur said, his stomach suddenly turning over.

"Not that good."

The Euripides Hotel that didn't exist, but that they always joked about because he didn't know who Euripides was.

"Don't let him take you to the Euripides," he said.

"I couldn't do that. It's a Greek place," she said. "For us Greeks."

Then, late one night in October, his doorbell rang.

"Who is it?" Arthur said.

"It's me."

He opened the door. She stood in the doorway with a smile that he saw had hesitation in it.

"Can I come in?"

"Sure, tootsula. Of course. Come in. What's happened, is something wrong?"

"There's nothing wrong, really. I just thought I would . . . come by."

The room was clean but somehow barren. He never sat in it and as much as read a book. He lived in the bedroom like a salesman. The curtains hadn't been washed in a long time.

"Here, sit down," he said.

She was walking a bit carefully. She had been drinking, he could see. She felt her way around a chair and sat.

"You want something? Coffee? I'll make some coffee."

She was looking around her.

"You know, I've never been here. This is the first time."

"It's not much of a place. I guess I could find something better."

"Is that the bedroom?"

"Yes," he said, but her gaze had drifted from it.

"I just wanted to talk."

"Sure. About what?"

He knew, or was afraid he did.

"We've known each other a long time. What has it been, three years?"

He felt nervous. The aimless way it was going. He didn't want to disappoint her. On the other hand, he was not sure what it was she wanted. Him? Now?

"You're pretty smart," she said.

"Me? Oh, God, no."

"You understand people. Can you really make some coffee? I think I'd like a cup."

While he busied himself, she sat quietly. He glanced briefly and saw her staring toward the window, beyond which were the lights of apartments in other buildings and the black, starless sky.

"So," she said, holding the coffee, "give me some advice. Bobby wants to get married."

Arthur was silent.

"He wants to marry me. The reason I was never serious about him, I was always making fun of him, his being so Italian, his big smile, the reason was that he was involved all that time with some Danish girl. Ode is her name."

"I figured something like that."

"What did you figure?"

"Ah, I could see something wasn't right."

"I never met her. I imagined her as being pretty and having this great accent. You know how you torture yourself."

"Ah, Noreen," he said. "There's nobody nicer than you."

"Anyway, yesterday he told me he'd broken up with her. It was all over. He did it because of me. He realized it was me he loved, and he wanted to marry me."

"Well, that's . . ."

Arthur didn't know what to say; his thoughts were skipping wildly, like scraps of paper in a wind. There is that fearful moment in the ceremony when it is asked if there is anyone who knows why these two should not be wed. This was that moment.

"What did you tell him?"

"I haven't told him."

A gulf was opening between them somehow. It was happening as they sat there.

"Do you have any feeling about it?" she asked.

"Yes, I mean, I'd like to think about it. It's kind of a surprise."

"It was to me, too."

She hadn't touched the coffee.

"You know, I could sit here for a long time," she said. "It's as comfortable as I'll ever feel anywhere. That's what's making me wonder. About what to tell him."

"I'm a little afraid," he said. "I can't explain it."

"Of course you are." Her voice had such understanding. "Really. I know."

"Your coffee's going to get cold," he said.

"Anyway, I just wanted to see your apartment," she said. Her voice suddenly sounded funny. She seemed not to want to go on.

He realized then, as she sat there, a woman in his apartment at night, a woman he knew he loved, that she was really giving him one last chance. He knew he should take it.

"Ah, Noreen," he said.

After that night, she vanished. Not suddenly, but it did not take long. She married Bobby. It was as simple as a death, but it lasted longer. It seemed it would never go away. She lingered in his thoughts. Did he exist in hers? he often wondered. Did she still feel, even if only a little, the way he felt? The years seemed to have no effect on it. She was in New Jersey somewhere, in some place he could not picture. Probably there was a family. Did she ever think of him? Ah, Noreen.

*

She had not changed. He could tell it from her voice, speaking, as always, to him alone.

"You probably have kids," he said as if casually.

"He didn't want them. Just one of the problems. Well, all that's *acqua passata*, as he liked to say. You didn't know I got divorced?"

"No."

"I more or less kept in touch with Marie up until she retired. She told me how you were doing. You're a big wheel now."

"Not really."

"I knew you would be. It would be nice to see you again. How long has it been?"

"Gee, a long time."

"You ever go out to Westhampton?"

"No, not for years."

"Goldie's?"

"He closed."

"I guess I knew that. Those were wonderful days."

It was the same, the ease of talking to her. He saw her great, winning smile, the well-being of it, her carefree walk.

"I'd love to see you," she said again.

They agreed to meet at the Plaza. She was going to be near there the next day.

He began walking up Fifth a little before five. He felt uncertain but tenderhearted, in the hands of a wondrous fate. The hotel stood before him, immense and vaguely white. He walked up the broad steps. There was a kind of foyer with a large table and flowers, the sound of people talking. As if, like an animal, he could detect the slightest noise, he seemed to make out the clink of cups and spoons.

There were flower boxes with pink flowers, the tall columns with their gilded tops, and in the Palm Court itself, which was crowded, through a glass panel he saw her sitting in a chair. For a moment he was not sure it was her. He moved away. Had she seen him?

He could not go in. He turned instead and went down the corridor to the men's room. An old man in black pants and a striped vest, the attendant, offered a towel as Arthur looked at himself in the long mirror to see if he had changed that much, too. He saw a man of fifty-five with the same Coney Island face he had always seen, half comic, kind. No worse than that. He gave the attendant a dollar and walked into the Palm Court, where, amid the chattering tables, the mock candelabra, and illuminated ceiling, Noreen was waiting. He was wearing his familiar dog's smile.

"Arthur, God, you look exactly the same. You haven't changed a bit," she said enthusiastically. "I wish I could say that."

It was hard to believe. She was twenty years older; she had gained weight, even her face showed it. She had been the most beautiful girl.

"You look great," he said. "I'd recognize you anywhere."

"Life's been good to you," she said.

"Well, I can't complain."

"I guess I can't either. What happened to everybody?"

"What do you mean?"

"Morris?"

"He died. Five or six years ago."

"That's too bad."

"They gave him a big dinner before that. He was all smiles."

"You know, I've wanted to talk to you so much. I wanted to call you, but I was involved in all this tedious divorce stuff. Anyway, I'm finally free. I should have taken your advice."

"What was that?"

"Not to marry him," she said.

"I said that?"

"No, but I could see you didn't like him."

"I was jealous of him."

"Truly?"

"Sure. I mean, let's face it."

She smiled at him.

"Isn't it funny," she said, "five minutes with you and it's as if none of it ever happened."

Her clothes, he noticed, even her clothes were hiding who she had been.

"Love never dies," he said.

"Do you mean that?"

"You know that."

"Listen, can you have dinner?"

"Ah, sweetheart," he said, "I'd love to, but I can't. I don't know if you knew this, but I'm engaged."

"Well, congratulations," she said. "I didn't know."

He had no idea what had made him say it. It was a word he had never used before in his life.

"That's wonderful," she said straightforwardly, smiling at him with such understanding that he was sure she had seen through him, but he could not imagine them walking into Clarke's, like an old couple, a couple from time past.

"I figured it's time to settle down," he said.

"Of course."

She was not looking at him. She was studying her hands. Then she smiled again. She was forgiving him, he felt. That was it. She always understood.

They talked on, but not about much.

He left through the same foyer with its worn mosaic tile and people coming in. It was still light outside, the pure full light before evening, the sun in a thousand windows facing the park. Walking along the street in their heels, alone or together, were girls such as Noreen had been, many of them. They were not really going to meet for lunch sometime. He thought of the love that had filled the great central chamber of his life and how he would not meet anyone like that again. He did not know what came over him, but on the street he broke into tears.

LOST SONS

All afternoon the cars, many with out-of-state plates, were coming along the road. The long row of lofty brick quarters appeared above. The grey walls began.

In the reception area a welcoming party was going on. There were faces that had hardly changed at all and others like Reemstma's whose name tag was read more than once. Someone with a camera and flash attachment was running around in a cadet bathrobe. Over in the barracks they were drinking. Doors were open. Voices spilled out.

"Hooknose will be here," Dunning promised loudly. There was a bottle on the desk near his feet. "He'll show, don't worry. I had a letter from him."

"A letter? Klingbeil never wrote a letter."

"His secretary wrote it," Dunning said. He looked like a judge, large and well fed. His glasses lent a dainty touch. "He's teaching her to write."

"Where's he living now?"

"Florida."

"Remember the time we were sneaking back to Buckner at two in the morning and all of a sudden a car came down the road?"

Dunning was trying to arrange a serious expression.

"We dove in the bushes. It turned out it was a taxi. It slammed on the brakes and backed up. The door opens and there's Klingbeil in the backseat, drunk as a lord. Get in, boys, he says."

Dunning roared. His blouse with its rows of colored ribbons was unbuttoned, gluteal power hinted by the width of his lap.

"Remember," he said, "when we threw Devereaux's Spanish book with all his notes in it out the window? Into the snow. He never found it. He went bananas. You bastards, I'll kill you!"

"He'd have been a star man if he hadn't been living with you."

"We tried to broaden him," Dunning explained.

They used to do the sinking of the *Bismarck* while he was studying. Klingbeil was the captain. They would jump up on the desks. *Der Schiff ist kaputt!* they shouted. They were firing the guns. The rudder was jammed, they were turning in circles. Devereaux sat head down with his hands pressed over his ears. Will you bastards shut up! he screamed.

Bush, Buford, Jap Andrus, Doane, and George Hilmo were sitting on the beds and windowsill. An uncertain face looked in the doorway.

"Who's that?"

It was Reemstma whom no one had seen for years. His hair had turned grey. He smiled awkwardly. "What's going on?"

They looked at him.

"Come in and have a drink," someone finally said.

He found himself next to Hilmo, who reached across to

shake hands with an iron grip. "How are you?" he said. The others went on talking. "You look great."

"You, too."

Hilmo seemed not to hear. "Where are you living?" he said.

"Rosemont. Rosemont, New Jersey. It's where my wife's family's from," Reemstma said. He spoke with a strange intensity. He had always been odd. Everyone wondered how he had ever made it through. He did all right in class but the image that lasted was of someone bewildered by close order drill which he seemed to master only after two years and then with the stiffness of a cat trying to swim. He had full lips which were the source of an unflattering nickname. He was also known as To The Rear March because of the disasters he caused at the command.

He was handed a used paper cup. "Whose bottle is this?" he asked.

"I don't know," Hilmo said. "Here."

"Are a lot of people coming?"

"Boy, you're full of questions," Hilmo said.

Reemstma fell silent. For half an hour they told stories. He sat by the window, sometimes looking in his cup. Outside, the clock with its black numerals began to brighten. West Point lay majestic in the early evening, its dignified foliage still. Below, the river was silent, mysterious islands floating in the dusk. Near the corner of the library a military policeman, his arm moving with precision, directed traffic past a sign for the reunion of 1960, a class on which Vietnam had fallen as stars fell on 1915 and 1931. In the distance was the faint sound of a train.

It was almost time for dinner. There were still occasional cries of greeting from below, people talking, voices. Feet were leisurely descending the stairs.

"Hey," someone said unexpectedly, "what the hell is that thing you're wearing?"

Reemstma looked down. It was a necktie of red, flowered cloth. His wife had made it. He changed it before going out.

"Hello, there."

Walking calmly alone was a white-haired figure with an armband that read 1930.

"What class are you?"

"Nineteen-sixty," Reemstma said.

"I was just thinking as I walked along, I was wondering what finally happened to everybody. It's hard to believe but when I was here we had men who simply packed up after a few weeks and went home without a word to anyone. Ever hear of anything like that? Nineteen-sixty, you say?"

"Yes, sir."

"You ever hear of Frank Kissner? I was his chief of staff. He was a tough guy. Regimental commander in Italy. One day Mark Clark drove up and said, Frank, come here a minute, I want to talk to you. Haven't got time, I'm too busy, Frank said."

"Really?"

"Mark Clark said, Frank, I want to make you a B.G. I've got time, Frank said."

The mess hall, in which the alumni dinner was being held, loomed before them, its doors open. Its scale had always been heroic. It seemed to have doubled in size and was filled with the white of tablecloths as far as one could see.

The bars were crowded, there were lines fifteen and twenty deep of men waiting patiently. Many of the women were in dinner dresses. Above it all was the echoing haze of conversation.

There were those with the definite look of success, like Hilmo who wore a grey summer suit with a metallic sheen and to whom everyone liked to talk although he was given to abrupt silences, and there were also the unfading heroes, those who had been cadet officers, come to life again. Early form had not always held. Among those now of high rank were men who in their schooldays had been relatively undistinguished. Reemstma, who had been out of touch, was somewhat surprised by this. For him the hierarchy had never been altered.

A terrifying face blotched with red suddenly appeared. It was Cramner, who had lived down the hall.

"Hey, Eddie, how's it going?"

He was holding two drinks. He had just retired a year ago, Cramner said. He was working for a law firm in Reading.

"Are you a lawyer?"

"I run the office," Cramner said. "You married? Is your wife here?"

"No."

"Why not?"

"She couldn't come," Reemstma said.

His wife had met him when he was thirty. Why would she want to go, she had asked? In a way he was glad she hadn't. She knew no one and given the chance she would often turn the conversation to religion. There would be two weird people instead of one. Of course, he did not really think of himself as weird, it was only in their eyes. Perhaps not even. He was being greeted, talked to. The women, especially, unaware of established judgments, were friendly. He found himself talking to the lively wife of a classmate he vaguely remembered, R. C. Walker, a lean man with a somewhat sardonic smile.

"You're a what?" she said in astonishment. "A painter? You mean an artist?" She had thick, naturally curly blonde hair and a pleasant softness to her cheeks. Her chin had a slight double fold. "I think that's fabulous!" She called to a friend, "Nita, you have to meet someone. It's Ed, isn't it?"

"Ed Reemstma."

"He's a painter," Kit Walker said exuberantly.

Reemstma was dazed by the attention. When they learned that he actually sold things they were even more interested.

"Do you make a living at it?"

"Well, I have a waiting list for paintings."

"You do!"

He began to describe the color and light—he painted landscapes—of the countryside near the Delaware, the shape of the earth, its furrows, hedges, how things changed slightly from year to year, little things, how hard it was to do the sky. He described the beautiful, glinting green of a hummingbird his wife had brought to him. She had found it in the garage; it was dead, of course.

"Dead?" Nita said.

"The eyes were closed. Except for that, you wouldn't have known."

He had an almost wistful smile. Nita nodded warily.

Later there was dancing. Reemstma would have liked to

go on talking but people drifted away. Tables broke up after dinner into groups of friends.

"Bye for now," Kit Walker said.

He saw her talking to Hilmo, who gave him a brief wave. He wandered about for a while. They were playing "Army Blue." A wave of sadness went through him, memories of parades, the end of dances, Christmas leave. Four years of it, the classes ahead leaving in pride and excitement, unknown faces filling in behind. It was finished, but no one turns his back on it completely. The life he might have led came back to him, almost whole.

Outside barracks, late at night, five or six figures were sitting on the steps, drinking and talking. Reemstma sat near them, not speaking, not wanting to break the spell. He was one of them again, as he had been on frantic evenings when they cleaned rifles and polished their shoes to a mirrorlike gleam. The haze of June lay over the great expanse that separated him from those endless tasks of years before. How deeply he had immersed himself in them. How ardently he had believed in the image of a soldier. He had known it as a faith, he had clung to it dumbly, as a cripple clings to God.

In the morning Hilmo trotted down the stairs, tennis shorts tight over his muscled legs, and disappeared through one of the sally ports for an early match. His insouciance was unchanged. They said that before the Penn State game when he had been first string the coach had pumped them up telling them they were not only going to beat Penn State, they were going to beat them by two touchdowns, then turning to Hilmo, "And who's going to be the greatest back in the East?"

"I don't know. Who?" Hilmo said.

Empty morning. As usual, except for sports there was little to do. Shortly after ten they formed up to march to a memorial ceremony at the corner of the Plain. Before a statue of Sylvanus Thayer they stood at attention, one tall maverick head in a cowboy hat, while the choir sang "The Corps." The thrilling voices, the solemn, staggered parts rose through the air. Behind Reemstma someone said quietly, "You know, the best friends I ever had or ever will have are the ones I had here."

Afterward they walked out to take their places on the parade ground. The superintendent, a trim lieutenant general, stood not far off with his staff and the oldest living graduate, who was in a wheelchair.

"Look at him," Dunning said. He was referring to the superintendent. "That's what's wrong with this place. That's what's wrong with the whole army."

Faint waves of band music beat toward them. It was warm. There were bees in the grass. The first miniature formations of cadets, bayonets glinting, began to move into view. Above, against the sky, a lone distinguished building, and that a replica, stood. The chapel. Many Sundays with their manly sermons on virtue and the glittering choir marching toward the door with graceful, halting tread, gold stripes shining on the sleeves of the leaders. Down below, partly hidden, the gymnasium, the ominous dark patina on everything within, the floor, the walls, the heavy boxing gloves. There were champions enshrined there who would never be unseated, maxims that would never be erased.

At the picnic it was announced that of the 550 original members, 529 were living and 176 present so far.

"Not counting Klingbeil!"

"Okay, one seventy-six plus a possible Klingbeil."

"An *im*possible Klingbeil," someone called out.

There was a brief cheer.

The tables were in a large, screened pavilion on the edge of the lake. Reemstma looked for Kit Walker. He'd caught sight of her earlier, in the food line, but now he could not find her. She seemed to have gone. The class president was speaking.

"We got a card from Joe Waltsak. Joe retired this year. He wanted to come but his daughter's graduating from high school. I don't know if you know this story. Joe lives in Palo Alto and there was a bill before the California legislature to change the name of any street an All-American lived on and name it after him. Joe lives on Parkwood Drive. They were going to call it Waltsak Drive, but the bill didn't pass, so instead they're calling him Joe Parkwood."

The elections were next. The class treasurer and the vice-president were not running again. There would have to be nominations for these.

"Let's have somebody different for a change," someone commented in a low voice.

"Somebody we know," Dunning said.

"You want to run, Mike?"

"Yeah, sure, that would be great," Dunning muttered.

"How about Reemstma?" It was Cramner, the blossoms of alcoholism ablaze in his face. The edges of his teeth were uneven as he smiled, as if eaten away.

"Good idea."

"Who, me?" Reemstma said. He was flustered. He looked around in surprise.

"How about it, Eddie?"

He could not tell if they were serious. It was all off-handed—the way Grant had been picked from obscurity one evening when he was sitting on a bench in St. Louis. He murmured something in protest. His face had become red.

Other names were being proposed. Reemstma felt his heart pounding. He had stopped saying, no, no, and sat there, mouth open a bit in bewilderment. He dared not look around him. He shook his head slightly, no. A hand went up, "I move that the nominations be closed."

Reemstma felt foolish. They had tricked him again. He felt as if he had been betrayed. No one was paying any attention to him. They were counting raised hands.

"Come on, you can't vote," someone said to his wife.

"I can't?" she said.

Wandering around as the afternoon ended Reemstma finally caught sight of Kit Walker. She acted a little strange. She didn't seem to recognize him at first. There was a grass stain on the back of her white skirt.

"Oh, hello," she said.

"I was looking for you."

"Would you do me a favor?" she said. "Would you mind getting me a drink? My husband seems to be ignoring me."

Though Reemstma did not see it, someone else was ignoring her, too. It was Hilmo, standing some way off. They had taken care to come back to the pavilion separately. Friends who would soon be parting were talking in small groups, their faces shadowy against the water that glistened behind them. Reemstma returned with some wine in a plastic glass.

"Here you are. Is anything wrong?"

"Thank you. No, why? You know, you're very nice," she said. She had noticed something over his shoulder. "Oh, dear."

"What?"

"Nothing. It looks like we're going."

"Do you have to?" he managed to say.

"Rick's over by the door. You know him, he hates to be kept waiting."

"I was hoping we could talk."

He turned. Walker was standing outside in the sunlight. He was wearing an aloha shirt and tan slacks. He seemed somewhat aloof. Reemstma was envious of him.

"We have to drive back to Belvoir tonight," she said.

"I guess it's a long way."

"It was very nice meeting you," she said.

She left the drink untouched on the corner of the table. Reemstma watched her make her way across the floor. She was not like the others, he thought. He saw them walking to their car. Did she have children? he found himself wondering. Did she really find him interesting?

In the hour before twilight, at six in the evening, he heard the noise and looked out. Crossing the area toward them was the unconquerable schoolboy, long-legged as a crane, the ex-infantry officer now with a small, well-rounded paunch, waving both arms.

Dunning was bellowing from a window, "Hooknose!"

"Look who I've got!" Klingbeil called back.

He was with Devereaux, the tormented scholar. Their arms were around each other's shoulders. They were crossing together, grinning, friends since cadet days, friends for life. They started up the stairs.

"Hooknose!" Dunning shouted.

Klingbeil threw open his arms in mocking joy.

He was the son of an army officer. As a boy he had sailed on the Matson Line and gone back and forth across the country. He told stories of seduction in the lower berth. My son, my son, she was moaning. He was irredeemable, he had the common touch, his men adored him. Promoted slowly, he had gotten out and become a land developer. He drove a green Cadillac famous in Tampa. He was a king of poker games, drinking, late nights.

She had probably not meant it, Reemstma was thinking. His experience had taught him that. He was not susceptible to lies.

"Oh," wives would say, "of course. I think I've heard my husband talk about you."

"I don't know your husband," Reemstma would say.

A moment of alarm.

"Of course, you do. Aren't you in the same class?"

He could hear them downstairs.

"*Der Schiff ist kaputt!*" they were shouting. "*Der Schiff ist kaputt!*"

VIA NEGATIVA

There is a kind of minor writer who is found in a room of the library signing his novel. His index finger is the color of tea, his smile filled with bad teeth. He knows literature, however. His sad bones are made of it. He knows what was written and where writers died. His opinions are cold but accurate. They are pure, at least there is that.

He's unknown, though not without a few admirers. They are really like marriage, uninteresting, but what else is there? His life is his journals. In them somewhere is a line from the astrologer: your natural companions are women. Occasionally, perhaps. No more than that. His hair is thin. His clothes are a little out of style. He is aware, however, that there is a great, a final glory which falls on certain figures barely noticed in their time, touches them in obscurity and recreates their lives. His heroes are Musil and, of course, Gerard Manley Hopkins. Bunin.

There are writers like P in an expensive suit and fine English shoes who come walking down the street in eye-splintering sunlight, the crowd seeming to part for them, to leave an opening like the eye of a storm.

"I hear you got a fortune for your book."

"What? Don't believe it," they say, though everyone knows. On close examination, the shoes are even handmade.

Their owner has a rich head of hair. His face is powerful, his brow, his long nose. A suffering face, strong as a door. He recognizes his questioner as someone who has published several stories. He only has a moment to talk.

"Money doesn't mean anything," he says. "Look at me. I can't even get a decent haircut."

He's serious. He doesn't smile. When he came back from London and was asked to endorse a novel by a young acquaintance he said, let him do it the way I did, on his own. They all want something, he said.

And there are old writers who owe their eminence to the *New Yorker* and travel in wealthy circles like W, who was famous at twenty. Some critics now feel his work is shallow and too derivative—he had been a friend of the greatest writer of our time, a writer who inspired countless imitators, perhaps it would be better to say one of the great writers, not everyone is in agreement, and I don't want to get into arguments. They broke up later anyway, W didn't like to say why.

His first, much-published story—everyone knows it—brought him at least fifty women over the years, he used to say. His wife was aware of it. In the end he broke with her, too. He was not a man who kept his looks. Small veins began to appear in his cheeks. His eyes became red. He insulted people, even waiters in restaurants. Still, in his youth he was said to have been very generous, very brave. He was against injustice. He gave money to the Loyalists in Spain.

Morning. The dentists are laying out their picks. In the doorways, as the sun hits them, the bums begin to groan. Nile went on the bus to visit his mother, the words of Victor Hugo about *all the armies in the world being unable to stop an idea whose time has come* on an advertisement above his head. His hair was uncombed. His face had the arrogance, the bruised lips of someone determined to live without money. His mother met him at the door and took this pale face in her hands. She stepped back to see better. She was trembling slightly with a steady, rhythmic movement.

"Your teeth," she said.

He covered them with his tongue. His aunt came from the kitchen to embrace him.

"Where have you been?" she cried. "Guess what we're having for lunch."

Like many fat women, she liked to laugh. She was twice a widow, but one drink was enough to make her dance. She went to set the table. Passing the window, she glanced out. There was a movie house across the street.

"Degenerates," she said.

Nile sat between them, pulling his chair close to the table with little scrapes. They had not bothered to dress. The warmth of family lunches when the only interest is food. He was always hungry when he came. He ate a slice of bread heavy with butter as he talked. There was scrod and sautéed onions on a huge dish. Voices everywhere—the television was going, the radio in the kitchen. His mouth was full as he answered their questions.

"It's a little flat," his mother announced. "Did you cook it the same way?"

"Exactly the same," his aunt said. She tasted it herself. "It may need salt."

"You don't put salt on seafood," his mother said.

Nile kept eating. The fish fell apart beneath his fork, moist and white, he could taste the faint iodine of the sea. He knew the very market where it had been displayed on ice, the Jewish owner who did not shave. His aunt was watching him.

"Do you know something?" she said.

"What?"

She was not speaking to him. She had made a discovery.

"For a minute then, while he was eating, he looked just like his father."

A sudden, sweet pause opened in the room, a depth that had not been there when they were talking only of immorality and the danger of the blacks. His mother looked at him reverently.

"Did you hear that?" she asked. Her voice was hushed, she longed for the myths of the past. Her eyes had darkness around them, her flesh was old.

"How do you look like him?" She wanted to hear it recited.

"I don't," he said.

They did not hear him. They were arguing about his childhood, various details of it, poems he had memorized, his beautiful hair. What a good student he had been. How grownup when he ate, the fork too large for his hand. His chin was like his father's, they said. The shape of his head.

"In the back," his aunt said.

"A beautiful head," his mother confirmed. "You have a perfect head, did you know that?"

Afterward he lay on the couch and listened as they cleared the dishes. He closed his eyes. Everything was familiar to him, phrases he had heard before, quarrels about the past, even the smell of the cushions beneath his head. In the bedroom was a collection of photographs in ill-fitting frames. In them, if one traced the progression, was a face growing older and older, more and more unpromising. Had he really written all those earnest letters preserved in shoe boxes together with schoolbooks and folded programs? He was sleeping in the museum of his life.

He left at four. The doorman was reading the newspaper, his collar unbuttoned, the air surrounding him rich with odors of cooking. He didn't bother to look up as Nile went out. He was absorbed in a description of two young women whose bound bodies had been found on the bank of a canal. There were no pictures, only those from a high-school year-book. It was June. The street was lined with cars, the gutters melting.

The shops were closed. In their windows, abandoned to afternoon, were displays of books, cosmetics, leather clothes. He lingered before them. A great longing for money, a thirst rose in him, a desire to be recognized. He was walking for the hundredth time on streets which in no way acknowledged him, past endless apartments, consulates, banks. He came to the fifties, behind the great hotels. The streets were dank, like servants' quarters. Paper lay everywhere, envelopes, empty packages of cigarettes.

In Jeanine's apartment it was better. The floor was polished. Her breath seemed sweet.

"Have you been out?" he asked her.

"No, not yet."

"The streets are melting," he said. "You weren't working, were you?"

"I was reading."

From her windows one could see the second-floor salon in the rear of the Plaza in which hairdressers worked. It was red, with mirrors that multiplied its secrets. Naked, on certain afternoons, they had watched its silent acts.

"What are you reading?" he asked.

"Gogol."

"Gogol . . ." He closed his eyes and began to recite, "*In the carriage sat a gentleman, not handsome but not bad-looking, not too stout and not too thin, not old, but not so very young . . .*"

"What a memory you have."

"Listen, what novel is this? *For a long time I used to go to bed early . . .*"

"That's too easy," she said.

She was sitting on the couch, her legs drawn up beneath her, the book near her hand.

"I guess it is," he said. "Did you know this about Gogol? He died a virgin."

"Is that true?"

"The Russians are a little curious that way," he said. "Chekhov himself thought once a year was sufficient for a writer."

He had told her that before, he realized.

"Not everyone agrees with that," he murmured. "You know who I saw on the street yesterday? Dressed like a banker. Even his shoes."

"Who?"

Nile described him. After a moment she knew who he must be talking about.

"He's written a new book," she said.

"So I hear. I thought he was going to hold out his ring for me to kiss. I said, listen, tell me one thing, honestly: all the money, the attention . . ."

"You didn't."

Nile smiled. The teeth his mother wept over were revealed.

"He was terrified. He knew what I was going to say. He had everything, everybody was talking about him, and all I had was a pin. A needle. If I pushed, it would go straight to the heart."

She had a boy's face and arms with a faint shadow of muscle. Her fingernails were bitten clean. The afternoon light which had somehow found its way into the room gleamed from her knees. She was from Montana. When they first met, Nile had seen her as complaisant, which excited him, even stupid, but he discovered it was only a vast distance, perhaps of childhood, which surrounded her. She revealed herself in simple, unexpected acts, like a farmboy undressing. As she sat on the couch, one arm was exposed beside her. Within its elbow he could see the long, rich artery curved down to her wrist. It was full. It lay without beating.

She had been married. Her past astonished him. Her body bore no trace of it, not even a memory, it seemed. All she had learned was how to live alone. In the bathroom were soaps with the name printed on them, soaps that had never been wet. There were fresh towels, flowers in a blue glass. The bed was flat and smooth. There were books, fruit, announcements stuck in the edge of the mirror.

"What did you actually ask him?" she said.

"Do you have any wine?" Nile said. While she was gone,

he continued in a louder voice, "He's afraid of me. He's afraid of me because I've accomplished nothing."

He looked up. Plaster was flaking from the ceiling.

"You know what Cocteau said," he called. "There's a fame worse than failure. I asked him if he thought he really deserved it all."

"And what did he say?"

"I don't remember. What's this?" He took the bottle of sea-colored glass she carried. The label was slightly stained. "A Pauillac. I don't remember this. Did I buy it?"

"No."

"I didn't think so." He smelled it. "Very good. Someone gave it to you," he suggested.

She filled his glass.

"Do you want to go to a film?" he asked.

"I don't think so."

He looked at the wine.

"No?" he said.

She was silent. After a moment she said, "I can't."

He began to inspect titles in the bookcase near him, many he had never read.

"How's your mother?" he asked. "I like your mother." He opened one of the books. "Do you write to her?"

"Sometimes."

"You know, Viking is interested in me," he said abruptly. "They're interested in my stories. They want me to expand *Lovenights*."

"I've always liked that story," she said.

"I'm already working. I'm getting up very early. They want me to have a photograph made."

"Who did you see at Viking?"

"I forget his name. He's, uh . . . dark hair, he's about my size. I should know his name. Well, what's the difference?"

She went into the bedroom to change her clothes. He started to follow her.

"Don't," she said.

He sat down again. He could hear occasional, ordinary sounds, drawers opening and being shut, periods of silence. It was as if she were packing.

"Where are you going?" he called, looking at the floor.

She was brushing her hair. He could hear the swift, rhythmic strokes. She was facing herself in the mirror, not even aware of him. He was like a letter lying on the table, the half-read Gogol, like the wine. When she emerged, he could not look at her. He sat slouched, like a passionate child.

"Jeanine," he said, "I know I've disappointed you. But it's true about Viking."

"I know."

"I'll be very busy. . . . Do you have to go just now?"

"I'm a bit late."

"No, you're not," he said. "Please."

She could not answer.

"Anyway, I have to go home and work," he said. "Where are you going?"

"I'll be back by eleven," she said. "Why don't you call me?"

She tried to touch his hair.

"There's more wine," she said. She no longer believed in him. In things he might say, yes, but not in him. She had lost her faith.

"Jeanine . . ."

"Good-bye, Nile," she said. It was the way she ended telephone calls.

She was going to the nineties, to dinner in an apartment she had not seen. Her arms were bare. Her face seemed very young.

When the door closed, panic seized him. He was suddenly desperate. His thoughts seemed to fly away, to scatter like birds. It was a deathlike hour. On television, the journalists were answering complex questions. The streets were still. He began to go through her things. First the closets. The drawers. He found her letters. He sat down to read them, letters from her brother, her lawyer, people he did not know. He began pulling forth everything, shirts, underclothes, long clinging weeds which were stockings. He kicked her shoes away, spilled open boxes. He broke her necklaces, pieces rained to the floor. The wildness, the release of a murderer filled him. As she sat there in the nineties, sometimes speaking a little, the men nearby uncertain, seeking to hold her glance, he whipped her like a yelping dog from room to room, pushing her into walls, tearing her clothes. She was stumbling, crying, he felt the horror of his acts. He had no right to them—why did this justify everything?

He was bathed in sweat, breathless, afraid to stay. He closed the door softly. There were old newspapers piled in the hall, the faint sounds from other apartments, children returning from errands to the store.

In the street he saw on every side, in darkening windows, in reflections, as if suddenly it were visible to him, a kind of chaos. It welcomed, it acclaimed him. The huge tires of buses roared past. It was the last hour of light. He felt the solitude of crime. He stopped, like an addict, in a phone booth. His legs were weak. No, beneath the weakness was something else. For a moment he saw unknown depths to himself, he glittered with images. It seemed he was attracting the glances of women who passed. They recognize me, he thought, they smell me in the dark like mares. He smiled at them with the cracked lips of an incorrigible. He cared nothing for them, only for the power to disturb. He was bending their love toward him, a stupid love, a love without which he could not breathe.

It was late when he arrived home. He closed the door. Darkness. He turned on the light. He had no sense of belonging there. He looked at himself in the bathroom mirror. There was a skylight over his head, the panes were black. He sat beneath the small, nude photograph of a girl he had once lived with, the edges were curled, and began to play, the G was sticking, the piano was out of tune. In Bach there was not only order and coherence but more, a code, a repetition which everything depended on. After a while he felt a pounding beneath his feet, the broom of the idiot on the floor below. He continued to play. The pounding grew louder. If he had a car . . . Suddenly the idea broke over him as if it were the one thing he had been trying to think of: a car. He would be speeding from the city to find himself at dawn on long, country roads. Vermont, no, further, Newfoundland, where the coast was still deserted. That was it, a car, he saw it plainly. He saw it parked in the gentle light of daybreak, its body stained from the journey, a faintly battered body that had survived some terrible, early crash.

All is chance or nothing is chance. That evening Jeanine

met a man who longed, he said, to perform an act of great and unending generosity, like Genet's in giving his house to a former lover.

"Did he do that?" she asked.

"They say."

It was P. The room was filled with people, and he was speaking to her, quite naturally, as if they had met before. She did not wonder what to say to him, she did not have to say anything. He was quite near. The fine wrinkles in his brow were visible, wrinkles not yet deepened.

"Generosity purifies," he said. He was later to tell her that words were no accident, their arrangement and choice was like another voice speaking, a voice which revealed everything. Vocabulary was like fingerprints, he said, like handwriting, like the body which revealed the invisible soul, which expressed it.

His face was dark, his features deep. He was part of another, a mysterious race. She was aware of how different her own face was with its wide mouth, its grey eyes, slow, curious, clear as a stream. She was aware also that the dress she wore, the depth of the chairs, the dimensions of this room afloat now in evening, all of these were part of an immersion into the flow of a great life. Her heart was beating slowly but hard. She had never felt so sure of herself, so bewildered by the ease with which it all was opening.

"I'm suspicious and grasping," he said. He was beginning his confessions. "I recognize that." Later he told her that in his entire life he had only been free for an hour, and that hour was always with her.

She asked no questions. She recognized him. In her own

apartment the lights were burning. The air of the city, bitter as acid, was absolutely still. She did not breathe it. She was breathing another air. She had not smiled once as yet. He later told her that this was the most powerful thing of all that had attracted him. Her breasts, he said, were like those of black tribal girls in the *National Geographic*.

FOREIGN SHORES

Mrs. Pence and her white shoes were gone. She had left two days before, and the room at the top of the stairs was empty, cosmetics no longer littering the dresser, the ironing board finally taken down. Only a few scattered hairpins and a dusting of talcum remained. The next day Truus came with two suitcases and splotched cheeks. It was March and cold. Christopher met her in the kitchen as if by accident. "Do you shoot people?" he asked.

She was Dutch and had no work permit, it turned out. The house was a mess. "I can pay you $135 a week," Gloria told her.

Christopher didn't like her at first, but soon the dishes piled on the counter were washed and put away, the floor was swept, and things were more or less returned to order—the cleaning girl came only once a week. Truus was slow but diligent. She did the laundry, which Mrs. Pence who was a registered nurse had always refused to do, shopped, cooked meals, and took care of Christopher. She was a hard worker, nineteen, and in sulky bloom. Gloria sent her to Elizabeth Arden's in Southampton to get her complexion cleared up and gave her Mondays and one night a week off.

Gradually Truus learned about things. The house, which was a large, converted carriage house, was rented. Gloria, who was twenty-nine, liked to sleep late, and burned spots sometimes appeared in the living room rug. Christopher's father lived in California, and Gloria had a boyfriend named Ned. "That son of a bitch," she often said, "might as well forget about seeing Christopher again until he pays me what he owes me."

"Absolutely," Ned said.

When the weather became warmer Truus could be seen in the village in one shop or another or walking along the street with Christopher in tow. She was somewhat drab. She had met another girl by then, a French girl, also an *au pair*, with whom she went to the movies. Beneath the trees with their new leaves the expensive cars glided along, more of them every week. Truus began taking Christopher to the beach. Gloria watched them go off. She was often still in her bathrobe. She waved and drank coffee. She was very lucky. All her friends told her and she knew it herself: Truus was a prize. She had made herself part of the family.

"Truus knows where to get pet mices," Christopher said.

"To get what?"

"Little mices."

"Mice," Gloria said.

He was watching her apply makeup, which fascinated him. Face nearly touching the mirror, intent, she stroked her long lashes upward. She had a great mass of blonde hair, a mole on her upper lip with a few untouched hairs growing from it, a small blemish on her forehead, but otherwise a beautiful face. Her first entrance was always stunning. Later you might notice the thin legs, aristocratic legs she called them, her mother had them, too. As the evening wore on her perfection diminished. The gloss disappeared from her lips, she misplaced earrings. The highway patrol all knew her. A few weeks before she had driven into a ditch on the way home from a party and walked down Georgica Road at three in the morning, breaking two panes of glass to get in the kitchen door.

"Her friend knows where to get them," Christopher said.

"Which friend?"

"Oh, just a friend," Truus said.

"We met him."

Gloria's eyes shifted from their own reflection to rest for a moment on that of Truus who was watching no less absorbed.

"Can I have some mices?" Christopher pleaded.

"Hmm?"

"Please."

"No, darling."

"Please!"

"No, we have enough of our own as it is."

"Where?"

"All over the house."

"Please!"

"No. Now stop it." To Truus she remarked casually, "Is it a boyfriend?"

"It's no one," Truus said. "Just someone I met."

"Well, just remember you have to watch yourself. You never know who you're meeting, you have to be careful." She drew back slightly and examined her eyes, large and black-rimmed. "Just thank God you're not in Italy," she said.

"Italy?"

"You can't even walk out on the street there. You can't even buy a pair of shoes, they're all over you, touching and pawing."

It happened outside Dean and De Luca's when Christopher insisted on carrying the bag and just past the door had dropped it.

"Oh, look at that," Truus said in irritation. "I told you not to drop it."

"I didn't drop it. It slipped."

"Don't touch it," she warned. "There's broken glass."

Christopher stared at the ground. He had a sturdy body, bobbed hair, and a cleft in his chin like his banished father's. People were walking past them. Truus was annoyed. It was hot, the store was crowded, she would have to go back inside.

"Looks like you had a little accident," a voice said. "Here, what'd you break? That's all right, they'll exchange it. I know the cashier."

When he came out again a few moments later he said to Christopher, "Think you can hold it this time?"

Christopher was silent.

"What's your name?"

"Well, tell him," Truus said. Then after a moment, "His name is Christopher."

"Too bad you weren't with me this morning, Christopher.

I went to a place where they had a lot of tame mice. Ever seen any?"

"Where?" Christopher said.

"They sit right in your hand."

"Where is it?"

"You can't have a mouse," Truus said.

"Yes, I can." He continued to repeat it as they walked along. "I can have anything I want," he said.

"Be quiet." They were talking above his head. Near the corner they stopped for a while. Christopher was silent as they went on talking. He felt his hair being tugged but did not look up.

"Say good-bye, Christopher."

He said nothing. He refused to lift his head.

In midafternoon the sun was like a furnace. Everything was dark against it, the horizon lost in haze. Far down the beach in front of one of the prominent houses a large flag was waving. With Christopher following her, Truus trudged through the sand. Finally she saw what she had been looking for. Up in the dunes a figure was sitting.

"Where are we going?" Christopher asked.

"Just up here."

Christopher soon saw where they were headed.

"I have mices," was the first thing he said.

"Is that right?"

"Do you want to know their names?" In fact they were two desperate gerbils in a tank of wood shavings. "Catman and Batty," he said.

"Catman?"

"He's the big one." Truus was spreading a towel, he noticed. "Do we have to stay here?"

"Yes."

"Why?" he asked. He wanted to go down near the water. Finally Truus agreed.

"But only if you stay where I can see you," she said.

The shovel fell out of his bucket as he ran off. She had to call him to make him come back. He went off again and she pretended to watch him.

"I'm really glad you came. You know, I don't know your name. I know his, but I don't know yours."

"Truus."

"I've never heard that name before. What is it, French?"

"It's Dutch."

"Oh, yeah?"

His name was Robbie Werner, "not half as nice," he said. He had an easy smile and pale blue eyes. There was something spoiled about him, like a student who has been expelled and is undisturbed by it. The sun was roaring down and striking Truus' shoulders beneath her shirt. She was wearing a blue one-piece bathing suit underneath. She was aware of being too heavy, of the heat, and of the thick, masculine legs stretched out near her.

"Do you live here?" she said.

"I'm just here on vacation."

"From where?"

"Try and guess."

"I don't know," she said. She wasn't good at that kind of thing.

"Saudi Arabia," he said. "It's about three times this hot."

He worked there, he explained. He had an apartment of his own and a free telephone. At first she did not believe him. She glanced at him as he talked and realized he was telling the truth. He got two months of vacation a year, he said, usually in Europe. She imagined it as sleeping in hotels and getting up late and going out to lunch. She did not want him to stop talking. She could not think of anything to say.

"How about you?" he said. "What do you do?"

"Oh, I'm just taking care of Christopher."

"Where's his mother?"

"She lives here. She's divorced," Truus said.

"It's terrible the way people get divorced," he said.

"I agree with you."

"I mean, why get married?" he said. "Are your parents still married?"

"Yes," she said, although they did not seem to be a good example. They had been married for nearly twenty-five years. They were worn out from marriage, her mother especially.

Suddenly Robbie raised himself slightly. "Uh-oh," he said.

"What is it?"

"Your kid. I don't see him."

Truus jumped up quickly, looked around, and began to run toward the water. There was a kind of shelf the tide had made which hid the ocean's edge. As she ran she finally saw, beyond it, the little blond head. She was calling his name.

"I told you to stay up where I could see you," she cried, out of breath, when she reached him. "I had to run all the way. Do you know how much you frightened me?"

Christopher slapped aimlessly at the sand with his shovel. He looked up and saw Robbie. "Do you want to build a castle?" he asked innocently.

"Sure," Robbie said after a moment. "Come on, let's go down a little further, closer to the water. Then we can have a moat. Do you want to help us build a castle?" he said to Truus.

"No," Christopher said, "she can't."

"Sure, she can. She's going to do a very important part of it for us."

"What?"

"You'll see." They were walking down the velvety slope dampened by the tide.

"What's your name?" Christopher asked.

"Robbie. Here's a good place." He kneeled and began scooping out large handfuls of sand.

"Do you have a penis?"

"Sure."

"I do, too," Christopher said.

She was preparing his dinner while he played outside on the terrace, banging on the slate with his shovel. It was hot. Her clothes were sticking to her and there was moisture on her upper lip, but afterward she would go up and shower. She had a room on the second floor—not the one Mrs. Pence had—a small guest room painted white with a crude patch on the door where the original lock had been removed. Just outside the window were trees and the thick hedge of the neighboring house. The room faced south and caught the breeze. Often in the morning Christopher would crawl into her bed, his legs cool and hair a little sour-smelling. The room was filled with molten light. She could feel sand in the sheets, the merest trace of it. She turned her head sleepily to look at her watch on the night table. Not yet six. The first birds were singing. Beside her, eyes closed, mouth parted to reveal a row of small teeth, lay this perfect boy.

He had begun digging in the border of flowers. He was piling dirt on the edge of the terrace.

"Don't, you'll hurt them," Truus said. "If you don't stop, I'm going to put you up in the tree, the one by the shed."

The telephone was ringing. Gloria picked it up in the other part of the house. After a moment, "It's for you," she called.

"Hello?" Truus said.

"Hi." It was Robbie.

"Hello," she said. She couldn't tell if Gloria had hung up. Then she heard a click.

"Are you going to be able to meet me tonight?"

"Yes, I can meet you," she said. Her heart felt extraordinarily light.

Christopher had begun to scrape his shovel across the screen. "Excuse me," she said, putting her hand over the mouthpiece. "Stop that," she commanded.

She turned to him after she hung up. He was watching from the door. "Are you hungry?" she asked.

"No."

"Come, let's wash your hands."

"Why are you going out?"

"Just for fun. Come on."

"Where are you going?"

"Oh, stop, will you?"

That night the air was still. The heat spread over one immediately, like a flush. In the thunderous cool of the Laundry,
past the darkened station, they sat near the bar which was
lined with men. It was noisy and crowded. Every so often
someone passing by would say hello.

"Some zoo, huh?" Robbie said.

Gloria came there often, she knew.

"What do you want to drink?"

"Beer," she said.

There were at least twenty men at the bar. She was aware
of occasional glances.

"You know, you don't look bad in a bathing suit," Robbie
said.

The opposite, she felt, was true.

"Have you ever thought of taking off a few pounds?" he
said. He had a calm, unhurried way of speaking. "It could
really help you."

"Yes, I know," she said.

"Have you ever thought of modeling?"

She would not look at him.

"I'm serious," he said. "You have a nice face."

"I'm not quite a model," she murmured.

"That's not the only thing. You also have a very nice ass,
you don't mind me saying that?"

She shook her head.

Later they drove past large, dark houses and down a road

which unexpectedly opened at the end like the vista she knew
was somehow opening to her. There were gently rolling fields
and distant lights. A street sign saying Egypt Lane—she was
too dizzy to read it—floated for an instant in the headlights.

"Do you know where we are?"

"No," she said.

"That's the Maidstone Club."

They crossed a small bridge and went on. Finally they
turned into a driveway. She could hear the ocean when he
shut off the ignition. There were two other cars parked
nearby.

"Is someone here?"

"No, they're all asleep," he whispered.

They walked on the grass to the other side of the house.
His room was in a kind of annex. There was a smell of damp-
ness. The dresser was strewn with clothes, shaving gear,
magazines. She saw all this vaguely when he struck a match
to light a candle.

"Are you sure no one's here?" she said.

"Don't worry."

It was all a little clumsy. Afterward they showered
together.

There was almost nothing on the menu Gloria was interested
in eating.

"What are you going to have?" she said.

"Crab salad," Ned said.

"I think I'll have the avocado," she decided.

The waiter took the menus.

"A pharmaceutical company, you say?"

"I think he works for some big one," she said.

"Which one?"

"I don't know. It's in Saudi Arabia."

"Saudi Arabia?" he said doubtfully.

"That's where all the money is, isn't it?" she said. "It certainly isn't here."

"How'd she meet this fellow?"

"Picked him up, I think."

"Typical," he said. He pushed his rimless glasses higher on his nose with one finger. He was wearing a string sweater with the sleeves pulled up. His hair was faded by the sun. He looked very boyish and handsome. He was thirty-three and had never been married. There were only two things wrong with him: his mother had all the money in a trust, and his back. Something was wrong with it. He had terrible spasms and sometimes had to lie for hours on the floor.

"Well, I'm sure he knows she's just a baby-sitter. He's here on vacation. I hope he doesn't break her heart," Gloria said. "Actually, I'm glad he showed up. It's better for Christopher. She's less likely to return the erotic feelings he has for her."

"The what?"

"Believe me, I'm not imagining it."

"Oh, come on, Gloria."

"There's something going on. Maybe she doesn't know it. He's in her bed all the time."

"He's only five."

"They can have erections at five," Gloria said.

"Oh, really."

"Darling, I've seen him with them."

"At five?"

"You'd be surprised," she said. "They're born with them.
You just don't remember, that's all."

She did not become lovesick, she did not brood. She was
more silent in the weeks that followed but also more settled,
not particularly sad. In the flat-heeled shoes which gave her
a slightly dumpy appearance she went shopping as usual.
The thought even crossed Gloria's mind that she might be
pregnant.

"Is everything all right?" she asked.

"Pardon?"

"Darling, do you feel all right? You know what I mean."

There were times when the two of them came back from
the beach and Truus patiently brushed the sand from
Christopher's feet that Gloria felt great sympathy for her and
understood why she was quiet. How much of fate lay in one's
appearance! Truus' face seemed empty, without expression,
except when she was playing with Christopher and then it
brightened. She was so like a child anyway, a bulky child, an
unimaginative playmate who in the course of things would
be forgotten. And the foolishness of her dreams! She wanted
to become a fashion designer, she said one day. She was
interested in designing clothes.

What she actually felt after her boyfriend left, no one
knew. She came in carrying the groceries, the screen door
banged behind her. She answered the phone, took messages.
In the evening she sat on the worn couch with Christopher

watching television upstairs. Sometimes they both laughed. The shelves were piled with games, plastic toys, children's books. Once in a while Christopher was told to bring one down so his mother could read him a story. It was very important that he like books, Gloria said.

It was a pale blue envelope with Arabic printing in the corner. Truus opened it standing at the kitchen counter and began to read the letter. The handwriting was childish and small. *Dear Truus*, it said. *Thank you for your letter. I was glad to receive it. You don't have to put so many stamps on letters to Saudi Arabia though. One U.S. airmail is enough. I'm glad to hear you miss me.* She looked up. Christopher was banging on something in the doorway.

"This won't work," he said.

He was dragging a toy car that had to be pumped with air to run.

"Here, let me see," she said. He seemed on the verge of tears. "This fits here, doesn't it?" She attached the small plastic hose. "There, now it will work."

"No, it won't," he said.

"No, it won't," she mimicked.

He watched gloomily as she pumped. When the handle grew stiff she put the car on the floor, pointed it, and let it go. It leapt across the room and crashed into the opposite wall. He went over and nudged it with his foot.

"Do you want to play with it?"

"No."

"Then pick it up and put it away."

He didn't move.

"Put . . . it . . . away . . ." she said, in a deep voice, coming toward him one step at a time. He watched from the corner of his eye. Another tottering step. "Or I eat you," she growled.

He ran for the stairs shrieking. She continued to chant, shuffling slowly toward the stairs. The dog was barking. Gloria came in the door, reaching down to pull off her shoes and kick them to one side. "Hi, any calls?" she asked.

Truus abandoned her performance. "No. No one."

Gloria had been visiting her mother, which was always tiresome. She looked around. Something was going on, she realized. "Where's Christopher?"

A glint of blond hair appeared above the landing.

"Hello, darling," she said. There was a pause. "Mummy said hello. What's wrong? What's happening?"

"We're just playing a game," Truus explained.

"Well, stop playing for a moment and come and kiss me."

She took him into the living room. Truus went upstairs. Sometime later she heard her name being called. She folded the letter which she had read for the fifth or sixth time and went to the head of the stairs. "Yes?"

"Can you come down?" Gloria called. "He's driving me crazy."

"He's impossible," she said, when Truus arrived. "He spilled his milk, he's kicked over the dog water. Look at this mess!"

"Let's go outside and play a game," Truus said to him, reaching for his hand which he pulled away. "Come. Or do you want to go on the pony?"

He stared at the floor. As if she were alone in the room

she got down on her hands and knees. She shook her hair loose and made a curious sound, a faint neigh, pure as the tinkle of glass. She turned to gaze indifferently at him over her shoulder. He was watching.

"Come," she said calmly. "Your pony is waiting."

After that when the letters arrived, Truus would fold them and slip them into her pocket while Gloria went through the mail: bills, gallery openings, urgent requests for payment, occasionally a letter. She wrote very few herself but always complained when she did not receive them. Comments on the logic of this only served to annoy her.

The fall was coming. Everything seemed to deny it. The days were still warm, the great, terminal sun poured down. The leaves, more luxuriant than ever, covered the trees. Behind the hedges, lawn mowers made a final racket. On the warm slate of the terrace, left behind, a grasshopper, a veteran in dark green and yellow, limped along. The birds had torn off one of his legs.

One morning Gloria was upstairs when something happened to catch her eye. The door to the little guest room was open and on the night table, folded, was a letter. It lay there in the silence, half of it raised like a wing in the air. The house was empty. Truus had gone to shop and pick up Christopher at nursery school. With the curiosity of a schoolgirl, Gloria sat down on the bed. She unfolded the envelope and took out the pages. The first thing her eye fell upon was a line just above the middle. It stunned her. For a moment she was dazed. She read the letter through nervously. She opened the drawer. There were others. She read them as well. Like love letters they were repetitious, but they were not love letters. He did more than work in an office, this man, much more. He went through Europe, city after city, looking for young people who in hotel rooms and cheap apartments— she was horrified by her images of it—stripped and were immersed in a river of sordid acts. The letters were like those of a high school boy, that was the most terrible part. They were letters of recruitment, so simple they might have been copied out by an illiterate.

Sitting there framed in the doorway, her hand nearly trembling, she could not think of what to do. She felt deeply upset, frightened, betrayed. She glanced out the window. She wondered if she should go immediately to the nursery school—she could be there in minutes—and take Christopher somewhere where he would be safe. No, that would be foolish. She hurried downstairs to the telephone.

"Ned," she said when she reached him—her voice was shaking. She was looking at one of the letters which asked a number of matter-of-fact questions.

"What is it? Is anything wrong?"

"Come right away. I need you. Something's happened."

For a while then she stood there with the letters in her hand. Looking around hurriedly, she put them in a drawer where garden seeds were kept. She began to calculate how long it would be before he would be there, driving out from the city.

She heard them come in. She was in her bedroom. She had regained her composure, but as she entered the kitchen she could feel her heart beating wildly. Truus was preparing lunch.

"Mummy, look at this," Christopher said. He held up a sheet of paper. "Do you see what this is?"

"Yes. It's very nice."

"This is the engine," he said. "These are the wings. These are the guns."

She tried to focus her attention on the scrawled outline with its garish colors, but she was conscious only of the girl at work behind the counter. As Truus brought the plates to the table, Gloria tried to look calmly at her face, a face she realized she had not seen before. In it she recognized for the first time depravity, and in Truus' limbs, their smoothness, their volume, she saw brutality and vice. Outside, in the ordinary daylight, were the trees along the side of the property, the roof of a house, the lawn, some scattered toys. It was a landscape that seemed ominous, too idyllic, too still.

"Don't use your fingers, Christopher," Truus said, sitting down with him. "Use your fork."

"It won't reach," he said.

She pushed the plate an inch or two toward him.

"Here, try now," she said.

Later, watching them play outside on the grass, Gloria could not help noticing a wild, almost a bestial aspect in her son's excitement, as if a crudeness were somehow becoming part of him, soiling him. A line from the many that lay writhing in her head came forth. *I hope you will be ready to take my big cock when I see you again. P.S. Have you had any big cocks lately? I miss you and think of you and it makes me very hard.* "Have you ever read anything like that?" Gloria asked.

"Not exactly."

"It's the most disgusting thing. I can't believe it."

"Of course, she didn't write them," Ned said.

"She kept them, that's worse."

He had them all in his hand. *If you came to Europe it would be great*, one said. *We would travel and you could help me. We could work together. I know you would be very good at it. The girls we would be looking for are between 13 and 18 years old. Also guys, a little older.*

"You have to go in there and tell her to leave," Gloria said. "Tell her she has to be out of the house."

He looked at the letters again. *Some of them are very well developed, you would be surprised. I think you know the type we are looking for.*

"I don't know . . . Maybe these are just a silly kind of love letter."

"Ned, I'm not kidding," she said.

Of course, there would be a lot of fucking, too.

"I'm going to call the FBI."

"No," he said, "that's all right. Here, take these. I'll go and tell her."

Truus was in the kitchen. As he spoke to her he tried to see in her grey eyes the boldness he had overlooked. There was only confusion. She did not seem to understand him. She went in to Gloria. She was nearly in tears. "But why?" she wanted to know.

"I found the letters," was all Gloria would say.

"What letters?"

They were lying on the desk. Gloria picked them up.

"They're mine," Truus protested. "They belong to me."

"I've called the FBI," Gloria said.

"Please, give them to me."

"I'm not giving them to you. I'm burning them."

"Please let me have them," Truus insisted.

She was confused and weeping. She passed Ned on her way upstairs. He thought he could see the attributes praised in the letters, the Saudi letters, as he later called them.

In her room Truus sat on the bed. She did not know what she would do or where she would go. She began to pack her clothes, hoping that somehow things might change if she took long enough. She moved very slowly.

"Where are you going?" Christopher said from the door.

She did not answer him. He asked again, coming into the room.

"I'm going to see my mother," she said.

"She's downstairs."

Truus shook her head.

"Yes, she is," he insisted.

"Go away. Don't bother me right now," she said in a flat voice.

He began kicking at the door with his foot. After a while he sat on the couch. Then he disappeared.

When the taxi came for her, he was hiding behind some trees out near the driveway. She had been looking for him at the end.

"Oh, there you are," she said. She put down her suitcases and kneeled to say good-bye. He stood with his head bent. From a distance it seemed a kind of submission.

"Look at that," Gloria said. She was in the house. Ned was standing behind her. "They always love sluts," she said.

Christopher stood beside the road after the taxi had gone. That night he came down to his mother's room. He was crying and she turned on the light.

"What is it?" she said. She tried to comfort him. "Don't cry, darling. Did something frighten you? Here, mummy will take you upstairs. Don't worry. Everything will be all right."

"Good night, Christopher," Ned said.

"Say good night, darling."

She went up, climbed into bed with him, and finally got him to sleep, but he kicked so much she came back down, holding her robe closed with her hand. Ned had left her a note: his back was giving him trouble, he had gone home.

Truus' place was taken by a Colombian woman who was very religious and did not drink or smoke. Then by a black girl named Mattie who did both but stayed for a long time.

One night in bed, reading *Town and Country*, Gloria came across something that stunned her. It was a photograph of a garden party in Brussels, only a small photograph but she recognized a face, she was absolutely certain of it, and with a terrible sinking feeling she moved the page closer to the light. She was without makeup and at her most vulnerable. She examined the picture closely. She was no longer talking to Ned, she hadn't seen him for over a year, but she was tempted to call him anyway. Then, reading the caption and looking at the picture again she decided she was mistaken. It wasn't Truus, just someone who resembled her, and anyway what did it matter? It all seemed long ago. Christopher had forgotten about her. He was in school now, doing very well, on the soccer team already, playing with eight- and nine-year-olds, bigger than them and bright. He would be six three. He would have girlfriends hanging all over him, girls whose families had houses in the Bahamas. He would devastate them.

Still, lying there with the magazine on her knees she could not help thinking of it. What had actually become of Truus? She looked at the photograph again. Had she found her way to Amsterdam or Paris and, making dirty movies or whatever, met someone? It was unbearable to think of her being invited to places, slimmer now, sitting in the brilliance of crowded restaurants with her complexion still bad beneath the makeup and the morals of a housefly. The idea that there is an unearned happiness, that certain people find their way to it, nearly made her sick. Like the girl Ned was marrying who used to work in the catering shop just off the highway near Bridgehampton. That had been a blow, that had been more than a blow. But then nothing, almost nothing, really made sense anymore.

CHARISMA

Men don't have to have looks. It's not that.

Cecily and her friend were talking about it, sitting on the couch together away from the party, with their legs tucked beneath them like two young girls. They were talking about men, Lucien Freud in particular. Cecily had seen him at the Met that morning, walking alone as if in meditation, not looking at the pictures, passing by them without interest and then suddenly stopping in front of a Rembrandt, simply stopping and standing for a long time staring at it.

"I'd love to know what he was thinking about," Cecily said. "I'd give anything to know."

"He just stood there?"

"He just stood very close to it, looking at it, incredibly intense. It was just coming off him in waves. His forehead."

"I know. He had an incredible forehead, the two sort of knobs on it. Did he look old?"

"Yes, but you know, not that kind of old."

"He's had tons of affairs, hasn't he? Fathered children left and right."

"Is that true?"

"I heard that one of his girlfriends was fourteen years old. Her brother tried to kill him."

"Fourteen. That's a little too much. That's still a child," Cecily said.

"I wonder how he would have met her."

"Probably the daughter of a friend. He wanted her to model. And it took a long time and he was very attentive."

"How old do you think he is, really?"

"I don't know."

"Seventy?"

"More than that."

"How does he do it all?"

"I don't know," Cecily admitted.

They thought about it.

"I'd fuck him, though," she said.

"You would?"

"In a minute."

"I would, too."

They were almost conspiring, away from everyone, confessing to each other amid the drinking and laughing.

Lucien Freud was actually seventy-nine. He was beyond age, with a deep ancestral face. At the museum he'd been wearing a dark velvety jacket over a Levi shirt. He no longer traveled. He would not have come to New York, not even for the opening, but his dealer had arranged a private jet for him. Cecily could imagine him sitting in one of the leather seats, his head more or less in profile, turned to one side as he stared out the round window at the dark sea, far below. He was thinking, as he later told someone, of fish and the plane passing over them. There were fish everywhere, in every separate river and sea, knowing nothing of each other, having no way to know. They lived in a continuum. They knew only their own lives, but how different was that? After a while he turned from the window and sat leafing through the pages of a magazine. He had pale blue eyes and could look nakedly at someone although he often turned his gaze aside. He was a fish himself, a piranha. He saw women and went after them, singling them out. So Cecily imagined. He had only two things he was interested in, his painting and women. They were intertwined.

The party was going on at the other end of the room. They were going to have to join it, that, or their husbands would come over.

Not far from there, amid the countless lights of other apartments at night, was the one that Leila Aaron shared with a roommate. Leila was a beautiful girl at the threshold of life. She came from a good family that she had disappointed by not going to college as expected—she could have gotten into any of them—and going to secretarial school instead, but she was so loving and generous that they soon accepted it. She was the youngest child and her parents forgave everything.

She was having dinner one night when a man I didn't know then, Paul Millard, Polo they called him, came into the restaurant with the wife of one of his friends and casually made his way through the crowd with her to where he could talk to the maître d' and if he had to, wait for a table. He was in a dark blue overcoat, unbuttoned despite the weather, and as he waited near Leila's table, he leaned down slightly and said something to her in a way that made her look up and smile. They say a woman's smile is the greatest thing she can possess, but in this case it was his, a brilliant wide smile that came naturally. Then the head waiter had a table for him.

"Who was that?"

"I don't know," she said.

You exchange looks and it's all written sometimes, although what happens remains to be known. When Leila and her date left she didn't look back but in her coat pocket she later found the folded piece of paper that the hatcheck girl had put there with the name Polo Millard and a telephone number on it.

The next day she was hesitant but something made her call.

A man answered the phone.

"Hello," he said.

"Polo?"

He understood immediately.

"Hi," he said.

"So, who are you, anyway?"

"I was hoping you'd call. I'm Paul Millard. They all call me Polo."

"I think you're a little too brash."

"I had to be."

She said nothing.

"Listen," he said idly, "I have two tickets to the opera. Want to come?"

"To the opera? When?"

"Tonight," he said.

That was how it began. It was chance, but as it happened, she was exactly to his taste, and she found herself irresistibly drawn to him. He was a convivial man. But to truly know him—they say that to really know anyone you must know what they fear, and in his case you wondered. It was hard to imagine him in fear. In gambling he had no fear. Like all real gamblers he didn't care about the money. He played backgammon for big stakes, thousands, even tens of thousands. The game was about doubling, doubling and redoubling. You needed nerve to stay with him because he had nerve and also the smile.

He left things at her door, bottles of whiskey, chocolates. He called her on the phone.

"I love you," he told her. "I'm absolutely mad for you."

"Oh, don't say that."

In the truest sense he was crazy, manic, really. He ignored ordinary reality, the kind everyone knows. That was his power and his charm. When you were with him you were in that world, too. What it was was hard to say.

"I want you to come to the Bahamas with me."

"Polo, I can't go to the Bahamas."

"Why not? Have you been there?"

She didn't go places with men—her family would know.

"Of course you can go," he said.

In the Bahamas she met some of his friends. They were men like him but not of his quality. He stayed up late gambling with them. He drank and did cocaine, but he was above any of the danger. She did cocaine for the first time there, but not as much. He wore a green shirt and white shorts. His face became broad and tan. They came in together from the sun.

"Don't bathe," he told her.

"Why not? What do you mean?"

"I want you to taste and smell like what you are."

"Which means?"

"God's fox," he said.

There was a photograph in which she was visible in a mirror, an almost incidental figure sitting on a bed with a stunned, nearly sullen expression on her face half-hidden by hair. He did things with her that I would have never dreamed of.

"Oh, God," she said softly.

Silence.

"Oh, my God."

He wrote about it afterwards in letters to her that she read with excitement. The letters still exist. Of course, she was not fourteen, she was twenty-three, but it was all frighteningly new.

The money came from his family, but a thing that disturbed Leila, puzzled her, was that he hated his mother, he wouldn't say why. He threw unopened letters from her into the trash.

"What is it about your mother?" she asked.

"She did some terrible things," he would say.

"What things?"

He changed the subject.

He went to Los Angeles for two weeks on business and slept with an actress he met. Leila suspected something but he denied it. She was concerned about the drinking. He would be abusive when he drank, and they would have violent quarrels but afterwards he apologized and it was as if nothing had happened. After making love they would sometimes read books together—not poetry, poets made you sad, he said—Lawrence Durrell and *Anna Karenina*. There were nights when he fell into bed from God knows where without explanation. He was making her live as his favorite, but she could not resist it. She felt herself succumbing to his life, he had taken possession of her. He was a liar, but half the time it was the truth.

She was afraid of what she was doing. What was next? She knew about California but she had surrendered herself.

"What's going to happen?" she asked him.

"What do you mean?"

"Tell the truth. What is it you want?"

"You know what's going to happen."

"What does that mean?" she said in despair.

He took her in his arms.

"Don't," she said. "Don't, please."

She turned away.

They had been married for three months when, after a series of arguments at a Thanksgiving dinner with friends, she opened a bedroom window and jumped to her death from the eighteenth floor. She had said nothing. She left no note.

Of course, that never happened. They were never married although later it seemed that they had been and for some unknown reason had separated. He was too unknowable for her to rely on, he was too faithless.

"We're going to get married," he told her.

"Polo, I don't think so."

"Yes, we will. We were predestined."

Much later he wrote to her somewhat wistfully, *Why did we fail to turn down the path we were meant to?*

The path. She had gone down it a long way. She had done things she could not imagine herself doing or being asked to do. She allowed herself to be whipped. It was like an unknown room you have somehow entered when, returning to bed in the dark without turning on the light, making your way past the doorway, the big chair, reaching for the familiar edge of the bed and, not finding it, reaching for the wall that is just across but not finding that either and finally, moving tentatively, touching something that should not be there, going along it with a cautious hand until there is a door-jamb—what doorjamb? the door to the room is behind somewhere—but it *is* a doorjamb and you are being led through it to a place you have never known.

It had been in the afternoon and she had steeled herself not to cry out or make a sound, but she could not prevent it. Afterwards they went down and had a drink. Her hand trembled and she felt an uncertain pride. She was afraid that her roommate would somehow see the marks. He wrote a long letter to her about it, and there were some photographs that she later destroyed.

His mother died leaving property in Santa Monica. He went to California several times to attend to it. He took Leila with him. They stayed in bed late and enjoyed the weather. They should have a child together, he told her.

He bought a house in the country, then sold it and bought another. He saw Leila less frequently. He fell in love with a sixteen-year-old Brazilian girl and even flew to Brazil to meet her family who politely rejected him. His friends knew about this but not the rejection.

Meanwhile, Leila had met someone. She was getting married, she told Polo.

"To who?"

"Alex Dereff."

"Who's that?"

"You don't know him. He's a musician."

"Don't do it, Leila. I don't want to lose you."

"I know," she said. "Anyway . . ."

"What's he like?"

"I don't know." Then, "He's a lot like you," she said.

No one was like him, his energy, his emanation. Merely seeing his head from a block away, you could say it was him. Standing unmistakably waiting for the elevator in the Four Seasons Hotel in a dark suit. There were other men like him but no one was really like him or like the intense pleasure he drew from life without coming to terms with it.

He never let go of her. He knew that in some way she was always his. He wrote to her from an inn in Connecticut where a certain Polo and Fermina—it was one of her names from *Love in the Time of Cholera*, a favorite book—had spent a night and Polo, passing by it, remembered what he had felt then and how much he yearned now for her company. *I know you will never visit places with me again.* He wrote to her that summer from Puerto Ercole, *There will be fireworks in town tonight. Writing to you dispels the torpor. I always imagine I'll catch sight of you in the hallway and we'll simply drive away together. You could send me a letter.*

He called from the ship just to describe to her what it was like as they came into the port of Genoa in the early morning, the mountains and mist, the stillness of the water as they moved through it and what it made him think of, waking with her, the beauty of days. The call woke her at almost one a.m. For a long time she listened without speaking with the receiver on the pillow close to her ear and her husband, not sleeping, lying quietly beside her.

He wrote to her from the Nile, passing along the great river in darkness, not a light to be seen, only the black sky and stars, five thousand years old.

When he left her life it was not the end of his. He lived as he had lived, even more elaborately. At his parties in the country were women in long gowns and Cambodian serving girls. Music was playing, women were sitting at tables talking and laughing, wanting to dance though their rich husbands ignored it. Polo was not Gatsby. He had held it in his hands from the beginning.

He always knew she would come, like Yeats' mistress had come, when he was dying. He thought about death every day but never spoke about it. In the end, as in myth, it came swiftly, the jealous gods struck him down. *Stay, stay but a little before you plunge into that vastness,* he'd written to her, *stay, stay until the day has run into the evensong.* He had esophageal cancer. She saw him for the last time three weeks before he died.

I heard he was buried in East Hampton, and when I was there, I went to visit his grave. It was in the spring and in the early morning the grass was still wet. There were trucks working near the entrance. I walked towards the rear of the cemetery where the grave was. Strangely, I couldn't find it.

That part of the cemetery seemed less arranged or well-tended, the ground was sunken in spots. An iron fence had some pieces broken off. The rear gate sagged.

For half an hour I wandered with a growing sense of disbelief. I was looking for a simple inscription. I'd had the grave described to me, on ground that sloped away so that it was a little apart, on a kind of knoll, but for all of that, I could not find it. It was barely nine in the morning. There were no other cars parked by the gate. I sat in mine for a long time wondering how it could be that I missed the grave, but it was just like him to have eluded me, in death as in life. To go where he could not be found. To escape the final questions.

GIVE

In the morning—it was my wife's birthday, her thirty-first—we slept a little late, and I was at the window looking down at Des in a bathrobe with his pale hair awry and a bamboo stick in his hand. He was deflecting and sometimes with a flourish making a lunge. Billy, who was six then, was hopping around in front of him. I could hear his shrieks of joy. Anna came up beside me.

"What are they doing now?"

"I can't tell. Billy is waving something over his head."

"I think it's a flyswatter," she said, disbelieving.

She was just thirty-one, the age when women are past foolishness though not unfeeling.

"Look at him," she said. "Don't you just love him?"

The grass was brown from summer and they were dancing around on it. Des was barefoot, I noticed. It was early for him to be up. He often slept until noon and then managed to slip gracefully into the rhythm of the household. That was his talent, to live as he liked, almost without concern, to live as if he would reach the desired end one way or another and not be bothered by whatever came between. It included being committed several times, once for wandering out on Moore Street naked. None of the psychiatrists had any idea who he was. None of them had ever read a damned thing, he said. Some of the patients had.

He was a poet, of course. He even *looked* like a poet, intelligent, lank. He'd won the Yale prize when he was twenty-five and went on from there. When you pictured him, it was wearing a gray herringbone jacket, khaki pants, and for some reason sandals. Doesn't fit together, but a lot of things about him were like that. Born in Galveston, ROTC in college, and even married while an undergraduate, although what became of that wife he never clearly explained. His real life came after that, and he had lived it ever since, teaching sometimes in community classes, traveling to Greece and Morocco, living there for a period, having a breakdown, and through it all writing the poem that had made his name. I read the poem, a third of it anyway, standing stunned in a bookshop in the Village. I remember the afternoon, cloudy and quiet, and I remember, too, almost leaving myself, the person I was, the ordinary way I felt about things, my perception of—there's no other word for it—the depth of life, and above all the thrill of successive lines. The poem was an aria, jagged and unending. Its tone was what set it apart—written as if from the shades. *There lay the delta, there the burning arms* . . . was the way it began, and immediately I felt it was not about rivers uncoiling but about desire. It revealed itself only slowly, like some kind of dream, *the light fluttering on the fronds*, with names and nouns, Naples, worn benches, Luxor and the kings, Salonika, small waves falling on the stones. There was repetition, even refrain. Lines that seemed unconnected gradually became part of a confession that had at its center rooms in the burning heat of August where something has taken place, clearly sexual, but it is also the vacant streets of rural Texas, roads, forgotten friends, the slap of hands on rifle slings and forked pennants limp at parades. There are condoms, sun-faded cars, soiled menus with misspellings, a kind of pyre on which he had laid his life. That was why he seemed so pure—he had given all. Everyone lies about their lives, but he had not lied about his. He had made of it a noble lament, through it always running this thing you have had, that you will always have, but can never have. *There stood Erechtheus, polished limbs and greaves . . . come to me, Hellas, I long for your touch.*

I had met him at a party and only managed to say, "I read your beautiful poem." He was unexpectedly open in a way that impressed me and straightforward in a way that was unflinching. In talking, he mentioned the title of a book or two and referred to some things he assumed I would, of course, know, and he was witty, all of that but something more; his language invited me to be joyous, to speak as the gods—I use the plural because it's hard to think of him as obedient to a single god—had intended. We were always speaking of things that it turned out, oddly enough, both of us knew about although he knew more. Lafcadio Hearn, yes, of course he knew who that was and even the name of the Japanese widow he married and the town they lived in, though he had never been to Japan himself. Arletty, Nestor Almendros, Jacques Brel, the Lawrenceville Stories, the *cordon sanitaire,* everything including his real interest, jazz, to which I only weakly responded. The Answer Man, Billy Cannon, the Hellespont, Stendhal on love, it was as if we had sat in the same classes and gone to the same cities. And there was Billy, swatting at his legs.

Billy loved him, he was almost a pal. He had an infectious laugh and was always ready to play. During the times he stayed with us, he made ships out of sofa cushions and swords and shields from whatever was in the garage. When he owned his car, the engine of which would cut out every so often, he claimed that turning the radio on and off would fix it, the circuits had been miswired or something. Billy was in charge of the radio.

"Oh, oh," Des would say, "there it goes. Radio!"

And Billy, with huge pleasure, would turn the radio on and off, on and off. How to explain why this worked? It was the power of a poet or maybe even a trick.

On Anna's birthday, at about noon a beautiful arrangement of flowers, lilies and yellow roses, was delivered. They were from him. That evening we had dinner with some friends at the Red Bar, always noisy but the table was in the small room past the bar. I hadn't ordered a birthday cake because we were going to have one back at the house, a rum cake, her favorite. Billy sat in her lap as she put her rings, one after another, carefully over separate candles, each ring for a wish.

"Will you help me blow them out?" she said to Billy, her face close to his hair.

"Too many," he said.

"Oh, God, you really know how to hurt a woman."

"Go ahead," Des told him. "If you don't have enough breath, I'll catch it and send it back."

"How do you do that?"

"I can do it. Haven't you heard of someone catching their breath?"

"They're burning down," Anna said. "Come on, one, two, three!"

The two of them blew them out. Billy wanted to know what her wishes had been, but she wouldn't tell.

We ate the cake, just the four of us, and I gave her the present I knew she would love. It was a wristwatch, very thin and square with Roman numerals and a small blue stone, I think tourmaline, embedded in the stem. There are not many things more beautiful than a watch lying new in its case.

"Oh, Jack!" she said. "It's gorgeous!"

She showed it to Billy and then to Des.

"Where did you get it?" Then, looking, "Cartier," she said.

"Yes."

"I *love* it."

Beatrice Hage, a woman we knew, had one like it that she had inherited from her mother. It had an elegance that defied the years and demands of fashion.

It was easy to find things she would like. Our taste was the same, it had been from the first. It would be impossible to live with someone otherwise. I've always thought it was the most important single thing, though people may not realize it. Perhaps it's transmitted to them in the way someone dresses or, for that matter, undresses, but taste is a thing no one is born with, it's learned, and at a certain point it can't be altered. We sometimes talked about that, what could and couldn't be altered. People were always saying something had completely changed them, some experience or book or man, but if you knew how they had been before, nothing much really had changed. When you found someone who was tremendously appealing but not quite perfect, you might believe you could change them after marriage, not everything, just a few things, but in truth the most you could expect was to change perhaps one thing and even that would eventually go back to what it had been.

The small things that could be overlooked at first but in time became annoying, we had a way of handling, of getting the pebble out of the shoe, so to speak. It was called a give, and it was agreed that it would last. The phrase that was overused, an eating habit, even a piece of favorite clothing, a give was a request to abandon it. You couldn't ask *for* something, only to stop something. The wide skirt of the bathroom sink was always wiped dry because of a give. Anna's little finger no longer extended when she drank from a cup. There might be more than one thing you would like to ask, and there was sometimes difficulty in choosing, but there was the satisfaction of knowing that once a year, without causing resentment, you would be able to ask your husband or wife to stop this one thing.

Des was downstairs when we put Billy to bed. I was in the hall when Anna came out holding her finger to her lips and having turned off the light.

"Is he asleep?"

"Yes."

"Well, happy birthday," I said.

"Yes."

There was something odd in the way she said it. She stood there, her long neck and blond hair.

"What is it, darling?"

She said nothing for a moment. Then she said,

"I want a give."

"All right," I said.

I don't know why, I felt nervous.

"What would you like?"

"I want you to stop it with Des," she said.

"Stop it? Stop what?"

My heart was skipping.

"Stop the sex," she said.

I knew she was going to say it. I had hoped something else, and the words were like a thick curtain tumbling down or a plate smashing on the floor.

"I don't know what you're talking about."

Her face was hard.

"Yes, you do. You know exactly what I'm talking about."

"Darling, you're mistaken. There's nothing going on with Des. He's a friend, he's my closest friend."

The tears began to run down her face.

"Don't," I said. "Please. Don't cry. You're wrong."

"I have to cry," she said, her voice unsteady. "Anyone would cry. You have to do it. You have to stop. We promised one another."

"Oh, God, you're imagining this."

"Please," she begged, "don't. Please, please, don't."

She was wiping her cheeks as if to make herself again presentable.

"You have to do what we promised," she said. "You have to give."

There are things you cannot give, that would simply crush your heart. It was half of life she was asking for, him slipping off his watch, holding him, having him in your possession, in indescribable happiness, in love with you. Nothing else could be like that. There was an apartment on Twelfth Street that we were able to use, the garden behind it, the dazzling chords of *Petroushka*—the record happened to be there and we used to play it—chords that would always, as long as I lived, bring me back to it, his pliancy and slow smile.

"I'm not doing anything with Des," I said. "I swear to you."

"You swear to me."

"Yes."

"And I'm supposed to believe you."

"I swear to you."

She looked away.

"All right," she said at last.

A great joy filled me. Then she said,

"All right. But he has to leave. For good. If you want me to believe you, that's what it takes."

"Anna . . ."

"No, that's the proof."

"How can I tell him to leave? What's the reason?"

"Make up something. I don't care."

In the morning he got up late and was in the kitchen, the smoothness of sleep still on him. Anna had gone off. My hands were trembling.

"Good morning," he said with a smile.

"Good morning."

I couldn't bring myself to it. All I could say was,

"Des . . ."

"Yes?"

"I don't know what to say."

"About what?"

"Us. It's over."

He seemed not to understand.

"What's over?"

"Everything. I feel like I'm coming apart inside."

"Ah," he said in a soft way. "I see. Maybe I see. What happened?"

"It's just that you can't stay."

"Anna," he guessed.

"Yes."

"She knows."

"Yes. I don't know what to do."

"Could I talk to her, do you think?"

"It wouldn't do any good. Believe me."

"But we've always gotten along. What difference does it make? Let me talk to her."

"She doesn't want to," I lied.

"When did all this happen?"

"Last night. Don't ask me how it came about. I don't know."

He sighed. He said something I didn't get. All I could hear was my own heart beating. He left later that day.

I felt the injustice for a long time. He'd brought only pleasure to us, and if to me particularly, that didn't diminish it. I had some photographs that I kept in a certain place, and of course I had the poems. I followed him from afar, the way a woman does a man she was never able to marry. The glittering blue water slid past as he made his way between the islands. There was Ios, white in the haze, where the dust of Homer lay, they said.

ARLINGTON

Newell had married a Czech girl and they were having trouble, they were drinking and fighting. This was in Kaiserslautern and families in the building had complained. Westerveldt, who was acting adjutant, was sent to straighten things out—he and Newell had been classmates, though Newell was not someone in the class you remembered. He was quiet and kept to himself. He had an odd appearance, with a high, domed forehead and pale eyes. Jana, the wife, had a downturned mouth and nice breasts. Westerveldt didn't really know her. He knew her by sight.

Newell was in the living room when Westerveldt came by. He seemed unsurprised by the visit.

"I thought I might talk to you a little," Westerveldt said.

There was a slight nod.

"Is your wife here?"

"I think she's in the kitchen."

"It's not really my business, but are the two of you having problems?"

Newell seemed to be considering.

"Nothing serious," he finally said.

In the kitchen the Czech wife had her shoes off and was painting her toenails. She looked up briefly when Westerveldt came in. He saw the exotic, European mouth.

"I wonder if we could talk for a minute."

"About what?" she said. There was uneaten food on the counter and unwashed dishes.

"Why don't you come into the living room?"

She said nothing.

"Just for a couple of minutes."

She looked closely at her feet, ignoring him. Westerveldt had grown up with three sisters and was at ease around women. He touched her elbow to coax her but she jerked it away.

"Who are you?" she said.

Westerveldt went back into the living room and talked to Newell like a brother. If this went on with him and his wife, it was jeopardizing his career.

Newell wanted to confide in Westerveldt. He sat silent, however, unable to begin. He was helplessly in love with this woman. When she dressed up she was simply beautiful. If you saw them together in the Wienerstube, his round white brow gleaming in the light and her across from him, smoking, you would wonder, how did he ever get her? She was insolent but there were times when she was not. To put your hand on the small of her naked back was to have all you ever hoped to possess.

"What is it that's bothering her?" Westerveldt wanted to know.

"She's had a terrible life," Newell said. "Everything will be all right."

Whatever else was said, Westerveldt didn't remember. What happened afterward erased it.

Newell was away on temporary duty somewhere and his

wife, who had no friends, was bored. She went to the movies and wandered around in town. She went to the officers' club and sat at the bar, drinking. On Saturday she was there, bare shouldered, still drinking when the bar closed. The club officer, Captain Dardy, noticed it and asked if she needed someone to drive her home. He told her to wait a few minutes until he was finished closing up.

Early in the morning, in the gray light, Dardy's car was still parked outside the quarters. Jana could see it and so could everyone else. She leaned over and shook him and told him he had to leave.

"What time is it?"

"I don't care. You have to go," she said.

Afterward she went to the military police and reported she had been raped.

In his long, admired career, Westerveldt had been like a figure in a novel. In the elephant grass near Pleiku he'd gotten a wide scar through one eyebrow where a mortar fragment, half an inch lower and a little closer, would have blinded or killed him. If anything, it enhanced his appearance. He'd had a long love affair with a woman in Naples when he'd been stationed there, a marquesa, in fact. If he resigned his commission and married her, she would buy him whatever he wanted. He could even have a mistress. That was just one episode. Women always liked him. In the end he married a woman from San Antonio, a divorcée with a child, and they had two more together. He was fifty-eight when he died from some kind of leukemia that began as a strange rash on his neck.

The chapel, an ordinary room with red wallpaper and benches, in the funeral home was crowded. Someone was delivering a eulogy, but in the corridor where many people stood it was hard to make out.

"Can you hear what he's saying?"

"Nobody can," the man in front of Newell said. It was Bressi, he realized, Bressi with his hair now white.

"Are you going to the cemetery?" Newell asked when the service was over.

"I'll give you a ride," Bressi told him.

They drove through Alexandria, the car full.

"There's the church that George Washington attended when he was president," Bressi said. A little later, he said, "There's Robert E. Lee's boyhood home."

Bressi and his wife lived in Alexandria in a white clapboard house with a narrow front porch and black shutters.

"Who said, 'Let us cross the river and rest in the shade of the trees'?" he asked them.

No one answered. Newell felt their disdain for him. They were looking away, out the car windows.

"Anybody know?" Bressi said. "Lee's greatest tactical commander."

"Shot by his own men," Newell said, almost inaudibly.

"Mistakenly."

"At Chancellorsville, in the dusk."

"It's not far from here, about thirty miles," Bressi said. He had been first in military history. He glanced in the rearview mirror. "How did you happen to know that? Where did you stand in military history?"

Newell didn't answer.

No one spoke.

There was a long line of cars moving slowly, going into the cemetery. People who had already parked walked alongside them. There were more gravestones than one could believe.

Bressi extended an arm and, waving lightly toward an area, said something Newell could not hear. Thill is in that section somewhere, Bressi had said, referring to a Medal of Honor winner.

They walked with many others, toward the end drawn by faint music as if coming from the ancient river itself, the last river, the boatman waiting. The band, in dark blue uniforms, had formed in a small valley. It was playing "Wagon Wheels," *Carry me home* . . . The grave was nearby, the fresh earth under a green tarpaulin.

Newell walked as if in a dream. He knew the men around him, but not really. He stopped at a gravestone for Westerveldt's father and mother, died thirty years apart, buried side by side.

There were faces he thought he recognized during the proceedings, which were long. A thick, folded flag was given to what must have been the widow and her children. Carrying yellow flowers with long stems they filed past the coffin, the family and also others. On an impulse, Newell followed them.

Volleys were being fired. A lone bugle, silvery and pure, began to play taps, the sound drifting over the hills. The retired generals and colonels stood, each with a hand held over his heart. They had served everywhere, though none of them had served time in prison as Newell had. The rape charge against Dardy had been dropped after an investigation, and with Westerveldt's help Newell had been transferred so he could make another start. Then Jana's parents in Czechoslovakia needed help and Newell, still a first lieutenant, finally managed to get the money to send to them. Her gratitude was heartfelt.

"Oh, God. I love you!" she said.

Naked she sat astride him and, caressing her own buttocks as he lay nearly fainting, began to ride. A night he would never forget. Later there was the charge of having sold radios taken from supply. He was silent at the court-martial. Above all he wished he hadn't had to be there in uniform, it was like a crown of thorns. He had traded it and the silver bars and class ring to possess her. Of the three letters to the court appealing for leniency and attesting to his character, one was from Westerveldt.

Though the sentence was only a year, Jana did not wait for him. She went off with a man named Rodriguez who owned some beauty parlors. She was still young, she said.

The woman Newell later married knew nothing of all that or almost nothing. She was older than he was with two grown children and bad feet, she could walk only short distances, from the car to the supermarket. She knew he had been in the army—there were some photographs of him in uniform, taken years before,

"This is you," she said. "So, what were you?"

Newell hadn't walked back with the others. He had no

excuse to do that. This was Arlington and here they all lay, formed up for the last time. He could almost hear the distant notes of adjutant's call. He walked in the direction of the road they had come in on. With a sound at first faint but then clopping rhythmically he heard the hooves of horses, a team of six black horses with three erect riders and the now-empty caisson that had carried the coffin, the large spoked wheels rattling on the road. The riders, in their dark caps, did not look at him. The gravestones in dense, unbroken lines curved along the hillsides and down toward the river, as far as he could see, all the same height with here and there a larger, gray stone like an officer, mounted, amid the ranks. In the fading light they seemed to be waiting, fateful, massed as if for some great assault. For a moment he felt exalted by it, by the thought of all these dead, the history of the nation, its people. It was hard to get into Arlington. He would never lie there; he had given that up long ago. He would never know the days with Jana again, either. He remembered her at that moment as she had been, when she was so slender and young. He was loyal to her. It was one-sided, but that was enough.

When at the end they had all stood with their hands over their hearts, Newell was to one side, alone, resolutely saluting, faithful, like the fool he had always been.

LAST NIGHT

Walter Such was a translator. He liked to write with a green fountain pen that he had a habit of raising in the air slightly after each sentence, almost as if his hand were a mechanical device. He could recite lines of Blok in Russian and then give Rilke's translation of them in German, pointing out their beauty. He was a sociable but also sometimes prickly man, who stuttered a little at first and who lived with his wife in a manner they liked. But Marit, his wife, was ill.

He was sitting with Susanna, a family friend. Finally, they heard Marit on the stairs, and she came into the room. She was wearing a red silk dress in which she had always been seductive, with her loose breasts and sleek, dark hair. In the white wire baskets in her closet were stacks of folded clothes, underwear, sport things, nightgowns, the shoes jumbled beneath on the floor. Things she would never again need. Also jewelry, bracelets and necklaces, and a lacquer box with all her rings. She had looked through the lacquer box at length and picked several. She didn't want her fingers, bony now, to be naked.

"You look re-really nice," her husband said.

"I feel as if it's my first date or something. Are you having a drink?"

"Yes."

"I think I'll have one. Lots of ice," she said.

She sat down.

"I have no energy," she said, "that's the most terrible part. It's gone. It doesn't come back. I don't even like to get up and walk around."

"It must be very difficult," Susanna said.

"You have no idea."

Walter came back with the drink and handed it to his wife.

"Well, happy days," she said. Then, as if suddenly remembering, she smiled at them. A frightening smile. It seemed to mean just the opposite.

It was the night they had decided would be the one. On a saucer in the refrigerator, the syringe lay. Her doctor had supplied the contents. But a farewell dinner first, if she were able. It should not be just the two of them, Marit had said. Her instinct. They had asked Susanna rather than someone closer and grief-filled, Marit's sister, for example, with whom she was not on good terms, anyway, or older friends. Susanna was younger. She had a wide face and high, pure forehead. She looked like the daughter of a professor or banker, slightly errant. Dirty girl, one of their friends had commented about her, with a degree of admiration.

Susanna, sitting in a short skirt, was already a little nervous. It was hard to pretend it would be just an ordinary dinner. It would be hard to be offhanded and herself. She had come as dusk was falling. The house with its lighted windows—every room seemed to be lit—had stood out from all the others like a place in which something festive was happening.

Marit gazed at things in the room, the photographs with

their silver frames, the lamps, the large books on Surrealism, landscape design, or country houses that she had always meant to sit down with and read, the chairs, even the rug with its beautiful faded color. She looked at it all as if she were somehow noting it, when in fact it all meant nothing. Susanna's long hair and freshness meant something, though she was not sure what.

Certain memories are what you long to take with you, she thought, memories from even before Walter, from when she was a girl. Home, not this one but the original one with her childhood bed, the window on the landing out of which she had watched the swirling storms of long-ago winters, her father bending over her to say good night, the lamplight in which her mother was holding out a wrist, trying to fasten a bracelet.

That home. The rest was less dense. The rest was a long novel so like your life; you were going through it without thinking and then one morning it ended: there were blood-stains.

"I've had a lot of these," Marit reflected.

"The drink?" Susanna said.

"Yes."

"Over the years, you mean."

"Yes, over the years. What time is it getting to be?"

"Quarter to eight," her husband said.

"Shall we go?"

"Whenever you like," he said. "No need to hurry."

"I don't want to hurry."

She had, in fact, little desire to go. It was one step closer.

"What time is the reservation?" she asked.

"Any time we like."

"Let's go, then."

It was in the uterus and had travelled from there to the lungs. In the end, she had accepted it. Above the square neckline of her dress the skin, pallid, seemed to emanate a darkness. She no longer resembled herself. What she had been was gone; it had been taken from her. The change was fearful, especially in her face. She had a face now that was for the afterlife and those she would meet there. It was hard for Walter to remember how she had once been. She was almost a different woman from the one to whom he had made a solemn promise to help when the time came.

Susanna sat in the back as they drove. The roads were empty. They passed houses showing a shifting, bluish light downstairs. Marit sat silent. She felt sadness but also a kind of confusion. She was trying to imagine all of it tomorrow, without her being here to see it. She could not imagine it. It was difficult to think the world would still be there.

At the hotel, they waited near the bar, which was noisy. Men without jackets, girls talking or laughing loudly, girls who knew nothing. On the walls were large French posters, old lithographs, in darkened frames.

"I don't recognize anyone," Marit commented. "Luckily," she added.

Walter had seen a talkative couple they knew, the Apthalls.

"Don't look," he said. "They haven't seen us. I'll get a table in the other room."

"Did they see us?" Marit asked as they were seated. "I don't feel like talking to anyone."

"We're all right," he said.

The waiter was wearing a white apron and black bow tie. He handed them the menu and a wine list.

"Can I get you something to drink?"

"Yes, definitely," Walter said.

He was looking at the list, on which the prices were in roughly ascending order. There was a Cheval Blanc for five hundred and seventy-five dollars.

"This Cheval Blanc, do you have this?"

"The 1989?" the waiter asked.

"Bring us a bottle of that."

"What is Cheval Blanc? Is it a white?" Susanna asked when the waiter had gone.

"No, it's a red," Walter said.

"You know, it was very nice of you to join us tonight," Marit said to Susanna. "It's quite a special evening."

"Yes."

"We don't usually order wine this good," she explained.

The two of them had often eaten here, usually near the bar, with its gleaming rows of bottles. They had never ordered wine that cost more than thirty-five dollars.

How was she feeling, Walter asked while they waited. Was she feeling OK?

"I don't know how to express how I'm feeling. I'm taking morphine," Marit told Susanna. "It's doing the job, but . . ." she stopped. "There are a lot of things that shouldn't happen to you," she said.

Dinner was quiet. It was difficult to talk casually. They had two bottles of the wine, however. He would never drink this well again, Walter could not help thinking. He poured the last of the second bottle into Susanna's glass.

"No, you should drink it," she said. "It's really for you."

"He's had enough," Marit said. "It was good, though, wasn't it?"

"Fabulously good."

"Makes you realize there are things . . . oh, I don't know, various things. It would be nice to have always drunk it." She said it in a way that was enormously touching.

They were all feeling better. They sat for a while and finally made their way out. The bar was still noisy.

Marit stared out the window as they drove. She was tired. They were going home now. The wind was moving in the tops of the shadowy trees. In the night sky there were brilliant blue clouds, shining as if in daylight.

"It's very beautiful tonight, isn't it?" Marit said. "I'm struck by that. Am I mistaken?"

"No." Walter cleared his throat. "It is beautiful."

"Have you noticed it?" she asked Susanna. "I'm sure you have. How old are you? I forget."

"Twenty-nine."

"Twenty-nine," Marit said. She was silent for a few moments. "We never had children," she said. "Do you wish you had children?"

"Oh, sometimes, I suppose. I haven't thought about it too much. It's one of those things you have to be married to really think about."

"You'll be married."

"Yes, perhaps."

"You could be married in a minute," Marit said.

She was tired when they reached the house. They sat together in the living room as if they had come from a big party but were not quite ready for bed. Walter was thinking of what lay ahead, the light that would come on in the refrigerator when the door was opened. The needle of the syringe was sharp, the stainless-steel point cut at an angle and like a razor. He was going to have to insert it into her vein. He tried not to dwell on it. He would manage somehow. He was becoming more and more nervous.

"I remember my mother," Marit said. "She wanted to tell me things at the end, things that had happened when I was young. Rae Mahin had gone to bed with Teddy Hudner. Anne Herring had, too. They were married women. Teddy Hudner wasn't married. He worked in advertising and was always playing golf. My mother went on like that, who slept with whom. That's what she wanted to tell me, finally. Of course, at the time, Rae Mahin was really something."

Then Marit said,

"I think I'll go upstairs."

She stood up.

"I'm all right," she told her husband. "Don't come up just yet. Good night, Susanna."

When there were just the two of them, Susanna said,

"I have to go."

"No, don't. Please don't go. Stay here."

She shook her head.

"I can't," she said.

"Please, you have to. I'm going to go upstairs in a little while, but when I come down I can't be alone. Please."

There was silence.

"Susanna."

They sat without speaking.

"I know you've thought all this out," she said.

"Yes, absolutely."

After a few minutes, Walter looked at his watch; he began to say something but then did not. A little later, he looked at it again, then left the room.

The kitchen was in the shape of an L, old-fashioned and unplanned, with a white enamel sink and wooden cabinets painted many times. In the summers they had made preserves here when boxes of strawberries were sold at the stairway going down to the train platform in the city, unforgettable strawberries, their fragrance like perfume. There were still some jars. He went to the refrigerator and opened the door.

There it was, the small etched lines on the side. There were ten ccs. He tried to think of a way not to go on. If he dropped the syringe, broke it somehow, and said his hand had been shaking . . .

He took the saucer and covered it with a dish towel. It was worse that way. He put it down and picked up the syringe, holding it in various ways—finally, almost concealed against his leg. He felt light as a sheet of paper, devoid of strength.

Marit had prepared herself. She had made up her eyes and put on an ivory satin nightgown, low in back. It was the gown she would be wearing in the next world. She had made an effort to believe in an afterworld. The crossing was by boat, something the ancients knew with certainty. Over her collarbones lay strands of a silver necklace. She was weary. The wine had had an effect, but she was not calm.

In the doorway, Walter stood, as if waiting for permission.

She looked at him without speaking. He had it in his hand, she saw. Her heart skidded nervously, but she was determined not to show it.

"Well, darling," she said.

He tried to reply. She had on fresh lipstick, he saw; her mouth looked dark. There were some photographs she had arranged around her on the bed.

"Come in."

"No, I'll be back," he managed to say.

He hurried downstairs. He was going to fail; he had to have a drink. The living room was empty. Susanna had gone. He had never felt more completely alone. He went into the kitchen and poured some vodka, odorless and clear, into a glass and quickly drank it. He went slowly upstairs again and sat on the bed near his wife. The vodka was making him drunk. He felt unlike himself.

"Walter," she said.

"Yes?"

"This is the right thing."

She reached to take his hand. Somehow it frightened him, as if it might mean an appeal to come with her.

"You know," she said evenly, "I've loved you as much as I've ever loved anyone in the world—I'm sounding maudlin, I know."

"Ah, Marit!" he cried.

"Did you love me?"

His stomach was churning in despair.

"Yes," he said. "Yes!"

"Take care of yourself."

"Yes."

He was in good health, as it happened, a little heavier than he might have been, but nevertheless . . . His roundish, scholarly stomach was covered with a layer of soft, dark hair, his hands and nails well cared for.

She leaned forward and embraced him. She kissed him. For a moment, she was not afraid. She would live again, be young again as she once had been. She held out her arm. On the inside, two veins the color of verdigris were visible. He began to press to make them rise. Her head was turned away.

"Do you remember," she said to him, "when I was working at Bates and we met that first time? I knew right away."

The needle was wavering as he tried to position it.

"I was lucky," she said. "I was very lucky."

He was barely breathing. He waited, but she did not say anything more. Hardly believing what he was doing he pushed the needle in—it was effortless—and slowly injected the contents. He heard her sigh. Her eyes were closed as she lay back. Her face was peaceful. She had embarked. My God, he thought, my God. He had known her when she was in her twenties, long-legged and innocent. Now he had slipped her, as in a burial at sea, beneath the flow of time. Her hand was still warm. He took it and held it to his lips. He pulled the bedspread up to cover her legs. The house was incredibly quiet. It had fallen into silence, the silence of a fatal act. He could not hear the wind.

He went slowly downstairs. A sense of relief came over him, enormous relief and sadness. Outside, the monumental blue clouds filled the night. He stood for a few minutes and then saw, sitting in her car, motionless, Susanna. She rolled down the window as he approached.

"You didn't go," he said.

"I couldn't stay in there."

"It's over," he said. "Come in. I'm going to get a drink."

She stood in the kitchen with him, her arms folded, a hand on each elbow.

"It wasn't terrible," he said. "It's just that I feel . . . I don't know."

They drank standing there.

"Did she really want me to come?" Susanna said.

"Darling, *she* suggested it. She didn't know a thing."

"I wonder."

"Believe me. Nothing."

She put down her drink.

"No, drink it," he said. "It'll help."

"I feel funny."

"Funny? You're not feeling sick?"

"I don't know."

"Don't be sick. Here, come with me. Wait, I'll get you some water."

She was concentrating on breathing evenly.

"You'd better lie down for a bit," he said.

"No, I'm all right."

"Come."

He led her, in her short skirt and blouse, to a room to one side of the front door and made her sit on the bed. She was taking slow breaths.

"Susanna."

"Yes."

"I need you."

She more or less heard him. Her head was thrown back like that of a woman longing for God.

"I shouldn't have drunk so much," she murmured.

He began to unbutton her blouse.

"No," she said, trying to rebutton it.

He was unfastening her brassiere. Her gorgeous breasts emerged. He could not take his eyes from them. He kissed them passionately. She felt herself moved to the side as he pulled down the cover of the white sheets. She tried to speak again, but he put his hand over her mouth and pushed her down. He devoured her, shuddering as if in fright at the end and holding her to him tightly. They fell into a profound sleep.

In earliest morning, light was clear and intensely bright. The house, standing in its path, became even whiter. It stood out from its neighbors, more pure and serene. The shadow of a tall elm beside it was traced on it as finely as if drawn by a pencil. The pale curtains hung unmoving. Nothing stirred within. In back was the wide lawn across which Susanna had been idly strolling as part of a garden tour on the day he had first seen her, shapely and tall. It was a vision he had not been able to erase, though the rest had started later, when she came to redo the garden with Marit.

They sat at the table drinking coffee. They were complicit, not long risen, and not regarding one another too closely. Walter was admiring her, however. Without makeup she was even more appealing. Her long hair was not combed. She seemed very approachable. There were calls that would have to be made, but he was not thinking of them. It was still too early. He was thinking past this day. Mornings to come. At first he hardly heard the sound behind him. It was a footstep and then, slowly, another—Susanna turned white—as Marit came unsteadily down the stairs. The makeup on her face was stale, and her dark lipstick showed fissures. He stared in disbelief.

"Something went wrong," she said.

"Are you all right?" he asked foolishly.

"No, you must have done it wrong."

"Oh, God," Walter murmured.

She sat weakly on the bottom step. She did not seem to notice Susanna.

"I thought you were going to help me," she said, and began to cry.

"I can't understand it," he said.

"It's all wrong," Marit was repeating. Then, to Susanna, "You're still here?"

"I was just leaving," Susanna said.

"I don't understand," Walter said again.

"I have to do it all over," Marit sobbed.

"I'm sorry," he said. "I'm so sorry."

He could think of nothing more to say. Susanna had gone to get her clothes. She left by the front door.

That was how she and Walter came to part, upon being discovered by his wife. They met two or three times afterward, at his insistence, but to no avail. Whatever holds people together was gone. She told him she could not help it. That was just the way it was.

Permissions Acknowledgments

Grateful acknowledgment is made to following publications, where these stories first appeared: the *Atlantic* for 'Charisma'; the *Carolina Quarterly* for 'Dirt'; *Esquire* for 'American Express', 'Comet', 'Dusk', 'Foreign Shores' and 'My Lord You'; *Grand Street* for 'Lost Sons', 'Akhnilo' and 'Twenty Minutes'; *Hartford Courant Literary Supplement* for 'Arlington'; the *New Yorker* for 'Last Night'; the *Paris Review* for 'Am Strande von Tanger', 'Bangkok', 'The Cinema', 'The Destruction of the Goetheanum' and 'Via Negativa'; *Tin House* for 'Give' and 'Such Fun'; and *Zeotrope* for 'Eyes of the Stars'.